LIGHT
THE
FIRE

Matt Biers-Ariel

Harold Frumkin Books

Harold Frumkin Books
Davis, California

First edition

Cover art: Ruth Santer

Library of Congress Cataloging-in-Publication Data

Biers-Ariel, Matt
  Light the fire / Matt Biers-Ariel

ISBN: 10:1536836540

Manufactured in the United States of America

To the memory of Nick McClellan
who exemplified the spirit of teaching

and

To my students
who provided the kindling

Chapter 1

THE BELL RANG and a caustic bubble rose from Mr. Samson's gut. He swallowed the bitterness down, stepped from his desk, and surveyed his fiefdom which exuded a sour milk aroma from its stained carpet. The clean surface of the teacher desk belied the impossibility of managing reams of essays, splayed books, and spilt coffee that would soon blanket it. The faux-wood desks stood in six rows and six columns conveying that students focus on the teacher and work alone. Just a few years back, students sat in groups of four to encourage collaboration. But that was then.

Despite his nausea, Mr. Samson smiled at the faded quotations he years ago peppered on the walls. The perennial student favorite was Groucho Marx's, "Outside of a dog, a book is man's best friend. Inside of a dog, it's too dark to read."

His eyes arrested on the framed certificate behind his desk: "2011 Yuba County Teacher of the Year." Mr. Samson stared into space and tried to summon that man back. He drained his coffee and opened the large cabinet. Shoved in the back were two one-quart steel pails, a jar of glass marbles, and a matchbox. He reached in, but the first students were at the threshold, so he closed the cabinet door.

In Advanced Placement English Literature, Mr. Samson led students through the classics; his success was framed for all to see. But that was then. Now it was all YouTube and Instagram. When he needed to badger Tier One students to read *Huckleberry Finn* instead of the SparkNotes, the party was over. He mulled this over for a moment and then his heart sank. What if the students were how they'd always been, and it was *he* who was different? At the age of 31, hadn't he simply become a cynical, burnt-out, and extraordinarily rotten teacher?

A hazel-eyed girl strode in wearing an orange Reagan High sweatshirt. She smiled broadly at Mr. Samson who unconsciously touched his wedding ring; many girls liked being in his class, for he had high cheekbones to go with his athletic physique. And the ponytail. Ponytails usually undermine masculinity, but his black-braided rope exuded virility. Occasionally he needed to remind a student that he was the teacher, she was the student, and a Mississippi River of hydrochloric acid separated the two. The ring was an additional Maginot Line of defense. Today he touched skin because he got divorced over the summer.

The first student was followed by a well-coifed dark-skinned girl. The two occupied desks in the front. "This is the first day I've been up before eleven in a month," the second girl complained to her companion. "It should be a felony to have an AP class at eight."

"Is there a seating chart?" a blue-haired girl sporting numerous piercings called from the doorway.

The questioner's style advertised rebellion, yet she was ready to sit where an adult commanded. Mr. Samson chuckled at the contradictory nature of teens. Though he despised what his job had become, he still liked kids.

5

"It's by height. Shortest front left, then snake around until you reach the tallest by the door." He pointed to indicate the pattern, and the students moved to where they thought they should sit. The second girl said to her friend, "See ya."

Mr. Samson felt hazel eyes on him. "You're kidding, right?"

Of course he was. But with the exception of one, the students complied with his nonsensical command. Bertrand Russell once said, "Men are born ignorant, not stupid. They are made stupid by education." Mr. Samson didn't think this was quite right; perhaps what was more true was that school took bright, hopeful kindergarteners and over a period of thirteen years turned them into automatons.

Two tall boys argued who would win the coveted seat closest to the door. Mr. Samson loudly cleared his throat. "Sit where you like, but not by someone who'll distract you, or by Friday you'll swear you've entered Dante's *Inferno*."

Maybe the magic was coming back; maybe the year would be okay.

"What's that?" a voice called.

"The video game," another replied. "Duh!"

After a generation of No Child Left Behind followed by the Common Core, and what did the brightest students know about Dante? He designed video games. Duh.

A t-shirt emblazoned with Jimi Hendrix entered the room on the torso of Bob Marley had Bob Marley been an Asian teen with acne to go with his dreads. He stumbled into the back row; likely he had stumbled into the wrong classroom. Mr. Samson's eyes lingered on the boy long enough to be a stare which the student caught and held with remarkably clear eyes.

"I heard there're no study guides in AP Lit."

True, Mr. Samson hated them. Students would read for themes and plot points picked by the teacher; the book's genius could not

6

emerge; the student's spirit untouched. But that was before his job was predicated on rising test scores. Study guides were research-based performance enhancers. They were "best practice."

"Well, not many."

The boy flung his backpack on the floor, yet another class to tolerate. The tardy bell rang; Mr. Samson closed his eyes and stood quietly in the front. Few students noticed; most continued their conversations until the vision of a silent teacher brought them to attention. Before losing them to laughter, Mr. Samson opened his eyes and recited:

"Introduction to Poetry" by Billy Collins

I ask them to take a poem
and hold it up to the light
like a color slide

or press an ear against its hive.

I say drop a mouse into a poem
and watch him probe his way out,
or walk inside the poem's room
and feel the walls for a light switch.

I want them to waterski
across the surface of a poem
waving at the author's name on the shore.

But all they want to do
is tie the poem to a chair with rope
and torture a confession out of it.

They begin beating it with a hose
to find out what it really means.

They looked engaged. Mr. Samson had hit a towering fly to deep left field. He clicked on the projector; the poem appeared on the screen.

"Perhaps one of you budding scholars can explain the poem?"

The students froze. Shouldn't he give hints, tell them what to look for? Wasn't that his job?

Mr. Samson offered nothing. This was a college-level class. The poem wasn't tough. The silence turned oppressive. Surreptitious texting ceased. His almost home run simply a routine fly out.

Mr. Samson sighed. "See, the poem is like a dilemma..."

The hazel-eyed girl raised her hand which Mr. Samson ignored. Invariably, when he was beginning to lecture, a student would ask to use the restroom. The timing was always the same. Let her wait.

"Teachers want you to love poetry. Poetry is life contemplated and distilled into a few verses of beautiful language. Yet school is more about analysis because that's what you're tested on..."

"Like torturing a poem?"

Mr. Samson stopped.

"What's your name?"

"Delphinia Westergard, but people call me Dell."

Mr. Samson addressed the class. "I want you to love literature, but many of you take this class because it looks good on your transcript. So I'm also going to teach you—as Dell suggests—to torture poems, so you can pass the AP test."

Dell asked, "Does 'press an ear against its hive' mean listen to its sound?"

"Exactly! The first part teaches how to love poetry. The second part is about analysis. When you analyze something, you destroy its magic and stop loving it. Maybe you'll pass the test, but what do you gain? Is society better off with citizens who analyze rather than love?"

"You aren't ruining my love for poetry," Dell's friend replied. "I'm here for the grade bump and college credit."

"What's your name?"

"Poonam Patel."

"I appreciate your honesty, Poonam." He turned to the class. "Raise your hand if you feel like Poonam."

Poonam raised hers and others shyly followed until the overwhelming majority were in solidarity against verse. The bell rang and the students got up to leave. Mr. Samson trudged to his desk, the beginning of another lousy year. Dell stayed behind.

"Miss Westergard?"

"I just want you to know that I like poetry a lot."

Mr. Samson smiled. With a half-dozen Dells, the year would be tolerable. She left and the first English 12 student walked in. Though both classes were for seniors, they were as different as Ted Williams was from Tennessee Williams.

25% of Reagan High students were on the AP track. Besides academics, these Tier One students immersed themselves in extracurriculars, sports, and volunteer work in order to build compelling college applications that four-year colleges and universities could not resist. The Tier Twos took English 12. Their grail was a high school diploma. Since the future demanded higher education, Mr. Samson had been rabid about tier-advancement, but even when he was Teacher of the Year, the number of Tier Twos who climbed to Tier One could barely field an outfield. Mr. Samson could sand and polish a student's veneer, but the rotted wood of dysfunctional family and poverty that lay below was mostly beyond his skills.

While both classes held nearly three dozen students in 750 square-feet, English 12 felt more crowded. Being within easy striking distance of each other made the class more fun. In the front row sat a girl whose primary distinguishing feature was a large cleavage which she modeled as if extending a hand to show off a two-carat diamond engagement ring. Mr. Samson did not bust her for dress code violation because male teachers were under scrutiny after a math teacher went to prison for sexual relations with a student. As he made his way around the classroom, he repeated male teacher Axiom #1: "Never look at a female student below her neck."

Instead of beginning the year with poetry, Mr. Samson paired students up and asked, "What's your favorite song?" They talked music for a minute and then switched partners.

"Next question: if you were an animal what would it be?"

"I'd be an eagle and fly out of this shit hole."

"I'd be a sloth and sleep all day."

"Dude, you're there. How many times did you sleep in Green's class?"

On the last round, Mr. Samson asked, "What was a meaningful book you've read?"

For a moment there was silence, and then, "Wasn't Tommy Lopez' two-kegger awesome? I don't remember a fuckin' thing!"

"Can you believe we're seniors!"

"We own this place!"

Books did not register on the Richter scale of their lives. If anyone said, "After reading *Night*, I learned not to scapegoat minorities," Mr. Samson would have pulled out one of the pails and lit the entire box of matches.

Mo Samson collapsed into his chair at the final bell, physically, mentally, emotionally drained—a typical first day. He wished he was going home to give Katherine the day's play-by-play, but the apartment would be empty. Though there had been no "Husband of the Year" framed above their bed, Mo and Katherine were once a good team. But his work troubles spilled into the marriage, and Katherine wanted a trade. If life was a baseball season, Mo started off leading the league in hits, but now the season wasn't even halfway over, and he couldn't get on base. He reflected that life might be too damn long, opened a can of beans, and made quesadillas.

After dinner, he checked email; like regular mail, it was mostly junk. He logged onto Facebook. He signed up when Katherine moved out. A half-dozen times was enough to realize it was another worthless time suck. Unlike most of his generation, he didn't live on the screen. Still, there might be something. His colleague Truck posted: *My last first day. 179 more until retirement. I see a Maui cabana on the horizon.*

Mo replied: *I didn't see a cabana, just tons of cleavage. This one senior Tracy Smith looks like her aspiration is to be a streetwalker.*

Mo pounded *Enter.* It was his first Facebook reply ever.

Chapter 2

MR. SAMSON FLUNG his planning book onto his desk, fired up the computer, and found a red-flagged email from Principal Dewey King: *See me asap.*

Dewey probably wanted to remind Mo that while he wasn't telling him to teach to the SBAC, the end of the year state test, Mo did need to bring up his scores and doing practice questions on a weekly basis would be prudent.

As he walked through the halls, students stared at him. Was it obvious to all that he hated his job? In the office, the registrar and two secretaries were working the phones and fielding questions from an endless line of students. A box of Starbucks coffee and a bowl of Noah's Bagels were in easy access. Though he already had his morning double, another cup couldn't hurt, but Dewey's secretary motioned him to enter his office. She, too, gave Mo a strange look.

Mo poked his head in. "You wanted to see me?"

"Come in and close the door."

Dewey returned to his computer. Had it not been for his shirt and tie, the principal could be mistaken for a Hell's Angel with his XXL body, bald head, and earring. With his starched white shirt, Dewey was the best dressed man on campus. His grey tie was filled with colorful, inspirational graffiti like, "Everything worth doing requires sweat." If a tie bestows power and authority on the wearer, what does one make of the male teacher's wardrobe? Career begins with button-down shirts and ties until one attains tenure. Then he loses the tie. A few more years and it's a button-down that needs ironing, then a short-sleeve pullover, and in the year of his retirement, he's wearing Hawaiian shirts and sandals.

"Okay," said Dewey.

The tone of "Okay" was similar to when Mo was about to deliver a detention. His armpits leaked.

"I'm assuming you haven't seen this." Dewey swung his computer screen, and there was Mo's Facebook post to Truck with a page of comments below: "Nice Mr. Samson sounds like a child predator. Is this the role model we want for our children?" and, "Haven't we been through enough? Get rid of this pervert."

"Shit."

"What the hell, Mo? I spent all last year dealing with the Robertson thing. And now you're talking about a student's tits on Facebook?"

"I thought it was just going to Truck."

"Are you kidding? If the original posting was public, so are the replies."

"I didn't know. I don't use Facebook."

Dewey stared at Mo, pursed his lips, and said nothing, his face inscrutable. Because of a single Facebook post, Mo's job was suddenly in jeopardy. This was more asinine than getting fired for crappy test scores.

"Am I fired?"

"Fired? No, you're not fired, but Mo, something like this happens again, and it'll be a notice of unprofessional conduct at a minimum, and we'd probably have a conversation of your future here. You're a smart guy; use your head." Dewey sighed. "It'd sure be nice if the football team got more media this year than one of our teachers."

"Sure, I get it." Mo got up to leave.

"One more thing. Sit. I know you hate the SBAC and don't do practice questions, but you need higher scores. For real."

"I know. I'm totally on board."

"Alright, fine." Dewey scrutinized Mo's shirt. "If you aren't going to iron, at least get permanent press. You're a professional. You should look it. That's it. Go teach."

As Mo was halfway out the door, Dewey added, "And I transferred Tracy Smith."

Mo exited the office. Maria Mendoza, a counselor, was waiting.

"You okay?"

"Dewey's comparing me to Robertson."

"Robertson? I doubt that; you must have misheard, but it's true that everyone's breathing down Dewey's neck. His job's as much on the line as yours. He didn't write you up for unprofessional conduct, did he?"

"No." Mo stared at his shoes. "I really blew it, huh?"

"Everyone's gone public on private things."

"Poor Tracy. If I apologize, would that help?"

"Only if you do it on Facebook," Maria said wryly.

"Ha-ha."

"But seriously, I spoke with Tracy and her parents. She's doing okay, though it didn't help that her dad said, 'I tell her all the time she dresses like a prostitute.'"

"Kids are going to think I'm a perv."

"Why don't you take the day off?"

"Maybe I should pull an Oedipus and blind myself."

"I've got a bobby-pin."

"Thanks."

"Why don't we grab tapas after the staff meeting?"

Mo squeezed Maria's hand, a true friend. As he was leaving, Vice-Principal Patricia Haman, The Hammer, stopped him. Short and trim with an abundant mane of dyed-blond hair, The Hammer was a former cheerleader who traded her short-skirted uniform for a business suit atop stilettos that clicked as she walked. During the school day, when the clicking echoed in the corridors, teachers tightened the reins in the classroom, and student posture improved. The student rumor that she painted her manicured and sharpened nails with arsenic-based nail polish was, of course, false.

"Mr. Samson, one moment please." About a third the size of the principal's office, the walls were bare but for a poster of a kitten hanging from a branch by a single claw with the caption, "Just Hang in There." Mo disliked all motivational posters, but this one he particularly despised due to its location.

"Mr. Samson, I want you to know that you are getting off easy. Because of the inappropriateness of your cavalier public remark regarding a student, I recommended a notice of unprofessional conduct."

"Trish, it's been a tough morning. I just got it from Dewey. I really don't need it from you."

"Mr. Samson, in case you have forgotten, you answer as much to me as to Principal King. I have my eye on you. I do not want to hear anything else involving you and female students."

"Don't insinuate that I act inappropriately. I made a Facebook mistake—that's all—and isn't enforcing the dress code your department?"

"It is a shared responsibility, Mr. Samson. If you have an issue with a student's dress, please send her or him to the office, and do not advertise it on the internet. Do you have any idea how your 'mistake' has affected your student? Your 'mistake' is cyber bullying. Her emotional distress is on your head. Good day, Mr. Samson." Mrs. Haman turned to her computer screen.

Mo stepped out of the office. After Maria dressed the wound, The Hammer ripped off the bandage and poured on the salt. The worst part was that she wasn't totally off-base. Their mutual dislike reached a new apex.

As he made his way to his classroom, he was mindful not to catch anyone's eye. His lesson plan involved a poem that dealt with a man who liked older women. "Great timing," he muttered. But the poem wasn't sexual, and it was the best way to teach the difference between "persona" and "poet," so he steeled himself for the day.

Chapter 3

VIOLET BROWN STOOD in front of her bathroom mirror finishing her face. She debated whether "Red Ocher" or "Scarlet Trouble" lip gloss would go best with "Panic Blue" hair.

"Feels dangerous today; better play it safe."

She applied Red Ocher and replaced her skull earring with one that read "Love." Even before the alarm went off, her phone had been buzzing about Samson's post.

"That's one big-time fuck-up," she told her reflection. She buttoned up her blouse one more.

Violet bounded down the stairs and hustled past the bowl and boxes of cereal her mother left out for her. Her union electrician father was out before dawn, and her mother had a long commute to an Elk Grove insurance office. As the only one of three girls still at home, she was used to being on her own. It felt like her parents were done raising kids. On one hand, she appreciated their being hands-off unlike Abby's helicopter mom who wanted Abby to text her after every class to tell her what she learned. On the other hand, Violet wished her parents cared a little about her life.

Violet grabbed a travel mug, poured herself leftover coffee, and climbed into her convertible VW bug. She texted as she drove. Tracy, of course, was incommunicado. She felt bad for her, but Samson was kind of right; Tracy totally flaunted her boobs. He probably wasn't another Robertson, but who knew? She saw a movie where this guy beat off to yearbook pictures, and Samson's post was worse than Ms. Cook's lecture about "single-cell orgasms."

Violet and Abby texted a dozen times before Violet picked her up.

"Think they'll fire him?" Abby asked as she climbed into the car with her coffee mug.

"Doubt it. Robertson slept with a freshman. Samson just said Tracy's got tig bitties."

"That freshman was total ratchet," said Abby.

"Yeah, well, Robertson was total perv."

"Love, nice," Abby pointed at Victoria's earring.

"It's all you need."

Violet pulled into the student parking lot. A multi-dented Toyota Corolla cut her off and slid into the parking spot she wanted.

"Fuck you, DeSean!" she yelled.

"I love you too, Violet!" He blew a kiss at her.

"He likes you," Abby said. "He's cute."

"More like Cro-Magnon."

Violet found another spot, killed the engine, and raised her coffee mug like it was a club. "Grog hit on head and mate you."

Both girls cracked up and walked onto campus. At Violet's classroom, Abby said, "Samson and AP Lit." She tugged at the top button on Violet's blouse. "One more can't hurt!"

"Bitch!" Violet laughed, knocked her hand away, and walked in. There was definitely a buzz in the air. Samson looked pale and distracted, definitely not the same guy from the day before.

Abby texted: *S. staring at your ta-tas?*

Samson passed out copies of Langston Hughes' poem "Preference."

18

Violet texted: *S. acting like nothing happened.*

Abby texted: *Tracy with t-shirt. lol.*

Samson asked, "Who can explain what a persona is?"

Silence.

Samson picked up a stack of index cards with student names. Violet remembered learning the word but couldn't remember what it meant. She was kind of impressed that Samson was in class. If it were her, she would have transferred schools.

"Javier Gomez?"

Javier shrugged. Samson had a look of disgust like, what the fuck are you doing in this class? Samson had a nasty edge, maybe even racist.

"Lupita Alvarez?"

"I don't know."

Handsome Hudson raised his hand. Violet sniggered at Handsome who was half kiss-ass and half jerk. It was obvious that Handsome was googling from his backpack. He wore a solid-red, A&F shirt to go with his gelled hair. If she ever found him asleep, she'd dye it "Electric Banana" with "Panic Blue" lightning bolts.

"Hudson?"

"A persona is a role or character adopted by an author."

"Good. Now zip up your backpack and explain what you mean."

Hah, Samson was onto Handsome.

"I believe it explains itself," Handsome retorted.

"Anyone else?"

Dell raised her hand.

"I think it means mask. A persona is like a mask an author puts on. We can't assume that the narrator and the author are the same."

Dell's such a freak. Samson looked blown away like in this class of morons, there's a genius.

"What do you think, Hudson?" Samson asked.

19

"That's what I said. It's like you have a murder story narrated by the murderer. That doesn't mean the author is a murderer. No offense, but it's pretty obvious. I thought this was supposed to be a tough class."

Handsome looked around to see who noticed his wit, but except for Olivia, no one cracked the tiniest smile. Samson said, "Okay, Hudson, how about reading the poem I passed out? Don't forget the title. It's key."

Violet picked up the poem and muttered, "Two classes, two poems. This could be an extremely boring year."

Handsome rustled the paper, cleared his throat, and read:

"Preferences" by Langston Hughes

I likes a woman
six or eight and ten years older'n myself.
I don't fool with those young girls.
Young girls'll say,
Daddy, I want so-and-so.
I needs this, that, and the other.
But a old woman'll say,
Honey, what does YOU need?
I just drawed my money tonight
and it's all your'n.
That's why I likes a older woman
who can appreciate me;
When she conversations you,
it ain't forever, Gimme!"

Samson commanded, "Shout out some words to describe the narrator."

Silence.

20

"An AP class that can't wait to engage in intellectual conversation."

Samson was sarcastic.

"Uneducated, definitely poor," said Dell.

"Thank you, Dell. Any other working minds this morning?"

Ouch. Violet did not like this teacher.

"Black," said Noah.

"Stupid," said Handsome.

"Good," Samson said, "neurons are firing. Now would a poor, ignorant, uneducated narrator name his poem 'Preference'? Poonam?"

"I don't know. Maybe something like, 'Who I likes.'"

"Now explain the difference between the poet and his persona in this poem."

An understanding of a different nature suddenly came to Violet. Her body could barely contain her insight; she jumped out of her seat and shouted, "His persona likes cougars! I'm right, right?" This was a great poem!

"Cougars?" Samson was confused.

"You know—middle-aged women who pick up college guys in bars. They wear tight jeans, boots, and low-cut tops to show off…their…uh…"

Victoria's face was hot. Samson's face turned scarlet. Silence erupted in the classroom.

Samson recovered with, "Okay, okay, I get it. Violet's right. Hughes' persona likes 'cougars.' The—uh—point is that Hughes is trying to paint a picture of a particular kind of man. But he is not that man. Hughes is educated and sophisticated. Does everyone see the difference between the poet and his persona?"

"We get it," Handsome spoke for the class.

"Okay, since everyone understands, we're going to move on…"

Violet raised her hand. "That was a great poem, Mr. Samson! Are we going to do more like it?"

Samson turned to the board. "...comma rules. Open your journals."

Chapter 4

THE DAY WAS out of Mr. Samson's control, like when the opposing team hits everything no matter who's pitching. At least English 12 would start with a short diagnostic; maybe he could regroup.

The diagnostic theoretically found holes in students' English skills. Perhaps someone had difficulty in reading comprehension. Another's deficit was writing strategies. A third, vocabulary. Following the diagnostic, Mr. Samson would analyze the results and create custom curricula to address the deficiencies, so by the time the SBAC came in the spring, the students would all test Proficient or Advanced, and Mr. Samson would continue to receive a paycheck. That was the idea.

But he wasn't going to create 150 individualized curricula. The next best thing would be to analyze the data for class trends and focus on common problems. Mr. Samson didn't do that either. For the first five years of his career, he spent hours poring over data and got the same news. Pedro couldn't understand what he read; Chloe wrote "i" not "I"; Cooper didn't know the word 'decimate.' He had to teach everything.

Mr. Samson gave the diagnostic not because it made him a more effective teacher; rather, The Hammer commanded him to send her the results. "Effective teaching must be data driven" was her mantra. Perhaps, but the data never changed.

While the students filled in bubbles at quarter-speed, Mr. Samson reread the Facebook posting. Writing that *Tracy Smith looks like her aspiration is to be a streetwalker* was idiotic, but it didn't indicate girls were unsafe in his presence. This wasn't another Robertson affair. He'd keep his job. But as students bubbled with one hand above the desk and perused social media with the other below, he hardly cared.

Following the diagnostic, they opened the textbook, a 1,200-page compendium of English literature. Mr. Samson bypassed the *Beowulf* excerpt because it was incomprehensible even to him and probably wouldn't be on the SBAC. He started with Geoffrey Chaucer's 14th century *Canterbury Tales*. That would be on the test, and he might be able to teach them satire. Back in the day, he had put together a presentation of modern satires. The Hammer came in one day while he showed a clip from *Monty Python and The Holy Grail*, and an argument ensued on the appropriateness of using "crass humor in the classroom that has a tenuous connection to the standards that must drive your curriculum."

Most students didn't get *Python* anyway, so now it was straight-up Chaucer with a No-Doz chaser.

Mr. Samson selected an index card.

"Cooper Henderson?" A stocky boy with dirty-blond hair atop a pasty, round face wearing a band t-shirt grunted. His sagging army surplus pants revealed lime green boxer shorts underneath. In the fashion of the day, the boy's Oakland A's hat still bore the hat-size sticker.

"Please, pick up from where I left off."

"Uh, where are we?"

The boy sitting behind Cooper was leaning back in his chair with the two front legs off the ground. His arms folded across his chest, his head encased in a Philadelphia Eagles' hoody. At Cooper's comment, he loudly brought the front legs to the floor, whacked his palm to his forehead, and guffawed, "What a dope!"

Mr. Samson looked at the seating chart and commanded, "Blake Thomas, you may not verbally attack another student. This is a warning." He paused to let the seriousness sink in on the freckled-faced redhead. Blake's face went blank, and Mr. Samson knew his words did not register. "Cooper, we're on line 54."

Blake rotated his head to view the rest of the class and loudly whispered, "He doesn't know where we're at because he's masturbating to Trac…"

"That's a detention!" Mr. Samson wanted to grab this Blake punk by his scruff and launch him out the door; being a student didn't give carte blanche to being a prick. He stormed over to the teacher desk and yanked open a drawer. He scribbled a detention and marched over to Blake. The class was silent. Mr. Samson tried to intimidate Blake with his size and anger, but Blake accepted the detention slip with a smirk which made Mr. Samson more livid. Both of them knew who won the round; Mr. Samson had violated a central teaching tenet; he let anger overwhelm him; he sank to the immaturity of a teen; he was no longer in charge.

In order to reestablish power, Mr. Samson moved Blake, but that did not stop him from taunting Cooper who was happy to give it back encouraging other boys to join in. Mr. Samson could not write fifteen detentions. He might no longer be Teacher of the Year, but at least he could prevent anarchy, or so he thought.

The seating chart that Mr. Samson depended on to provide structure for managing English 12 was as effective in controlling this class as a Little League pitcher against the heart of the New York Yankees lineup. Sure, Tracy Smith provided the spark. But tinder was needed; it came from the fact that in Tier Two classes, boys usually outnumbered girls; this class had 26 boys and 8 girls. The tiers were gender imbalanced because being a successful Tier One student required the ability to critically read, coherently write, and quietly sit. The stereotypical teen boy didn't want to analyze a piece of literature or talk about feelings. He wanted to do stuff. Intellectually, Mr. Samson knew it wasn't Blake's fault he wasn't in a vocational class because most had been cut to ensure all students were exposed to four years of Chaucer, Shakespeare, and Emily Dickinson instead of taking auto shop or learning how to install photovoltaic panels. Blake and his peers acted out because public education had left them behind.

Through force of will, Mr. Samson compelled the class to continue Chaucer. When the bell rang, Blake politely asked, "Wasn't Tracy Smith in this class?"

From across the classroom, Cooper yelled, "Don't be a fucking douche-bag!"

Mr. Samson did not give him a detention.

His *Inferno* day finished, Mo opened his stash of Hershey Kisses and was one chocolate the wrong side of a stomachache when he remembered the staff meeting and hustled across campus.

"Budget cuts," Mick "Truck" McGuire groused as Mo entered the multipurpose room. When Mick McGuire was listening to literary classics on tape during his years as a long distance trucker, his trucker pals called him Professor. At age 33, he started night school and went on to earn a doctorate in English literature, but he was too old and uncultured for academia, so he took a position at Reagan High where the Shakespeare scholar went by Truck to his colleagues, Dr. Truck to his students. Truck pointed at the table which held five decimated doughnut boxes containing a single plain doughnut in the midst of crumbs from more satisfying varieties. A coffee urn reeking of a weak, institutional blend shared the table. Packets of tea, sugar, and sugar substitute were shoved into a small bowl, and a container of non-dairy creamer stood next to it. The counter was littered with plastic swizzle sticks and empty sweetener packets amid the drops and rivulets of creamer.

Pouring himself a cup of coffee was the 64-year-old wearing a Hawaiian shirt, shorts, and sandals. "How the mighty have fallen," he shook his hoary head. "What was it last year? Carnitas and ice cream sundaes?"

"You've got Alzheimer's. Carnitas was three years ago."

Truck dumped a packet of sugar substitute into his Styrofoam cup. "Doc says I got to cut down." He stirred his coffee, took a sip, and snarled, "Gimmie death," while pouring in two sugar packets. "Thank God, this is my last year."

For the first time all day, Mo laughed. "Last year, first day of school, Dr. Truck, and I quote, 'Thank God, this is my last year. I've had it with the little bastards who pride themselves in their ignorance.'"

"Yeah, well, this year they're giving the golden handshake to us old-timers to make room for the cheap newbies. Add my pension and trucker's retirement, and I can scrape by as long as I die by 70."

Before Mo could manage a quip, Dewey boomed, "We've had a great two days of school! It's going to be an *awesome* year!"

The Hammer passed out binders with emergency information, calendar, and the staff development plan. Mo counted 5 proximate teachers texting while Dewey reviewed the contents. The difference between student and teacher texting was that students hid theirs in backpacks, laps, and sweatshirt pockets. Teachers shamelessly texted in the open.

"Take five to look over everything; let me or Mrs. Haman know of any questions, concerns, comments."

Mo scanned the staff development plan; this year was going to focus on raising the achievement level for Hispanic, African-American, and low income students. Every staff development in Mo's career dealt with decreasing the achievement gap. Some years the gap was slightly wider, some years slightly narrower, but as a whole, the difference between well-to-do whites and Asians versus the rest was more stable than any marriage he knew.

Dewey said, "As we launch into another school year, I am once again reminded that we have the most important job in the world..."

Maria texted Mo: *more important than oncologists*

Mo: *aerospace engineers*

Maria: *don't forget tapas*

"...the awesome responsibility of shaping the next generation of political leaders, innovators, professionals, tradespeople. Now while I do not judge our school, or our teachers by test scores, and I would never tell you to teach to the test, we did not make our state-mandated goals last year. But I have absolute confidence in the professionalism of this staff; we will make this year's target."

The Hammer stood up. "As you are aware, we must reach 60% Proficiency in Math, Science, and English Language Arts. If we fail to achieve this, we will be sanctioned, and there will be repercussions. Teachers who experience negative growth for a third straight year will be non-reelected rehires."

Mo's scores were down two years running; he knew he had to teach to the test to save his job. Even though Mo was sickened by this, the job market was lousy. He'd suck it up and get through the year.

Truck, however, spoke. "With all due respect, Trish, there's a lot of Kool-Aid drinking if you think we can get to 60% Proficiency. This is the wet dream of conservatives who want to destroy public education and fund parochial schools where they can teach Creationism. Pardon my language, but it is pure, unadulterated bullshit to tie job security on some snot-nosed freshman gang-banger knowing what the word 'loquacious' means."

28

A smattering of applause and a mild "that's right!" broke out. The Hammer ignored the others and zeroed in on Truck.

"With all due respect, Mr. McGuire, both Principal King and I know that if we work hard and apply research-based pedagogical techniques we can and will make our target."

"Pass the Kool-Aid, and—by the way—it's *Dr.* McGuire." Mo felt the same as Truck, but he said nothing because it was pointless to argue with The Hammer. Besides he wanted out.

No one had anything to add, so Dewey said, "That's it. Get some rest."

Counselors dealt with student schedules and mental health. Their doors were always open for those in crisis. For Tier Ones whose parents didn't attend college, they found scholarships. They badgered Tier Two slackers to pull their grades up. They were empathetic ears for burnt out teachers. From the first moment Mo and Maria hit it off. She was insightful, non-judgmental, and made Mo laugh.

They met at Tapas World. Mo liked the décor and falling into one of the overstuffed couches was the perfect way to end a tough day, but Mo took offense at $6.50 for a draft beer.

"Why do you care?" asked Maria. "You don't drink. So, how'd you survive the day?"

"Think post-Blitz London."

"I can imagine. This hasn't been the best of times."

Mo shrugged. He didn't have the energy to give Maria the full story. The truth was that even before the Facebook debacle, he was terrified about where his life seemed to be heading with his divorce and now his career taking a similar trajectory.

A waitress came by.

"Hiya, Ms. Mendoza, Mr. Samson. Can I get you something?"

"Ashondra," Maria answered, "how are you? How's Nicole?"

"Great, she'll be three in October. And I'm taking Intro to Bio at Lincoln Community College. I'm going to be a nurse."

"That's wonderful. You'll make a terrific nurse. How about a plate of olives, cheese empanadas, and…" glancing at Mo…"patron peppers?" Mo nodded. "And a glass of merlot."

"And I'll have a root beer, please."

Maria sighed as Ashondra went to the kitchen. "She took Intro to Bio last year. I just don't see it."

"Waitressing isn't the worst profession in the world."

"No, of course not. Oh well. She wouldn't be the first student to get derailed by a baby." Maria sipped her wine. "So besides the fact that people want to tar and feather and run you out of town, how's it going?"

"Grad school teach you to get the client to open up with humor?"

"Of course, but I'm not your therapist. I'm your friend, and even during last week's inservice you seemed unhappy."

There was a long moment of silence, the same awkward discomfort as when Mo asked a class to explicate a text.

"Okay," Maria said. "New subject. Dating. Did you go out with anyone this summer?"

"A woman at the Sacramento Jazz Festival caught my eye. I smiled at her and she smiled back, and then next thing I know, she's standing next to me. We chit-chatted for a minute, and she gave the ponytail this once-over, like 'Can I introduce this guy to my friends?' That didn't feel great. Anyway, I don't think I'm ready to date."

"Coming out of a divorce is hard. But why not cut that ponytail? You know, a new beginning."

"I've told you like twenty times."

"No you haven't."

"Sure I have."

Maria shook her head and Mo reached down his back lifting the braided black hair that reached past the small of his back.

30

"I was a catcher in Little League because I was fat. In high school I worked out and dedicated my life to baseball. By junior year I was starting catcher and all-league. My nickname was Beast because I batted clean-up. Professional football players were wearing dreadlocks, so I started a ponytail in honor of my Nez Perce grandfather. It was the section championship game, and we stood along the baseline between home plate and first base. As each player was introduced, he doffed his cap. Prior to the play-offs, everyone got crew cuts. I was going to too, but Lumpy, our captain, said, 'Beasts don't cut their hair.' So I didn't. I was on fire throughout the playoffs, batting over .500. When I doffed my cap during the introduction, some jerk from the stands yelled, 'Get a haircut, Injun!' My guys spontaneously chanted, 'Beast! Beast! Beast!'

"I hit two doubles, a single, and knocked in five runs. We were up 7-6 in the bottom of the seventh. There were two outs, and a player from Lincoln tried scoring from second on a single to center. Lumpy's throw beat the runner, and the guy bowled me over to dislodge the ball, but I hung on, and we were champs. My teammates hoisted me in the air, and I vowed I'd be like my namesake and never cut my hair."

Maria gaped at Mo as he sipped his root beer. "That's a great story. I can't believe you never told me. But seriously, Mo, everybody breaks vows. Every New Year I vow to go to the gym."

"And every year I vow to be nice to The Hammer. I don't know why this is different."

"You know in the end it didn't work out for your namesake."

"I don't know; he took out a couple thousand Philistines when he went out."

"Mo, the martyr. Alliterative. You going to take out the Department of Education on your way down?"

With Maria, Mo didn't have to watch what he said and how he said it like with Katherine. They just talked. Maybe he should tell her that he was losing it. He was pretty scared.

"And then you played in the minor leagues, right?"

Talking about a bitter remembrance was easier than discussing his present turmoil. "I got drafted out of college and played for the Portland Sea Dogs. The beauty of baseball is how everyone pulls together as a team. I'd lay down my life for my high school and college teammates. But the Sea Dogs? We weren't a team. If stabbing your roommate in the back would get you a step closer to The Bigs, that's what you did. I felt like a jilted lover. One night after a game, I sat in a hotel room and broke down. Baseball was my first love, and now there was nothing I hated more. The next morning I took my gear bag and walked the streets of Trenton. A kid with a Baltimore Orioles hat and jersey was sitting on a porch. I gave him the bag, bought a Greyhound ticket to Sacramento, and here I am." Mo laughed bitterly. "Maybe I should quit teaching too."

"You might not get the chance. One more year of negative test scores, and you'll get fired"

"I know, but Truck's right. There's no way we're going to get Tier Twos to 60% proficiency. Why don't they demand students sprout wings and fly? Or oil companies formulate gasoline that doesn't emit carbon dioxide? It's an impossible mandate. How stupid are they?"

Mo finished his root beer.

"Mo, you don't need to get everyone to 60%; you just have to raise your scores. You've got to teach to the test, at least a little. Everyone does."

"I know. I'm going to, but I didn't become a teacher to teach kids how to bubble."

"You're a great teacher, Mo Samson. Don't throw it away."

"Used to be. I used to be a great teacher, used to be a great baseball player, used to be a decent husband. I can't even use Facebook without screwing up."

"You might consider a little therapy."

"Yeah, maybe. Look, I'm pretty beat. I'll see you tomorrow. Today's on me." Mo threw $30 on the bar and left.

Chapter 5

THE TEACHERS' ROOM was their clubhouse. A teacher could drink a cup of coffee, collaborate with a colleague, or lick wounds before reentering the fray. More often than not, the room was not a retreat but a subatomic orbital of jumpiness, especially 15 minutes before the first bell when teachers mobbed the copiers. Mo observed that the chance one of the machines jamming was directly correlated to the number of teachers in line. Both machines broke down only on the mornings of final exams.

"How you doing, kid?" Truck asked as he and Mo stood alone at the one working copier. Truck was running off Shakespeare quizzes.

"Surviving."

"Ever see Katherine?"

"Not really. It's not like we had kids. I saw her at a party with a guy from her office."

"You dating?"

"Not done whipping myself for screwing up the marriage."

Truck fed another sheet into the copier. "Don't get me wrong, Katherine is beautiful and competent and with a couple of chardonnays under her belt reasonably funny. But she couldn't have been easy to live with."

"It wasn't bad."

"Mo, you don't have to defend her. All of us do things that could wreck our marriages if our marriages are ready to be wrecked."

"Yeah, okay."

"I get that you're not ready to get involved, but as your friend, I advise you to at least get laid."

Mo didn't say anything, and Truck picked up his copies. "At least that Tracy Smith thing blew over."

"I was such an idiot."

"Gotta let it go."

"You done?"

"Yep."

Mo punched in his code, but it flashed he was out of copies.

"Are you kidding me? It's the middle of the month, and I'm out!"

"Here." Truck punched in a number. "The Hammer's TA left her code on the machine last week. Copy your derrière and Instagram it to her."

Mo copied a study guide for the poem, "The World is Too Much With Us."

"Would you look at that?" Truck nodded to a flyer above the copier advertising *Dr. Jeff Lebowski's Effective Teacher Workshop.* "Same old bullshit. Some academic or 'master' teacher makes a PowerPoint that'll fix your teaching in one short seminar. A bargain at $500."

Mo eyed the flyer. "The district pays you a $250 stipend."

"Whoop-de-fucking-do. I'd rather watch paint dry. Neither Dr. Lebowski, nor you, nor me, nor any of us, know jack about effective teaching. Every ten years, we get new reforms based on the 'latest research.' If these worked, our kids would be getting smarter and

35

smarter. But our valedictorian knows less than I did when I graduated high school with a 2.3 GPA. And that's only because I aced auto shop. Fact is we don't know shit about how to take five-year-old kids, educate them for 13 years, and turn them into critical-thinking, empathetic adults knowledgeable in culture, science, and social skills who will become good citizens but stand up against societal bullshit."

"Maybe you should run for the Board of Education. 'Vote for Dr. Truck. He don't know shit.'"

Truck picked up his briefcase. "Ha-ha. Maybe you should do stand-up. You know what really gets my goat. It's all the goddamn lip-service, 'Teaching is such a *noble* profession.' If we were actually valued, teachers would drive Porsches and bond traders would have 15-year-old Toyotas with cracked windshields. See ya."

"This teaching to the test is killing me. I'm thinking of quitting."

Truck stopped.

"Maybe I'll drive truck. What do you think?"

"Great idea. A lot of intellectual stimulation, and you don't even need an apartment; you can sleep in your cab. Course after driving 9 straight hours powering down amphetamines, you'll need to mainline Ambien. Don't forget the salary cut. Mo, you're a damn good teacher..."

"Was..." Mo interrupted but Truck cut him off.

"*Are* a damn good teacher. Quit feeling so goddamn sorry for yourself. You got hosed. Who hasn't? Just play along with the testing bullshit for a year and get your scores up. Forget what I said about workshops and Porsches. Teaching *is* fucking noble. Stay sane by teaching how you want once a week. What's that?" Truck pointed at Mo's pile of study guides.

"Didn't you once lecture me these were the spawn of Satan? Isn't your teaching style to let the poem speak for itself?"

Mo shrugged and Truck took the pile of guides and dumped them into the recycling box.

36

"This is your day to teach."

Mo grinned. Dr. Truck fixed him. As the good doctor went out the door, he said, "And get laid," just as first year teacher Jennifer Hamilton walked into the room. She smiled at Mo. Mo averted his eyes and grinned.

AP Lit students took their seats, and Mr. Samson pointed to the white board which indicated the page in the literature book he wanted them to turn to. He closed his eyes. He could feel the slowing of his pulse; the poem stood before him like a fat fastball right down the middle. He swung:

> "The World Is Too Much With Us"
> William Wordsworth, 1802
>
> The world is too much with us; late and soon,
> Getting and spending, we lay waste our powers;—
> Little we see in Nature that is ours;
> We have given our hearts away, a sordid boon!
> This Sea that bares her bosom to the moon;
> The winds that will be howling at all hours,
> And are up-gathered now like sleeping flowers;
> For this, for everything, we are out of tune;
> It moves us not. Great God! I'd rather be
> A Pagan suckled in a creed outworn;
> So might I, standing on this pleasant lea,
> Have glimpses that would make me less forlorn;
> Have sight of Proteus rising from the sea;
> Or hear old Triton blow his wreathèd horn.

By Jove, the poem was genius. In 14 short lines Wordsworth summed up the problem with consumerism and humanity's estrangement from the natural world. He wanted to savor it as long as he could like when he slowly trotted around the bases. No tying the poem to a chair to torture a confession out of it. Let the poem speak for itself. Let it become part of you.

With a conspiratorial grin, Mr. Samson unclasped his hands from in front of his belly and opened them wide, palms facing the class. "Well? What do you think? What does it say to you? How does it make you feel?"

Mr. Samson's new found enthusiasm for poetry qua poetry found no takers. Befuddlement not amazement settled over the students.

"Nobody?" He tried not to sound disappointed, but it probably leaked through. "As Billy Collins said, walk into the poem's room and look for a light switch. Take five minutes."

Mr. Samson walked around the classroom to see if he could be of service, but no one called him over, so he went to his desk and looked back at the students. There was no enthusiasm; rather, they were dutifully going through the motions. Poonam was right. They hated poetry. What had he been thinking? What had Truck been smoking? On one side, he was trying to keep his job by teaching to the test. On the other side, he was trying to engender a love for poetry. On both sides, he was losing. Why even bother? He'd been thinking about perusing Craig's List Help Wanted section for the past week. He clicked on *Education* and found: *pre-school assistant, autistic child aide*, and *school crossing guard*. Were Triton and Proteus telling him that he was done with education? He peeked around the computer monitor; they were still putting in the time, so he perused *Writing/Editing*. He found *freelance writer for food blog*. At $25/blog, he'd need to write 6 articles a day for 360 days a year to equal his not so stellar current salary. Plus no medical, no retirement.

The students were finished, so Mr. Samson navigated away from Craig's List and announced, "Who will enlighten us?"

Silence.

"Noah?"

He shook his head.

"Dell?"

"I need another minute."

"Violet?"

"I don't know."

"Hudson?"

Hudson tossed his pencil on the desk, spread his arms, palms facing the ceiling, and leaned back in his chair as if announcing the task was too difficult, and what did Mr. Samson expect.

And suddenly Mr. Samson was livid. He said loudly, aggressively, "You want me to tell you? Is that the job of the teacher? Do you not have brains?" The students looked scared. Good. Maybe fear would jar them awake. "Well?"

Mr. Samson guffawed, marched to the file cabinet, almost tore the doors from the hinges, and noisily grabbed one of the two steel pails and a fistful of marbles. He slammed both pail and marbles onto his desk.

"You think the job of the teacher is to fill your bucket." He picked up a marble. "Okay, here it is. In 1802, that's over 200 years ago, for the mathematically challenged, William Wordsworth realized that all people give a damn about is materialism." Mr. Samson plunked the marble into the quart pail. "We don't see and definitely don't appreciate the beauty of the natural world." He dropped in another marble. "Monotheistic religions claim that they are superior to paganism. But the poem claims that being a pagan is better because, unlike monotheists, pagans aren't cut off from nature." Ping. "The poem is 14-lines which makes it a sonnet." Ping. "Questions? Comments?"

His rampage had run its course. He felt purged and he slightly softened. "William Wordsworth wrote a poem that was so profound and true to the human spirit that we still read it 200 years later. You have the rest of the period to write something, anything, that contains something you think is true about your world. It can be a poem or a mini-essay or a rap. I don't care. Be original; write something worth reading."

Mr. Samson returned to his desk. He wasn't happy with himself or with the students or with anything. The students whispered to each other. He gave them a minute and then, "Your insights are due at the end of the period. I'm going to grade them."

They began scribbling. If this is what it took to get them to work, then so be it. Thomas Hobbes said that but for the fear of government, people would kill each other. The Samson addendum was: but for the fear of grades, students wouldn't do a damn thing. At the bell, the students passed in their work. Samson glanced at one. Worthless. Of course it was Samson's fault for not giving them enough time or guidance. It was a stupid assignment. Dell stayed behind.

"I'm trying to write a sonnet, but I need more time. Should I turn in what I've got, or would it be okay to work on it and turn it in later?"

"Later would be fine." He felt bad about Dell; she was the one decent student surrounded by mediocrity.

The English 12 students filed into the classroom eating each other's chips and cookies while swapping germs by trading swigs off 22-ounce cans of energy drinks. Mr. Samson opened the literature book to begin where they left off in the *Canterbury Tales*. He went through the tales methodically, passionlessly. The class read them aloud and then discussed the imagery, the vocabulary, the irony. The discussions were mostly Mr. Samson asking leading questions which were answered by shrugs or monosyllabic replies followed by Mr. Samson answering his own questions and requesting students take notes. They took out their journals but never wrote anything down; he never expected they would. Following each story, students answered the questions the book editors thought were important.. Some measured reading comprehension, but most focused on higher level thinking requiring complete paragraphs. The average number of words on the sheets they turned in was about 50. This would have been sufficient to answer a single question in some depth; however, there were ten questions.

Mr. Samson knew that not a single student enjoyed the stories; perhaps a half-dozen who weren't texting understood them. Though Mr. Samson liked Chaucer, it was ridiculous to teach him. But they needed to know about the father of English poetry for the SBAC test. End of discussion.

"Open to page 245. We left off right before 'The Pardoner.'"

"I hope it's as good as the last one, the one about...what was it about again?" Blake announced and his pals clad in assorted hoodies and baseball caps cackled.

In the month since the start of school, Blake had established himself as class prick. Mr. Samson had been unable to assert authority over him, and Blake ran amok.

"Blake, would you please begin to read."

"I don't feel well."

"You look fine."

"Looks are deceiving." He gave a fake cough. "Isn't that a theme of *Can't Bury My Tail*?"

"DeSean."

DeSean Williams was a bodybuilder and middle linebacker on the football team. He was handsome enough to be employed at the local Abercrombie and Fitch store. He wore only A&F muscle shirts in school. DeSean's cologne, which always preceded him, sometimes caused Mr. Samson to gag. He did not view DeSean as scholar material.

DeSean put his head on his desk and mumbled, "Pass."

"Quentin."

A skinny, pale-faced kid wearing a Golden State Warriors jersey and a New York Yankees cap had been hunched over a calculator amusing himself. He peaked at the page in his neighbor's book, made a show of yanking open his closed literature book, and read, "My-lords, said-he, in-churches-when-I-preach I-take-great-pains-to-have-a-haughty-speech And-ring-it-out-as-roundly-as-a-bell; I-know-it-all-by-heart, what-I've-to-tell.

"Quentin, would you mind slowing down a bit. It's not a race."

"I'm done," he said flashing Mr. Samson a smug look that showed he was smarter than everyone in the classroom, including the ex-jock, has-been teacher. Quentin was reasonably intelligent, but when Mr. Samson asked why he didn't take AP Lit, he replied, "Fiction is stupid." He was going to be a game designer and would better spend his evenings playing video games than reading and writing about a "bunch of whining literary losers." He ignored Mr. Samson's comments on his first written assignment, so by the end of the second week, Mr. Samson had written him off.

"Fine, Pedro? How about it?"

Pedro Ochoa was a Mexican immigrant whose spoken English was decent, but his reading was at a third-grade level.

"My theme's...always...the same...and ever was..."

By the end of the first line, Mr. Samson was ready to call in a relief reader because he had mistakenly assigned Pedro 10 lines before there was a text break. Mr. Samson didn't want to be a jerk and stop him midstream, especially since Pedro was one of the few who tried. If Quentin read as if an army of crystal meth molecules stormed his central nervous system, Pedro read like he had just inhaled a blunt of medical-grade marijuana.

Mr. Samson glanced around the room as Pedro inflicted the Chaucer water torture on the students, dripping one word of the poet on them every few seconds. By the end of the second line, scores of fingers were in backpacks not so secretly texting, Facebooking,

Twittering, ordering pizza. Mr. Samson didn't stop them because it was his fault, and given how the day was going, he didn't even care. The students were done learning. He was done teaching. Everyone was done.

In the middle of the third line, Pedro took a long pause before the word "patriarchs," and Esther Lopez, without permission, took up the reading. Boys mostly shrank in the presence of Esther because while she was a beauty whose face appeared to be the chiseled features of an Aztec princess, her withering tongue could reduce the wittiest big man on campus to an incoherent infant. She put out the vibe that she was older and more sexually experienced than her peers. Mr. Samson was wary around her.

Neither Mr. Samson nor Pedro complained about Esther's hijacking, and she not only perfectly read Pedro's lines, but continued to the end of the story about the avaricious Pardoner who sold worthless religious relics to naïve penitents who thought the relics would absolve them of their sins.

"What's the point Chaucer is making through 'The Pardoner'?" Mr. Samson asked.

Esther said, "He's a hypocrite. He pretends to be all holy and everything, but he's like those priests who rape little kids."

"He's only a crook," Abby Rinelli said. "Priests who rape kids should get their…you know…chopped off."

"I totally agree; give me a blade and I'll gladly do the chopping." Esther replied. The boys were uncharacteristically quiet. "But what I'm saying is this guy is like the priests because they're all hypocrites. Priests don't let us use birth control or get abortions, but then they go and rape little kids. That's my point."

Mr. Samson was taken aback. After the earlier disaster with "The World Is Too Much With Us," here were Tier Twos engaging in literature! He was about to jump in with a question to take the discussion to the next level when Blake yelled, "Cooper's got AIDS!"

Samson slammed the two-pound book shut. "Blake! Out!" He hoped Blake would argue because he had a lot more to tell the little prick. But Blake pretended contrition, and as he departed, he said, "I'm sorry I disturbed the class, Mr. Samson."

The magic of the Chaucer discussion was gone; students had already moved on talking about other matters and tweeting how Blake owned Samson. Mr. Samson surveyed the classroom. To reestablish authority, he commanded, "Do questions one through ten following the story." Not a single student changed what he or she was doing. He was totally inconsequential to their lives, so he added, "I'm collecting and grading them at the end of the period." Still there was no movement toward the task, so he upped the threat. "Those who don't turn in completed work will get a 30-minute detention. Answers need to be in complete sentences." Glacially, journals opened and pens came out. Mr. Samson was miserable. If he had had himself as an English professor, he would have majored in biology.

School ended and Mo slumped into Maria's office, an eight-foot-by-eight-foot room dominated by a couch which Mo fell into. He'd wait for her to finish, and then the two would go to Tapas World where he'd drown his sorrows in a pint of root beer.

"Rough day?" Maria asked looking up from her computer.

"Year."

"What's up?"

"Everything. School, students, the SBAC."

"You're taking teach-to-the-test way too seriously. You already focus on critical reading the way the Common Core is set up, so you don't have to alter your curriculum much. Just add in some questions a couple of times a week and give them a few opportunities to practice the test format. That's it."

"The problem is they can't figure out anything unless I spoon feed it to them. I practically have to help them chew."

"There must have been something good today."

Mo shook his head and then, "You know Esther Lopez?"

Maria nodded.

"I had no idea she was so smart..."

"Pretty girls can't be smart?" Maria interrupted.

"You know what I mean. She was spot on in a discussion about the hypocrisy of priests and Chaucer's characters. I mean, you should see this class. One of my all-time 'we-don't-give-a-shit' groups, and here's this Esther Lopez, coming out of nowhere, reading like she's a book-on-tape and then analyzing the crap out of Chaucer and comparing it to the modern priest sex scandal. She killed it."

"That's great, but, Mo, don't get too enamored with her."

"What?" Was Maria implying that he was planning something inappropriate with a student?

"I'm not saying anything. I'd tell any teacher after a divorce the same thing. Esther is a very attractive and mature young woman. That's all. I'm not implying you're acting or thinking unethically."

"Sure," Mo was not happy with this conversation. He had come for their end of the week tapas, not for a lecture on how to behave with adolescent girls. "How much longer til you're done? I need like ten plates of patron peppers."

"Didn't you get my text? I can't make it today."

"You're dumping me too?"

"Course not, but I've kind of got a date."

"You've kind of got a date? With whom?"

"I'd rather not say."

"Someone I know?"

"I'd rather not say."

Mo got up to leave.

"Okay, well, I hope you kind of have a good time."

"Mo, you should be happy for me."

"I am, it's just...I don't know."

"Mo, this has nothing to do with us. Next Friday for sure. Tapas on me."

"Sure. Great. Have fun."

"Really?"

"Yeah."

On his way home, Mo stopped to buy tortillas, beans, and salsa. As he walked the aisles, he paused in front of the beer.

"A lot more choice than when I last had one." When Mo made the high school varsity baseball team, he wanted to fit in and went to some of their parties. It didn't take long before he was drinking a large quantity of beer. He liked drinking, and his friends told him that he was "totally outrageous" after a sixer. One night he came home and barfed on the front steps. Because his mother watched her father drink himself to death, she never touched alcohol. Though Mo was only a quarter Native American, she believed he had inherited the Indian alcohol curse. His mother enlisted an older cousin to party with Mo. The two of them shared a pint of Southern Comfort. The cousin only pretended to drink, so Mo drank the entire bottle. His mother's cure was to get Mo so sick that he would forever abstain. For at least a year, the taste or smell of alcohol made him want to retch, and he decided that along with the nausea, alcohol was not conducive to sports and that was it. The cure worked. He never had the desire to drink since.

Now was different. Sports was a thing of the past. His marriage was over. He sucked as a teacher. Maria abandoned him. He needed something to get out of his slump. What harm could a beer do?

"Need help?" a clerk appeared at his side.

"There're too many choices."

"What do you like? Stout? A lager? Something bitter?"

"Bitter? Perfect. What's your bitterest?"

"This baby here. You'll love it."

The clerk put a 22-ounce Arrogant Bastard bottle in Mo's hand.

"That's kind of big."

The clerk nodded and pointed to a six-pack of 12-ounce beer. "That's a good one too."

Mo bought the sixer and opened a bottle as he sat down to his quesadilla. He poured it into a glass and considered. What was the big deal? It was just a beer. He raised the glass, tilted it back, and the sweet bitterness made its way down. He felt better and considered a second, but he was disciplined. One was enough.

Chapter 6

NOT ANOTHER MULTIPLE choice!" Poonam whined as Mr. Samson passed out the day's assignment.

"You're the one taking the class for the AP credit, so that's what we're doing, training for the test."

"But it's only October. Five more months of this?"

"Try seven," said Hudson.

"Have some pity on us," Violet said.

"We could do some practice timed writing if you prefer. The writing in this class is terrible. Do you whine to your coaches when they give you drills?"

"At least sports are fun," Poonam said.

There was way too much complaining as far as Mr. Samson was concerned. They had taken it upon themselves to do a course of college rigor. They were unmotivated and not terribly gifted.

"My job is not to entertain. Not everything in life is fun. If you learn that, you can thank me."

"Thank you," Hudson said. "A hundred times thank you."

Mr. Samson returned to his desk, so the students sighed and began on the poem and its questions. He sighed as well, but the best way to prepare for the test was for students to learn how to read indecipherable poems followed by nitpicking questions.

"A Valediction Forbidding Mourning"
By John Donne (1611)

As virtuous men pass mildly away,
And whisper to their souls to go,
Whilst some of their sad friends do say,
The breath goes now, and some say, No:

So let us melt, and make no noise,
No tear-floods, nor sigh-tempests move;
'Twere profanation of our joys
To tell the laity our love

Moving of th' earth brings harms and fears,
Men reckon what it did, and meant;
But trepidation of the spheres,
Though greater far, is innocent...

1. The line "virtuous men pass mildly away" means
    a. Good men die
    b. Don't fight against the end of life
    c. Suffering is part of nobility
    d. How lovers should part
2. "tear-floods" is an:
    a. Oxymoron
    b. Hyperbole
    c. Allusion
    d. Alliteration

49

3. A motif in the third stanza is:
   a. The heavens
   b. Fearful men
   c. The innocence of love
   d. All of the above
4. The word "trepidation" means...

This poem was not going to engender love of poetry, but it was exactly what the AP test would offer. Mr. Samson circulated through the classroom, and with a perverse glee, he pointed out tear-floods of wrong answers.

When students weren't reading metaphysical poems, they were writing essays or reading James Joyce's *A Portrait of the Artist as a Young Man*. Even though many critics called this novel one of the top five of the 20th century, the students hated it and had given up trying to understand it. Since Mr. Samson had to explain everything, the steel pail was quickly filling with marbles.

Principal King had stopped by his classroom and put a note in his box applauding his, "teaching difficult texts with proper scaffolding, just as the Common Core requires." A week later his classes fared better than all the others on a surprise practice multiple-choice test that The Hammer sprang on the English department. The Hammer herself called him out at the next staff meeting as "Teacher of the Month" and presented him with a certificate. Luckily, he had chewed three Altoids to mask the bourbon he drank following the last period of the day. When he brought the bottle to work a week before, he vowed it would last a month. Since it was half empty, he would need to stop washing down his peanut butter and jelly with a double shot.

"Okay, any one not finished?" The students looked glassy-eyed. "Good. Number 1. Who's got an answer? Hudson?"

"D."

"Good. Number 2, Javier?"

"Uh, C?"

"Sorry. Dell?"

"I got B."

"How many of you got B? Let's see hands."

About a third of the class raised their hands.

"B's right. Javier, do you see why it's B?"

"Uh, sort of."

"Want me to explain?"

"I'm good."

And so it went.

At the end of the questions, Mr. Samson said, "If you're getting less than 70%, you might consider extra practice at home. Let's turn to *A Portrait of the Artist as a Young Man.* Take out your study guides."

The students moved in slow motion as they took out their work. Real time was reestablished when they violently slammed the novel onto their desks. Mr. Samson knew that they didn't need to read *Portrait* to do well on the AP test, but the disgust he felt toward himself should be shared. Suffer the little children.

"Noah?"

"On the first day of class, you said you rarely did study guides."

"This is a hard book; they're just to help you. Poonam?"

"This book doesn't make any sense. Just give us the test, so we can fail and get on to something better," and she muttered loud enough for the class to hear, "if that's possible."

Mr. Samson ignored the comment. "This is a college-level text. I don't see what the problem is. You have a study guide and a teacher to help you. If it was easy, you wouldn't need a class. That's why we don't read *Harry Potter* or *The Hunger Games.*"

"At least those are good," Poonam persisted.

"Poonam, please answer the first question on the study guide."

At the end of class, Dell approached Mr. Samson's desk.

"Mr. Samson?"

"Yes?"

"I was talking to my cousin Sarah Lipshutz; she had you a few years ago. And—well—I told her about class, and she told me it was really different. And I was kind of wondering why?"

Dell's eyes were sympathetic, not disdainful. He owed her more than a bullshit reply, but she was a student, so he couldn't be completely forthcoming.

"Dell, we live in an age where schools and teachers are evaluated on test scores. The most effective way to raise scores is to teach what's going to be on the test and practice test questions. I'm sorry."

"But if you taught us how you taught Sarah's class, I know we'd do well on the tests."

"Unfortunately, my students' scores haven't done well teaching like that."

Mr. Samson had to look away.

"Is that why you're so sad?"

Though her question obviously came from a place of empathy, Mo recoiled as if he had been slapped in the face. He could come up with nothing to say to a true insight except for a banal, "We all carry some sadness."

"Sure. Have a better day, Mr. Samson."

Married to his sadness was a self-loathing multiplied by alcohol. He knew it was destroying him, but he didn't care; he welcomed it. He deserved it.

As for Dell, Mr. Samson would transfer her to a better teacher second semester.

English 12 students were equally unmotivated by Mr. Samson's curriculum, but after weeks of worksheets and drills, some finally knew the difference between passive and active verbs, most could explain the difference between *its* and *it's,* and Cooper now capitalized the word *I*.

He escorted them to the library to get reading books. Sustained, silent reading (SSR) was predicated on the idea that allowing students to read books of their own choice was more likely to turn them into readers than Chaucer or Joyce. Mr. Samson would have bet his paycheck that it was more likely for a team to rally from a 12-0 deficit in the bottom of the 9th than it was for an English 12 vidiot to be turned into a reader, but he welcomed SSR because it allowed him a break from the curriculum that was killing him.

Upon entering the library, the students went straight to the computers to check Instagram and watch YouTube videos. When Mr. Samson approached, they scattered. Mt. Samson walked around the library refocusing those who found comfy chairs to nap in. He discovered a group of boys in a study room with their smart phones out.

"Put those away," Mr. Samson commanded. They slowly complied. "You need to get books."

DeSean said, "I've got one at home."

"Yeah? What's it called?"

"I don't know. It's like a Harry Potter book."

"Is it a Harry Potter book?"

"Isn't that what I just said?"

"Bring it next class, or you'll get a detention."

"That's kind of harsh, don't you think?"

"What about you?" He turned to Ryan Dowling, the six-foot, three-inch school jock. Ryan was the baseball and football MVP of the North Valley Region. He played quarterback and centerfield. Ryan had a calmness and maturity that other students looked up to. Ryan was one of the more polite students, but there were stories of him binge drinking at weekend parties. Mr. Samson wondered if anyone suspected that he himself was binge drinking every day.

Ryan said, "I've got one at home too."

"What's its name?"

Ryan smiled, got up, and started perusing the aisles. DeSean joined him. Mr. Samson moved to Cooper who had his phone back out.

"Go get a book."

Cooper slipped his phone under a magazine as if Mr. Samson was a two-year old and hadn't reached the developmental stage of object permanence.

"Books are boring."

"They're boring," Mr. Samson repeated. That summed up this generation. Reading was boring. Nature was boring. They couldn't exist without first-person shooter video games. "You know, Cooper, when you read, you learn about ideas that go beyond the obvious, beyond what you and your friends talk about. If you don't read, you're saying, 'At 17-years-old, I pretty much know everything I need to know.'"

"I learn lots of stuff online."

"It's not the same. It's the difference between grabbing a burger at McDonalds versus going to a five-star restaurant where the chef buys at the local farmers' market, spends hours marinating the meat, and barbeques it, so it melts in your mouth—the perfect steak. Care goes into books. People online write down the first thing that comes to their minds. There's no craft, no reflection."

Cooper said, "I like Big Macs."

Mr. Samson took Cooper's phone. "You get this back when you show me the book you checked out." Cooper got up and Mr. Samson continued patrolling. DeSean and Ryan were now gabbing on a couch in the magazine section. He didn't have the energy to herd them toward the shelves. He walked into an aisle and found Esther with a book. She looked up and said, "Can you help me find something good?"

"What do you have?"

She held up *100 Years of Solitude* by Gabriel Garcia Marquez.

"That's a classic. The author won the Nobel Prize."

"The first page is too weird."

"Sometimes you've got to give a book time."

"Can you recommend something else?"

Mr. Samson perused the M section and found Melville's *Moby Dick*, Mitchell's *Gone With the Wind*, and Morrison's *Beloved*. He put them in her hands and then took *Moby Dick* back. As he returned it to the shelf, another book caught his eye.

"What?" Esther asked.

"What?" Mr. Samson replied.

"You stared at a book. That's the one I want. Is it this?" She pulled out Joyce Carol Oates *The Gravedigger's Daughter*.

Mr. Samson shook his head. "It was nothing." He started down the aisle.

"You don't even have to take it off the shelf. Just point at it."

Mr. Samson turned to face Esther; she was practically the only student involved in class. She was brighter than most Tier Ones. And she was pleasing to look at which of course didn't matter at all. He tapped the spine of Nabokov's *Lolita*. Esther took it from the shelf. It had the picture of an adolescent girl in a bikini on the cover.

"What's it about?"

"Illicit love."

"What's illicit?"

"If I have to explain that, you won't understand the book. It has an advanced vocabulary and lots of French."

"I took French 2." Esther opened the book and read aloud: *Lolita, light of my life, fire of my loins. My sin, my soul. Lo-lee-ta: the tip of the tongue taking a trip of three steps down the palate to tap, at three, on the teeth. Lo. Lee. Ta.*

"Doesn't sound hard."

Cooper came back with a copy of *Holes,* a book for sixth graders. He put out his hand for his phone.

"You never read *Holes*?"

"I read it like five times. I always read it. It's a good book."

Mr. Samson gave Cooper his phone. Lolita was gone.

The bell rang. "This won't end well," and he followed the students out of the library.

Chapter 7

MO DRANK THREE 22-ounce bottles of Arrogant Bastard Ale the night before, so the morning alarm was unduly harsh. There were no clean shirts in his closet; he hadn't done laundry in two weeks. He picked up a couple shirts from the floor, smelled them, and decided on the least offensive. A shower made him feel better though the three-day facial stubble advertised homeless person. Maybe a sharp blade wouldn't be such a good idea this morning; he'd shave the next day, just as he told himself the day before. And then…disaster! He had forgotten to buy coffee. Alcohol might have made his days tolerable, but it was caffeine that got him to work. He stumbled out the door with the back half of his shirt hanging over his belt and drove to the coffee shop.

"The pail's filling fast," he muttered to himself as he stood in line. "When it's full, I'll get a motorcycle and drive off a cliff."

Mo was at the counter and pulled his wallet out of his back pocket with so little coordination that it fell to the floor behind him. He turned to pick it up and there was Dell Westergard standing two people behind him. Mr. Samson was mortified. Had she heard his suicidal mumble? Did she realize he was hung-over? Did she avoid saying hello because she was embarrassed to be seen with him? Did she despise him for being the world's worst teacher?

He fabricated chipperness. "Oh hi, Dell. I guess that wasn't very coordinated."

Dell gave a small smile. She knew. At least Mr. Samson's alcoholic grandfather was beloved by his community. Mr. Samson was simply a loser. The motorcycle idea was too romantic for him. A gun would be better. Quicker, more efficient, more appropriate.

He turned to the front, ordered, and waited for his double cappuccino. A moment later, Dell stood nearby waiting for her drink. He couldn't stand there and pretend he didn't know her. He was the adult. It was on him to say something. He just needed to kill a minute and he'd be free. He'd have his coffee and be straight and get to school and teach something well, and he wouldn't drink. He would not touch the bottle all day. For real. He could do it.

Dell rustled through her backpack probably to avoid having to interact with her pathetic teacher. Mr. Sampson would say something honest. She would appreciate that.

"Dell," he started. She looked up. "I'm afraid you've caught me a bit...uh...discombobulated, and..."

"It's okay, Mr. Samson."

"I, well, I didn't sleep too good...I mean...well. I didn't sleep well..."

"It's okay, Mr. Samson. I have something for you. Here."

Dell handed Mr. Samson a sheet of typed paper she slipped out of a folder. "I've been meaning to turn this in. Awhile back you asked us to write something true. This is it."

Mr. Samson took the sheet; his coffee was ready. "I look forward to reading it. See you in class." He got into his car, placed the coffee in the cup-holder, belted up, turned the ignition key, put his arm atop the passenger seat, and started to swivel his head to check for traffic behind. He glanced down at what Dell gave him as he swiveled; the title arrested his movement, and he cut the engine in order to read, "The English Teacher."

Sarah told me about the English Teacher

Who recited poems, played games, taught thinking
And helped kids navigate life's difficult paths.
I counted the days until I'd sit in his class.

Winnie-the-Pooh once said that the honey
Is always sweetest before the first bite.
For a teddy bear filled only with fluff
He had wisdom; he had the smart stuff.

Some honey can be bitter as the cud.
The English Teacher is hurting something bad.
Maybe his boulder is too hard to bear,
For he makes out like he doesn't care;

To waste the gifts given to one freely
Is a life one can't live with easily.

Mo tried to take up his coffee, but his hand shook the hot liquid
through the opening, and he returned it to the holder. Then the tears
came, and he put his hands atop the steering wheel, so he could sob
against them. Mo Samson had doused his inner fire with bucket upon
bucket of water and then clubbed the smoldering wood with a
baseball bat. He would see his spirit dead but for a 17-year-old kid
yanking the bat from his hands; she took the barely glowing ember,
gently placed a piece of kindling, and softly blew on the nascent
flame.

A car alarm aroused him, and Mo wiped his eyes, found a napkin
under the passenger seat, blew his nose, and headed to school.

A light, warm breeze surprised the late October day. Wisps of
cirrus clouds drifted across the heavens. A red-tail hawk rode the
updrafts high above the school. At the top of a large oak tree, a

59

mockingbird sang. And there was Mr. Samson crammed into a stuffy classroom with 34 students jammed in columns and rows, toe to heel, elbow to elbow. Lately, he kept the blinds down because even a robin flitting from one tree to another had the capacity to take students off the task at hand which the day before was analyzing a passage from "Nature," Ralph Waldo Emerson's love letter to the natural world. The plan for this day was to read "Song of Myself #52" by Walt Whitman, answer some analysis questions, compare it to "Nature" in a Venn diagram, and do a compare/contrast timed essay. Not the most inspired lesson.

Mr. Samson tucked the pile of poems under his arm and raised the blinds. "Many great thinkers believed that knowledge comes from contemplating the natural world. Moses, Mohammed, and Buddha all reached enlightenment in the outdoors by a burning bush, in a cave, and under a tree, never enclosed in a room. Jesus took a month long wilderness adventure before starting his ministry. Einstein is reputed to have had his ah-ha moment regarding relativity by watching the waves at the beach. So why don't we take students outside more?"

Mr. Samson didn't wait for an answer. "Because students become unfocused, and standardized tests don't measure the ability to contemplate the beauty of a flower."

Violet raised her hand, "I vote we go outside and contemplate flowers." She left her hand in the air. "Who's with me?"

En masse 34 students raised hands.

"Sorry, we have a poem to read and an essay to write. This is AP literature not nature awareness."

The students looked disgusted; why did he mention the outdoors if they were going to do the same stupid shit? But for the first time in a long while, Mr. Samson grinned and walked out the door. He ducked his head back in. "C'mon." The students followed and made a circle on the quad's lawn. Mr. Samson picked a dandelion, stared intently at it and blew. The students watched the seeds helicopter away. After they dissipated, Mr. Samson said, "This is the final poem in Walt Whitman's collection he titled, 'Song of Myself.'" He closed his eyes which was the sign that he was about to recite, something he hadn't done in ages. For this one he left eyes shut.

The spotted hawk swoops by and accuses me, he complains of my gab and my loitering.

I too am not a bit tamed, I too am untranslatable,
I sound my barbaric yawp over the roofs of the world.

The last scud of day holds back for me,
It flings my likeness after the rest and true as any on the shadow'd wilds,
It coaxes me to the vapor and the dusk.

I depart as air, I shake my white locks at the runaway sun,
I effuse my flesh in eddies, and drift it in lacy jags.

I bequeath myself to the dirt to grow from the grass I love,
If you want me again look for me under your boot-soles.

You will hardly know who I am or what I mean,
But I shall be good health to you nevertheless,
And filter and fibre your blood.

Failing to fetch me at first keep encouraged,
Missing me one place search another,
I stop somewhere waiting for you.

When Mr. Samson opened his eyes, he was greeted by smiling students. His eyes lingered for a two-second eternity on Dell. He could have kissed her. "Okay. Reread the poem with a partner and try to figure out what the poet is trying to say." After a pause. "Don't worry, you won't be writing an essay or filling out a study guide."

Seemingly on cue, the mockingbird in the oak began to cycle through its song repertoire. The bird sang and the students studied. Mr. Samson wanted to unleash a barbaric yawp. This was why he became a teacher.

"Time's up. Who can enlighten us?"

No one spoke, but rather than anger, tell them the answer he was looking for, and toss a marble into the pail, Mr. Samson said, "This is the last poem in the collection. He's writing it at the end of a day. The word 'day' might symbolize something else."

In a quiet voice that belied her morbidly obese body, Lupita Alvarez volunteered a response for the first time all year. "Maybe the end of day means the end of life. My abuelo died last month, so I've been thinking a lot about him. Maybe the poem's saying that when someone we love dies, he doesn't disappear. He's with us when we look for him, when we need him." Lupita looked up at the mockingbird. "He loved mockingbirds. He liked to play duets with them by blowing on blades of grass."

The mockingbird began a new song and all eyes riveted on the small, non-descript grey and white bird. After two songs, Lupita addressed the bird. "Abuelito, I know you're with me."

Mr. Samson beat down a choke in his throat that threatened to overwhelm him and said, "The thing about this poem is that it begins by contemplating nature and then ends with a statement about human existence. Your homework is to choose a place in nature where you can comfortably sit for 15 minutes. Contemplate the area around you. You can take in the entire view, or you can focus on one individual item, like a flower. Pay attention to what's going on inside of you as well. After 15 minutes, write a poem."

"Does it have to rhyme?"

"Does Whitman's?"

A maintenance worker on a tractor lawnmower started in on the lawn, the mockingbird flew off, and the class retreated back to the classroom.

Mr. Samson marched to the metal file cabinet, opened it, and brought out a box of safety matches along with a second one-quart steel pail; this one was filled almost to the brim with sand. He placed it on the small table at the front of the classroom where the first steel pail sat, half filled with marbles.

"Lupita, would you please come up here and light a match? It represents the fire you lit in all of us today."

Lupita hesitated, but Mr. Samson held the proffered match. He wasn't going to let this moment slip away. She shyly came to the front, took the match and box, looked at Mr. Samson, and then at her peers who viewed her with a respect Mr. Samson had not seen her given all year, perhaps her entire life. The scratching match sparked into a tiny flame. She held it aloft like the Olympic torch. It was a religious moment.

"When you're ready, put the match out in the sand."

Mr. Samson held the bucket of sand. Lupita watched the match burn down and then slowly snuffed it out, leaving a half-inch of match-wood sticking out of the sand.

At the end of class, Dell was the last to leave.

"That was a great class, Mr. Samson!" Her face glowed. Mr. Samson lit a match.

"This one's for you."

Chapter 8

THREE LOUD BLOWS threatened to knock the bedroom door down.

"Blake, you gonna be late if you don't get your lazy-ass outta bed!"

"Go away!" he yelled to his stepmother.

"I gotta go! You gotta get Ashley's breakfast!"

She opened the door and turned on the lights. "Let's go, Blake."

Blake bolted up in bed, a sheet wrapped around his body. "How about some privacy?"

"Right," she guffawed. "You want Burger King or KFC tonight?"

"Here's an idea: real food."

His stepmother ignored his comment. As she stepped out of the room, she turned back, "Your father's coming home in two weeks. It'd be nice if you call him."

"It'd be nice if he stopped being an asshole drunk and getting locked up for punching a bartender."

She charged back into the room and raised her hand above his face.

"Don't talk like that about your father!"

"Don't you gotta get to work?"

She left the bedroom door open and stormed out the front door.

Blake savored the day's one quiet moment and surveyed his room. A half-filled case of Red Bulls sat on the dresser along with his cell phone, wallet, and keys; its open drawers leaked shirts and socks. A 42-inch flatscreen was bolted to the wall; the blue screen on; the diodes on its bottom left corner out. On the floor was a smattering of video games, three game controllers, and dirty and clean laundry in a ground-covering amalgam of blue, orange, gray, and black shirts, shorts, underwear, and socks along with one Philadelphia Eagles' jersey. A poster of actress Megan Fox astride a motorcycle was tacked above the bed. A torn poster of former Eagles quarterback Michael Vick was on the door. Two cases of Bud were stacked in the closet.

Blake picked up a shirt, smelled it, and slung it over his arm. He went to the dresser, removed a pair of underwear, grabbed a pair of pants hanging over the chair, and took a shower. With shampoo in his hair, the hot water ended.

"Fucking bitch!"

Blake quickly rinsed, toweled off, put on his clothes, and knocked on his half-sister's door.

"Ashley, get up!"

"I know. Mom woke me before she left."

"Well, come on."

Blake wanted eggs but there were only two in the fridge. He cursed his step-mother again and scrambled them for Ashley. He threw two pieces of bread into the toaster and poured Ashley a glass of milk. He went to his room and brought out a Red Bull. Ashley was picking at her eggs.

"Eat your eggs."

"I'm not hungry," and Ashley pushed the plate away.

Blake pushed it back.

"Eat 'em."

"No."

Had this been anyone else, Blake would have picked up the plate and thrown the eggs, along with the plate, into the trash.

"You want to be like me and mess up your life? You're smart and do good in school. Eat your eggs. When you get a big job, you can bail me out of jail."

"You're not going to jail, right?" Ashley asked.

"Course not. But you got to eat your eggs." She picked up her fork. Blake buttered the two pieces of toast. He gave one to Ashley and ate the other between swigs of Red Bull. Ashley finished and put her plate and glass in the sink to join the dishes from the previous night.

"Brush your teeth and let's go."

Blake pulled his truck into the student lot and gunned it at Cooper who sidestepped the vehicle and gave it a whack on the driver's door.

"Whaz up, fool?" Cooper greeted Blake when he stepped out of the truck.

"Your mother was good last night."

"Your stepmother did the football team," Cooper came back.

Blake laughed. "I don't know who I'd feel sorrier for. That bitch used up all the hot water in the shower. My nuts shrank to raisins."

"Grew to raisins."

"Let's go. You don't need another detention."

"You don't need another detention."

Cooper and Blake slid into the classroom as the bell rang. Blake sank into his seat just in time for Samson to begin his daily rant, "Q, put your phone away. Chloe, put your chips away! I'm serious! Q, last warning on phone! Take out your journals!"

Blake knew Samson had a shitty job babysitting a class of teens who didn't give a shit about English. It was Blake's job to teach this to the teacher. Given how Samson was becoming more of a prick every day, Blake's job was just about done. Soon there'd be a long-term sub greeting the class with, *"Mr. Samson? He's been institutionalized."*

"DeSean, sit down!"

"Samson, chill, I'm blowing my nose. You burn something in here?"

"Let's go! Journals out! That means writing utensils too!"

"Samson, you ain't got no more tissues," DeSean said. "Can I go to the office?"

"Can't you wait?"

"I got allergies. I think I'm allergic to English."

Some people chuckled, but Blake could not let DeSean challenge him for class clown.

Blake stood up and rubbed his butt. "Can I go to the office too? English gives me hemorrhoids."

"Boys!"

DeSean said, "Serious, Samson, I need tissues. Can I go?"

"Okay, go. Everyone else, eyes up here."

Blake watched about a quarter of the class text. His phone vibrated twice.

"Chloe, I'm going to confiscate your chips." Samson said.

"They're not chips." Chloe held up a bag. "They're Hot Cheetos. Want one?"

"No and put them away."

i want some of C's Hot Cheetos, Blake texted Cooper.

i'll tell L. he'll beat your ass.

i'll beat your ass.

"Blake, take out a pencil."

"I'm out. Got any extra?" he asked with his hand grasping a pencil in his backpack.

"In the cabinet. Top left. Okay, you have five minutes to write on this: Describe a time in which you were jealous of someone. How did you respond? Okay? Any questions?"

"Yeah, I don't get it," Cooper said as Blake walked toward the cabinet.

Blake stopped midstride and loudly proclaimed, "I told you he was a dope!"

"Outside!" Samson commanded.

"I'm jealous of Cooper's intellect," Blake said as he opened the door just as DeSean entered with two towers of tissues, five boxes per tower. Blake faked like he was going to tackle DeSean; the twin towers crumbled onto the floor. The class erupted.

Blake stood outside and could hear muffled sounds before all was quiet. Samson opened the door.

"Why are you so disruptive?"

"I'm sorry. Can I come back in?"

"You're like this all the time. This can't continue."

"I'm sorry. For real. Can I come back in? I want to write."

"You've got to control yourself. And what's up between you and Cooper?"

"We just mess around."

"If you don't mess around, you're welcome back in. One more outburst, and it's the office."

Blake saluted and returned to class. Everyone was writing except Chloe who sat next to Blake. Samson walked up to Chloe and whispered,

"What's the problem?"

"I can't think of anything to write."

"You've never been jealous of one of your friends?"

"I can't think of anything."

"Why don't you write about how you think you'd feel if you were jealous."

68

"That's kinda stupid."

Blake put down his pencil to applaud, but Samson shot him the evil eye, so he started to write how he was jealous of people who had families that didn't scream at each other and didn't have dads who couldn't keep jobs because they were violent, alcoholic, drug-addicted assholes who were usually in jail.

Samson called out, "One more minute!"

Blake wrote furiously.

"Time! Any volunteers?"

Esther raised her hand. Even though Blake wasn't partial to browns, there was no doubt that she was hot. He stared at her black, spaghetti-strap top paired with a brightly-colored, flowered short skirt and thought about how it would be to pollinate her.

"My sister is a registered nurse. I'm jealous that she's smarter than me and has her sh…life more together than mine."

"Has your jealously ever made you do anything mean to her?" Samson asked.

The girl gave a short snort. "When I was little, I stole my mom's jewelry box and hid it under her pillow, and I'm the one who got beat!"

The class laughed.

"Jealousy can make us do pretty silly things…" Samson began.

"Are you calling me silly, Mr. Samson?"

Samson's face went red. Blake texted Cooper: *S has Hot Cheetos 4 E.*

A few others read their journals, and then Samson said, "Anyone else?"

Blake looked around and started to raise his hand. Cooper grinned at him with the anticipation of a good joke coming, but Blake didn't want to tell a joke. He put his hand down. Samson asked, "Blake do you want to read something?"

Blake didn't look up from his journal. "I'm jealous of everyone who doesn't have an asshole dad. It'd be cool to have a dad who asked how was your day instead of 'get me a beer.'"

Blake felt everyone stare at him. He hated pity. "JK. My dad's A-1 awesome. The thing I'm really jealous of is Cooper's boxers. Are those little whales on them?"

"Ducks," replied Cooper. "Little yellow ducks."

The class cracked up, but attention quickly left Cooper and Blake to Samson. He lit a match, and said, "For the honesty a lot of you wrote about in your journals." He held up the burning match and then snuffed it out in a second steel pail. Blake was tempted to say something that would put Samson over the edge because Samson had clearly lost it. But Samson was staring at Blake, and he appeared sane for the first time in a long while. He lit a second match and addressed Blake. "This is for you, for taking a risk."

Even though it was totally stupid, the fire did something to Blake, something he couldn't explain, and then Samson put the match out in the pail.

As the smoke rose, Blake said, "Because I'm jealous of Cooper's boxers?"

"Because you're jealous of Cooper's boxers," Samson replied.

Chapter 9

BY WEEK'S END, there were many matches in the sand; the marbles hadn't moved.

"It's been forever," Maria said when she and Mo met at Tapas World.

"You've been blowing me off for your new boyfriend, Mr. Anonymous."

"You canceled the last three times, Mr. God-Does-My-Memory-Suck. Maybe you're the one with a new girlfriend."

Mo laughed. "To get a girlfriend, you have to date."

"Still obsessing about how you killed your marriage?"

"This week was a watershed."

"So you're ready?"

"Got any sisters?"

"Only brothers," she laughed. "How about online dating?"

"Are you kidding?"

"That's how it's done these days."

"I don't know. I'm not so graceful with the internet."

"Okay, new subject. You haven't been by my office in a month. Where've you been?"

Mo moved his gaze from Maria to the pull handles on the draft beer. He sighed. He did like those bitter IPAs.

"I've been kind of out of it."

Maria made a face. "According to Dewey, you've been the model teacher. And The Hammer gave you Teacher of the Month. How weird is that?"

"Weird because I totally sucked as a teacher until this week."

Ashondra was tending bar and brought out plates of Marcona almonds and Kalamata olives. She slid a pair of beer coasters in front of the two. "Ms. Mendoza? A glass of merlot?"

"How about a nice zin. And…" she looked at Mo, "what do you feel like eating?"

"Let's start with the empanada plate."

Ashondra brought Maria the wine then turned to the beer taps and pulled a pint which she placed in front of Mo.

"You're going to like this one, Mr. Samson. Double Dry Hopped IPA from Stone Brewery. It's awesome."

Maria's eyebrows arched. "I'm afraid there's a mistake."

Ashondra looked confused.

"For as long as I've known him, Mr. Samson has never touched alcohol."

"Mr. Samson?"

Mo watched the tiny carbon dioxide bubbles climb the glass to the top where the gravity defying foam took over and ever so slowly climbed a bit more above the rim. The beer was alive. A spirit. Mo brought the beer to his nose. Ashondra was right. The aroma was intense. He was reminded of Iago, *Othello*'s villain: *good wine is a good familiar creature, if it be well used.* Iago was right despite the fact that he used the familiar creature to destroy Cassio. Mo considered: I am my own Iago and nearly destroyed myself with the golden elixir in front of me.

Tapas World was empty save a man sat at the end of the bar.

"Ms. Mendoza is right. I'll have a root beer, but it would be a shame to waste this lovely beer. Please ask that gentleman if he'd like it."

Mo turned to Maria, "It was a hard month."

"You've been drinking?"

Mo was ashamed.

"Let's leave it a mystery. You've got one as well. Cheers."

Mo raised his root beer to his lips.

"Dewey."

"Dewey what?"

"Mr. Anonymous."

Luckily, Mo had not taken a sip, or he would have spewed root beer over himself and Maria.

"You are kidding me."

"Like I told you, it's nothing serious. It's just...you know. So...what about you?"

This was too much. Maria was banging their boss?

"Dewey?"

"This is exactly why I didn't tell you. You're so judgmental. He's a good guy." Maria did not look pleased.

"Okay, okay. Sorry." Mo took a sip from his root beer and gazed down the bar at the half-empty pint in front of the man who touched the brim of his baseball cap to Mo. Maria looked at him expectantly. She'd pump Ashondra for info anyway.

"I needed to fall into the abyss, you know, the hero's journey myth. Though I'm clearly no hero."

"Maybe a tragic hero."

"I was holding on to the abyss wall by a single, mossy, slippery stone. Alcohol pretended to be my pal, but in reality, it was stomping on my fingers. Just as I was about to let go, someone threw down a rope, and I climbed out."

Mo's audience doubled as Ashondra wiped a spot on the bar over and over in order to listen.

"You were drinking *here*?"

Both Ashondra and Mo looked abashed.

"And at home," Mo added. He didn't mention school. There were things even a good friend could not forgive.

"Who threw the rope?"

Mo glanced at Ashondra who quickly made her way down to the end of the bar to pick up the empty pint glass.

"It doesn't matter. What matters is I'm back. I'm a teacher again. And my first proclamation is, 'Screw the tests.'" Mo lifted his glass to Maria.

"Is that wise? If you focus on the Common Core, and your scores don't rise, at least you can argue you were a team player. If you don't, it's like you're giving them the finger."

Mo said, "Do you know that of the ten Common Core anchor reading standards, not one deals with enjoyment or appreciation of literature? Not one. It's all analyze this and analyze that. All of them."

"Once you get fired it won't matter what you think about the Common Core. Why won't you make modest changes so you can keep your job?"

Mo shrugged. "Someone has to take a stand."

"So that martyr thing's real."

"No. It's just that I'm guessing my test scores have just as much chance going up whichever way I teach. Anyway, I'd rather lose my job than my soul."

"Your soul?" Maria looked incredulous. "You don't even believe in a soul."

"Touché."

Mo had nothing more to say. Maria was angry but only because she cared about him. He tried imagining Dewey and Maria. It would never last. He wondered if there was a woman like Maria that he could be attracted to. That would be the woman for him. He daydreamed about a woman who looked like Katherine but had Maria's spirit when she said, "I hear you're recommending *Lolita* to female students."

74

Mo got hot in the face. How did Maria know? If The Hammer found out, he might earn himself a notice of unprofessional conduct. He wasn't a pervert or pedophile, but wherever Mo turned, he was doing something stupid regarding girls.

"I didn't recommend it."

"No?"

"She insisted I show it to her. And since when are you vetting books?"

"Esther was in my office; I noticed it."

"I told her the vocabulary would be too hard."

"I picked it up and couldn't get through the first page without a dictionary. I don't know who decides something's a classic, but I'll take John Green any day. I gave her my copy of *The Fault in our Stars*."

"So we're good?" Mo ventured.

"It wasn't Esther who threw the rope?"

"Esther? No."

Maria relaxed. "We're good."

Chapter 10

MR. SAMSON SIPPED orange juice as he drove past the coffee shop. Satisfying teaching was enough of a morning jolt to get him to work. He practically sprang through the empty pre-school corridors, and he considered joining an adult baseball league ending his decade-long antipathy toward the game. In the classroom, Green Day was cranked as he danced to the white board and wrote the day's agendas. He wasn't embarrassed when the first students entered, but he turned the speakers down.

AP Lit was about to start Kate Chopin's *The Awakening,* a late 19th century novella critiquing the state of women in America. For her trouble, Chopin was castigated and the public reaction to the future classic probably drove her to an early grave and possibly accelerated women's rights. If anyone doubted the power of literature, here was the answer. It also inoculated him from any undercurrent that he was anti-woman based on the Facebook faux pas.

Before opening page one, he wanted the class to understand the genesis of the western view of women, so he brought out excerpts of Genesis.

"Anyone heard of a sacred cow?' Mr. Samson asked. His new found enthusiasm had been mirrored back by the students. His questions were no longer treated as rhetorical.

Hudson answered, "It has something to do with India. They're all vegetarians; eating a Whopper is like a capital crime."

"They only chop off a hand," Mr. Samson corrected. Olivia, Hudson's girlfriend, turned pale. "Kidding," Mr. Samson grinned, "but Hudson is right. Cows are sacred in Hinduism which gave rise to the term: *sacred cow* which is an idea that a people in a society will not question. Who can give an example?"

Violet said, "In America it's a sacred cow to not eat dog. It's okay to eat cows and pigs and chicken, but dog meat is supposed to be gross or something. Like eating a cow isn't totally disgusting."

"Are you a vegetarian?" Mr. Samson asked.

"Vegetarians are weak sauce; I'm vegan!" Violet lifted her coffee mug that was printed with: *Love Animals, Don't Eat Them.*

Mr. Samson said, "How about sacred cows not related to food?"

"America is the best country in the world." Noah said.

"We are the best country," Poonam said.

"Then how come we have more gun murders than anywhere else?"

Poonam turned to face Noah. "If you don't like America, then why don't you go back to China?"

"I was born in Sacramento, and I'm Vietnamese. Not all Asians are Chinese."

"Yeah, duh, I'm Asian too in case you haven't noticed."

Mr. Samson positioned himself between Poonam and Noah. He said, "Here's a sacred cow for about 50% of America. The Bible is the Word of God. Half of us think God wrote or inspired the Bible. They don't question its validity making it a sacred cow. Many of those who don't think the Bible is the Word of God have a related sacred cow. They believe the Bible is the root of the world's problems."

"It's true," Noah said.

"You are totally ignorant," Poonam replied.

77

Mr. Samson cut them off. "Whether or not you think the Bible is one kind of sacred cow or another, you need to know what's in it because you can't be literate without knowing its stories."

Mr. Samson passed the first chapters of Genesis.

Noah said, "You can't teach religion in a public school."

"I can teach the Bible as literature, but I can't preach it as religion," Mr. Samson amended. "I want to understand gender roles. The Bible lays these roles out."

The class read Genesis One where God creates Adam and Eve at the same time on the sixth day after creating all other life. Then the class turned to Genesis Two where God creates them a second time: Adam first, then the animals, and finally God fashions Eve from one of Adam's ribs.

Though it wasn't germane to gender roles, Mr. Samson took the discussion into a different direction.

"If God created humans and the animals in Genesis One, why create them again in Genesis Two?"

Noah said, "It's because the Bible comes from different sources. It's called the Documentary Hypothesis."

Olivia said, "I think it's the same story just told differently for God to teach different lessons. It's like the two blind men and the elephant. One feels the trunk and says it's a snake, the other one feels the leg and says it's a tree. It's the same with the Bible."

Dell lifted her head from the text and said, "Did anyone else notice that God is called God in the first story but Lord God in the second story? That could support the different sources idea."

"Okay," said Mr. Samson. "Suppose that question is going to be on the SBAC. Which of the three answers is right?" Mr. Samson answered himself. "It turns out that Noah's Documentary Hypothesis answer is correct because it's the theory accepted by biblical scholars. Congratulations, Noah, you remembered and regurgitated a fact that was poured into your pail."

Mr. Samson took a marble and tossed it into the steel pail. Noah did not look pleased. Mr. Samson turned to Olivia.

"Olivia, don't despair. You didn't know about the Documentary Hypothesis or maybe you just don't agree with it. The thing about your answer is that it shows critical thought by putting the two Creation stories in a framework you know about, that different points of view can make the same story appear different. You didn't get the 'right' answer, but you exercised critical thought; your fire was clearly lit. Would you like to light a match?"

Olivia shook her head, so Mr. Samson did it for her, watched it burn for a moment and put it out in the sand.

"Next we come to Dell who analyzed the text and discovered on her own what the biblical scholars of the 19th century discovered, namely the vocabulary of different biblical stories was different indicating that they came from different sources. Well done, Dell, you figured out the Documentary Hypothesis. The only problem is that the SBAC with its multiple choice and short answer questions read by a computer might have a hard time recognizing an 'ah-ha!' insight."

"Would you like to light a match?"

Dell came to the front, took the match, and lit it.

She held the match arm's length out to Mr. Samson. "Do you think you could put this out with your ponytail or would your hair burn?"

"A challenge," he said. "I'll probably strike out."

Mr. Samson measured the distance by taking the end of his ponytail in his hand and holding it tantalizingly close to the flame. Dell held the match at the end to give the flame more time. Mr. Samson threw his ponytail as he swung his body around. The ponytail went well below Dell's hand, and Hudson yelled, "Strike one!" Mr. Samson made exaggerated adjustments to his feet, bent his knees, and tried a second time. The ponytail hit the match and sent it flying out of Dell's hand extinguishing the fire and bringing applause from the students. Dell retrieved the match. The burnt end had disappeared; Dell held the stub in her hand.

Mr. Samson held out the pail for her. She put in the match, and as she removed her hand, it grazed Mr. Samson's hand holding the pail. He felt the touch travel up his arm, up his neck, to his face. Dell smiled and returned to her seat.

Violet said, "Samson, can we get back to women and gender roles? The point of the second Creation story is that women are second class people. And that's weak sauce because a woman can do anything a man can."

Olivia said, "My pastor said a man and a woman are two parts of the same soul. They complete each other. That's what marriage is."

Dell said, "The idea that a man needs a woman and vice-versa sounds so natural and right. Our bodies are meant to fit into each other, right? But it's not always like that. Look at homosexuality or look at great men or women who don't need to be "completed." Like Leonardo Da Vinci or even Jesus."

Mr. Samson liked the Jesus comment because even though it was said innocently, it forced the religious among the class to stop and consider Jesus differently. He also liked that beyond her obvious intellectual gifts there was a bit of play and revolution in Dell. On the other hand, the hand touch was not good at all.

In anticipation of the bell, the students began to pack up their belongings.

"What are you going to do with those pails?" Noah asked. Most students stopped. What was Samson going to do with his weirdness?

"The marbles will be recycled and used again. That's what happens with most information you learn in school. The teacher fills your pail with stuff you can use for *Jeopardy* and impressing people at parties, but not so much else. On the other hand, the matches, the sparks of insight, well, one of you can come up with an insightful thing to do with them."

Noah nodded.

"Anyone who has an idea just needs to submit it in triplicate with a ten-dollar bill attached for consideration."

"Ha, ha," Violet said. "You're a riot."

The bell rang. Dell approached Mr. Samson's desk.

"That was fun."

"It was," Mr. Samson agreed. He was guarded but masked it with, "How did you come up with putting out the match with my hair?"

"A spark of insight."

"Touché."

"Have you ever considered the rib story comes from the floating rib?"

"Floating rib?"

"You know, your lower ribs aren't attached to the sternum. There are people who are missing one of these floating ribs. Maybe someone saw a male skeleton back then that was missing a rib and came up with the story."

"I've never heard that before." Mr. Samson grinned. "You could be a biblical scholar."

"Religion's not for me. But I do have a favor to ask. Would you be able to read my personal essay for college?"

"My pleasure."

Dell slipped a folder out of her backpack, put it on his desk, and walked out. Mr. Samson opened his desk drawer to replenish his stapler and found the bottle of bourbon that he forgot he had. He picked the bottle up, stuffed it into his briefcase, and thought about the abyss Dell had pulled him out of. He'd do what he could to help Dell get into an elite college.

And it was time to sign up for online dating.

81

Chapter 11

NEITHER COOPER NOR Q had a first period class, so they often met next to a field on the northern edge of town. On the edge of the field stood the remaining oak that Dos Robles was named after. To a certain crowd, it was known as Match Tree; thousands of used matches littered the ground under the canopy.

Cooper kept his pipe, weed, Visine, and Altoids in a Simon and Garfunkel, 3-CD, Greatest Hits collection that he had emptied of CDs and plastic inserts. He packed the one-hit pipe and handed it to Q. Q drew smoke, held it, and exhaled.

"Smooth. Notes of lemon and skunk."

Cooper laughed. "What kind of shit is Chief Freak going to start today?"

"Couldn't be worse than that Canterbury crap."

"That was funny when you read in class."

Q laughed. "And when Samson kicked Blake out for yelling you had AIDS."

"That's because I do!" Both boys laughed harder.

"Can you imagine doing school straight?" Q was already blazed. "Another hit and I'll sneak behind Samson and cut off his fag ponytail."

"Dude, that would be awesome! You should totally do it! Here!"

Cooper offered the pipe, but Q waved him off. Cooper shrugged. "Can't let it go to waste," and took a hit. The boys applied the Visine and Altoids treatment and went to school. Cooper was near the bottom of the senior class, but as long as he passed government and English, he'd graduate. That was enough. His mom was always on his case to do better in school, but why bother? His dad worked construction in North Dakota and made a shit-ton of money. He'd get Cooper a job. His mom warned that his dad was a liar, but she was just sore because he left her. Cooper didn't blame him because his mom was totally insane, especially after his grandpa died. Her meds didn't help. He tried them; they didn't do nothing but give him a raging headache.

The boys stumbled into English. Cooper survived the world's lamest class because of Blake, Q, and his other pals. When Blake was on, the class was better than Comedy Central.

The bell rang, and with a big show, Samson wrote "_ _ _ _ _ _ _ _ _ _ _" across the entire whiteboard. Next to it, he drew a gallows. Most of the students were out of their seats, talking to their friends, texting, or eating.

"Let's get started! Who's got a letter?"

No one said anything. It was a burn that no one wanted to play his stupid game. Cooper learned nothing in this class.

"Quentin, a letter please."

"Q."

Samson made a show of looking for a Q along the dashes and then drew a circle under the top of the gallows.

Blake yelled, "Z!" and Samson drew a vertical line to show the body.

Cooper and just about everyone else picked up the strategy and shouted: X, V, K, Y, F, J, U, W.

The gallows grew a head, two eyes, nose, mouth, body, two arms, and two legs.

"We won!" Leon shouted. Leon was the guy Cooper knew even Chief Freak wouldn't mess with. Samson was scared of him. Who wasn't? Leon wore tank top shirts that showed off his muscles and tattoos of a cross, a skull, and a lion's head. He competed in MMA, and once when Cooper was really stoned he realized that Leon was like a human Doberman, lean muscles and always jumpy, ready to fight. Maybe Cooper should take bets and try to start something between Leon and Samson. But there'd be no bets against Leon.

"Congratulations!" Samson said. "I've never seen a group so spectacularly not get a single letter. Let's try something different. Try and guess a letter that fits."

Kimi raised her hand. She was decent. Cooper gave her a 7.

"S?"

Samson put an S at the start and one in the middle.

Esther shouted, "T!"

That girl was a 9-plus. He'd love to hook up with her, but he was fat and didn't play sports. His most redeeming quality was access to fine cannabis. Samson gave the figure hair.

People yelled, "E!" "B!" "A!" "C!"

The hangman grew eyebrows; the board read: S _ A _ E S _ E A _ E.

Cooper thought he might know the answer, but he wasn't positive.

"A letter, DeSean."

"D?"

A moustache went on the face.

"Samson, you put me on blast." DeSean put his head down on the desk.

"It's 'Shakespeare,'" Q said.

"Give the boy a prize," Samson said.

Cooper groaned. There had been potential, but it was just Shakespeare. Wasn't *Romeo and Juliet* torture enough? Why were teachers so in love with that fool? If they were going to study poetry and shit, why not Lil' Wayne or Eminem? Or Tupac?

"We'll be reading and performing Shakespeare's great tragedy *Othello*. Take out your journals. I'm going to give you a PowerPoint with some background information."

This was Cooper's cue to turn off his brain. He didn't move a muscle toward his journal. He teetered on the edge of a self-induced coma.

"Cooper, your journal. DeSean, how about waking up?"

Except for a couple of words at the top of the first five or six pages, his journal was blank.

"And pen."

The first slide of the PowerPoint had a picture of Shakespeare. A giant red question mark flew onto the page across his face.

S learns ppt! Q texted. *He's beyond FB!*

Cooper laughed. Samson looked his way, but Cooper was able to control himself. Samson walked by and might be smelling him. Cooper faked like he was looking for something in his backpack and took a whiff. He was good. Samson started droning about Shakespeare. Cooper had only heard this same stupid shit like ten times, so he didn't bother writing anything.

"There is a controversy about whether or not Shakespeare wrote his plays. Has anyone heard this?"

Chloe raised her hand. Samson looked excited that someone was going to answer his lame question, but she wanted to go to the bathroom. Burn. The only thing preventing Cooper from falling asleep was the fun of not getting caught texting. But that wasn't true for everyone. Samson was yammering about some shit, when DeSean snored loud enough to stop the class.

Unbelievably, Samson didn't wake him and tried to be all cool with, "Research suggests that teens have a different circadian rhythm than adults. According to your biological clocks, teens aren't ready to

85

sleep until past midnight, so I can understand why DeSean is tired. Normally I'd let him sleep, but DeSean isn't sawing logs, he's clear-cutting a forest. Let's take a Shakespeare break for a group challenge. You have to come up with a solution to DeSean's snoring without waking him."

"Put his hand in warm water," Q said.

"Lame," said Leon.

"What's your idea?" asked Q.

"Nothing, but the hand thing is lame."

Esther said, "Maybe we can make kind of a box around him."

Samson said, "There's an idea."

Getting stoned made Cooper lazy, but it also made him observant. And damn if Samson wasn't looking, no, more like staring at Esther. Cooper was in Robertson's class the year before because he had failed Algebra. It was the same look Robertson used to give Tanya. Samson was probably fucking Esther. He started to text Q and Blake, but Blake and Esther began moving desks to make a circle around DeSean. Once the first level was established, they started stacking desks on top to make a second level, and Cooper totally got what they were doing. He and others joined in. Then Blake picked up the four-foot-wide roll of butcher paper. Esther held one end and Blake and Ryan wrapped the roll around the desks making a cocoon around DeSean. Once it was finished, DeSean woke up, grunted, and then went to sleep without snoring.

Samson lit one of his stupid matches and Q texted: *fertility ritual.*

Cooper texted: *4 Esther.*

"Why do you keep lighting matches?" Chloe asked. "It smells."

"I light one whenever you guys do something cool."

Esther asked, "What about the marbles?"

"These are for when I teach you something you could learn on your own."

Everyone rolled their eyes.

"We're seniors, Samson," said Blake. "We're not supposed to learn anything."

Samson gave a creepy smile and said, "Time to get back to Shakespeare." Two sentences accidentally leaked into Cooper's brain before he turned it off. He wrote in his journal, "Othello tragic hero. Tragic hero has tragic flaw."

With a couple of minutes before the end of class, Samson turned off the PowerPoint and told everyone to write down something they learned during the lesson. Samson walked by Cooper and chuckled when he read in Cooper's journal, "DeSeans tragic flaw is two many concussions."

Chapter 12

NOAH CHU WAS singing "I Shot the Sheriff" along with his i-Pod as he rode his fixed-gear bicycle to school. He knew he looked deranged, not because he was singing, but because he was wearing his football helmet and carrying an oversized coat hanger with pads and jersey draped over it. By high school, most of his peers had traded in their two-wheels for four, but when he was in sixth grade, his science teacher had a poster of a bicycle that read, "For every mile of driving, one pound of CO2 is added to the atmosphere." He vowed never to own a car; he figured if Bob Marley were alive, he'd be writing songs about the global climate change. He even considered going vegan like Violet, but he loved steak. Noah didn't drive, so he had enough environmental karma to spend on meat.

The school bike rack was relatively empty. Out of the 1,600 students, no more than 30 rode bikes. Of the cyclists, about 10 had no other transport. The others were environmentalists like Noah or rode fixies because they were cool. Noah didn't exactly fit into the environmentalist group because he was a carnivore, and he didn't wear skinny jeans like the fixie crowd. Noah didn't belong to any group; he was on the periphery of many. He played football but didn't worship the ground Ryan Dowling walked on. He wore dreadlocks but didn't get high. And he took AP classes but wasn't planning on going to college. No one could pigeon-hole him. He was his own man.

As Noah locked up his bicycle, he sized up the long line of cars honking and jockeying around the student parking lot. He turned to the sparsely populated bike racks and muttered, "We are so screwed."

Noah removed his helmet and went to the gym to store his gear, but the doors were locked. Since he didn't have a car, he couldn't stash it there. He went to his first class, AP Lit. The classroom was empty save Mr. Samson who was writing on the whiteboard.

"Hey, Mr. Samson, can I keep my gear here until after school?"

Mr. Samson turned and his eyes widened. "Noah Chu plays football?"

"Vietnamese can't be dumb jocks?"

"No, it's the hair that advertises dumb stoner."

Noah bristled, but Mr. Samson grinned to show he wasn't serious.

"You know I'm half all-American. My mom was a good Texas Baptist until she met my dad. Then her dad told her she was dead in his eyes."

"I'm sorry to hear that."

Noah shrugged. "Who wants to be related to a bunch of crackers anyway?"

There was an awkward silence; maybe the "cracker" comment sounded racist, so he added, "You know a lot of kids in the stoner crowd aren't dumb."

"The smartest kid at my high school got baked every day."

Noah liked that Mr. Samson was also impossible to put into a box; few teachers openly spoke about pot. Mr. Samson pointed behind his desk. "Leave it there."

Noah dumped his gear, and Mr. Samson asked, "So Mr. Anti-establishment, how did you come to play America's game?"

"I'm fast and I can catch, so I play wide out."

"I never would have thought. One more question: after you graduate and presumably hang up your pads, do you have any plans?"

Usually Noah shrugged off the incessant "after you graduate" question that all adults asked and gave them a bullshit answer like "go to community college and get my gen ed before transferring to a four-year." But he liked Mr. Samson, so he said, "I don't know, some kind of adventure, maybe bike across the country. If you're thinking about recommending college, don't bother. I'm not signing a death sentence if I don't go. My brother's a Berkeley grad and sells insurance. Great job. Anyway, it doesn't matter what I do. We're pretty much doomed by global warming and population overload. I'm just going to have a good time while I can."

Noah tried to gauge Mr. Samson's reaction. Noah couldn't read his face, so he continued. "Let's say I go to college and then spend 50 weeks a year in a cubicle staring at a computer screen dealing with junk I couldn't care less about. And then I won't be able to retire because Social Security's going to be bankrupt. You're the one who tells us to think. Don't you think that it makes more sense to enjoy life while you can instead of waiting 50 years for something that probably won't happen?"

Mr. Samson nodded. "I can't argue with your logic, but if you do get a college education, you'll have more opportunities than sitting in a cubicle. What about getting involved in climate change? That's something you could sink your teeth in. Learn the science. Be an environmental entrepreneur. Organize the students."

Noah had already thought about all this. "Look around you, Mr. Samson. Students couldn't care less. And those are the ones who believe it's real. We're going to fry. It's already starting. Besides, like I said, it doesn't matter. Nothing really matters. Isn't that the point of *Ecclesiastes*?"

"You read *Ecclesiastes*?"

"Not in church; that's for sure. I google for enlightenment. One day I found, "The Devil can cite scripture for his purpose..."

"Shakespeare."

"Yeah, and then I thought what if an atheist could cite scripture, and then I found Ecclesiastes. Here, look."

He pulled out his journal and read, "'Utter futility, all is futile;' 'What value is there for man, in all the gains he makes under the sun.' See even the Bible says nothing matters. In the end, we're all worm meat. That's what Mercutio said in *Romeo and Juliet*."

Students started entering the classroom, Noah put his journal away and started feeling that Mr. Samson was more a colleague than a teacher. He respected that.

The bell hadn't rung and Mr. Samson called to Noah, "Ecclesiastes is right; nothing really matters except one thing: looking in the mirror each day. As long as you're happy with what you see, you're good."

Noah asked, "What happened to that kid from your high school?"

"Prosecutor for the DEA."

"Joke, right?"

"Irony isn't always fiction." Mr. Samson smiled. "You never know what the future is going to hold; that's why keeping doors open is good."

The bell rang.

"Pass up your essays," Mr. Samson said.

Noah sent his forward. He didn't think much of *The Awakening*; little action, way too many symbols, flat characters. Except for Dell, no one liked it. He raised his hand.

"Is the next book going to be...uh...better?"

Poonam shot Noah a quick glare and said, "Though I hate to admit that Noah is right, he's right. It was boring and the main character Edna was totally immature and self-centered. If you don't want to get married and have kids, then don't? You can't abandon your kids."

It was as if Noah saw Poonam for the first time beyond her cheerleader persona; there was something there, a fire in her eyes.

Mr. Samson answered, "Edna wanted to be her own person but was trapped in a loveless marriage. It was the first American novel that gave voice to the dissatisfaction women felt regarding their place in society."

Poonam said, "She had way too much self-pity. C'mon, girl, who doesn't have problems! I broke up with my boyfriend last week, so I'm going to drown myself? Get a divorce like everyone else and pull it together."

Noah agreed with Poonam and was going to add something, but Mr. Samson wanted the last word. He said, "You can't project today's social norms on the America a century ago. Divorce wasn't an option. And don't forget the Bible loomed over everything. Edna was just a rib of her husband; she was powerless; women's suffrage was a generation away. Edna couldn't leave her marriage. Kate Chopin was an early feminist. Partly because of women like her, women today can get out of bad marriages. All of you, males included, stand on their shoulders. Let me ask you this. Raise your hand if you're a feminist."

Even though Noah didn't like the book, his mother, a biochemist for the USDA, had drilled into his head equality between the sexes. Since this was the core of feminism, he figured he must be one; he was incredulous that only he, Dell, and Violet raised their hands. His eyes rested on Poonam an extra second hoping she would raise hers. But she was a conservative cheerleader and totally girly. The "fire in her eyes" was gone.

Violet said, "Feminism isn't about hating men or not shaving your armpits. Before feminism, we couldn't get real jobs, and there wasn't birth control. If you wanted an abortion, you went to a back alley, and got mutilated or died."

Mr. Samson nodded. "Alongside *The Awakening*, we've tracked the evolution of American feminism through poetry. One last poem and then feminism is finished. It was written in 2000. 'What Do Women Want' by Kim Addonizio is better for a female voice. Violet?"

"Sure."

> I want a red dress.
> I want it flimsy and cheap,
> I want it too tight...

"Wait a second. Can I start over? I want to get her voice right."

Mr. Samson nodded. This time Violet spoke in a husky voice, slowed her cadence, and emphasized 'want.'

> I want a red dress.
> I want it flimsy and cheap,
> I want it too tight, I want to wear it
> until someone tears it off me
> I want it sleeveless and backless,
> this dress, so no one has to guess
> what's underneath. I want to walk down
> the street past Thrifty's and the hardware store
> with all those keys glittering in the window,
> past Mr. and Mrs. Wong selling day-old
> donuts in their café, past the Guerra brothers
> slinging pigs from the truck and onto the dolly,
> hoisting the slick snouts over their shoulders.
> I want to walk like I'm the only
> woman on earth and I can have my pick.
> I want that red dress bad.
> I want it to confirm

93

your worst fears about me,
to show you how little I care about you
or anything except what
I want. When I find it, I'll pull that garment
from its hanger like I'm choosing a body
to carry me into this world, through
the birth-cries and the love-cries too,
and I'll wear it like bones, like skin,
it'll be the goddamned
dress they bury me in.

"That is so not a feminist poem," Poonam said.

"She's a skank," Hudson agreed. Noah chuckled. If Hudson was a girl, he'd be a skank because he'd do anything to get what he wanted.

"Why do you think she's a 'skank'?" Mr. Samson asked.

"She sleeps around."

"If she were a guy, you'd call him a player," Violet said. "You'd think he was the shit."

"No I wouldn't."

"Right," Noah said, "show me a guy who doesn't want to get laid. And a guy who gets laid a lot is a player."

Poonam turned around and stared at Noah. "No one would accuse *you* of that." Noah felt the adrenalin rush sort of like right before catching a kick-off. Poonam's words were an insult, but her delivery made them a compliment.

"It's a feminist poem because it's about power," Dell said. "Red equals power…"

"And sex…" said Hudson.

"It's not about sex," countered Dell. "Sex is a tool. She wants power, and sex is the way to get it."

94

"That's what I'm saying," Hudson said. "Women have always used sex as a way to power. That play we read last year Lysistrada, and in the Bible you have—what's her name— Del-something."

"Del...Lilah. But those are different; this narrator relishes in the power of her sexuality," Dell said. "Kate Chopin couldn't have written this in the 1890s. This is feminism today. It's a great poem."

Following the discussion, Mr. Samson lit four matches. The first couple of times he did the match thing, it had been cool. Now it was getting old. Leave it to an adult to do something cool and then beat it to death until it became a kind of dumb. And speaking of dumb, Mr. Samson held four lit matches while standing under the smoke detector.

"Uh, Mr. Samson," he said pointing to the ceiling.

"Damn!" Mr. Samson yelled, shook out the flames, grabbed Poonam's journal, and fanned the air.

The bell rang, and Noah lingered at his desk for a minute until he saw Poonam making her way out; he quickly gathered his stuff, so he and Poonam could accidentally exit together.

"Hey," he said.

"Hey," she said. "Samson and his fire. It's like an opium den. He should be committed. So you're really a feminist?"

"And you're really a 1950s housewife wannabe?"

"From India. Maybe I'll get me a beehive hairdo." She laughed. "Think how funny it would look next to your dreads."

Noah smiled and they walked down the hall.

Chapter 13

MR. SAMSON STOOD at his desk watching the students leave. Dell was gathering her books. He called her over.

"I've got your college essay. I made a few comments, but overall it's excellent and fits with what we've been talking about in class." He handed her the essay. She stood looking like she wanted him to say more, but Mr. Samson never felt completely comfortable as the repository of teen secrets that often found their ways into essays, poems, and short stories. On one hand, he was gladdened when a student trusted him, and he enjoyed knowing a secret as much as anyone; on the other hand, he never knew what to say without sounding like an idiot. He settled on, "I was sorry to read about your father. That must be hard."

Dell appeared strong except for biting her lower lip. "Having a second family is obviously morally corrupt, but then dumping my mom and me when we found out was a coward's way out. Anyway, maybe I should thank him for making me realize that women don't need men. It's a new world. We're outperforming boys in school, and we're going to hold power in America with or without red dresses. I'm going to be part of that. No offense, but men created the world's problems, so they aren't the ones who are going to fix them."

"No offense taken."

She looked like she was about to cry. He held a box of tissues for her. She took one to dab her eyes.

"He still wants to be my dad, but I won't see him."

Mr. Samson said, "I know that you feel you don't need your dad, or any man for that matter, but if you ever want to talk, my door is open."

"Thanks, Mr. Samson. I'm definitely going to take you up on that. Maybe coffee some morning. Double cappuccino, right?"

Again his face was warm. No doubt about it. Here he was offering to be a willing ear, but at his animal level, was he kind of checking her out? What the hell was he doing? Talk about morally corrupt. He hoped that Dell didn't notice, or worse, way, way, *way* worse, was *she* interested? Thankfully, he had signed up for the online dating service OkCupid and had a date Friday night.

In as casual voice as he could muster, he said, "A cup of tea seems to do it these days," and then he added, "Thanks to you."

He had no idea why he added those three words, but by doing so, he inadvertently stepped across the teacher/student border.

Dell blushed scarlet. "Thanks for the feedback. See you."

Mr. Samson watched Dell as she walked out. "Do not be a perv," he commanded himself.

As he watched the door, he thought it was his heart pounding, but beating a drum was a pair of heels carrying Vice-Principal Haman.

"Mr. Samson, would you please explain which state standard this lesson is targeted at?"

The Hammer held her phone for Mr. Samson to watch a short video of DeSean being mummified in butcher paper. Mr. Samson could have kissed her for bringing him back to school. He unsuccessfully tried to suppress a smile.

"It was a lesson on creative problem solving."

"I do not believe there is a standard in the Common Core English Language Arts curriculum on 'creative problem solving.'"

"There should be. It was a great lesson."

"Mr. Samson, your job is to deliver a curriculum that meets the anchor standards mandated by the Common Core. This is a disturbing development. For the next month, you will hand me your week-long lesson plans at the beginning of each week."

"You're kidding."

"Monday mornings prior to first period."

The Hammer turned and minced her way out of the classroom.

Mr. Samson silently cursed his enemy and wondered who fed her the video.

For two minutes, Chloe had been nominally looking through her bag for a writing utensil. Of course she was texting, but Mr. Samson had no desire to stop her. If a 17-year-old young woman thought her time was better spent texting a friend about how unfair her bitchy mother was for taking away her car keys because she came home at two a.m., rather than writing down the grammatical anomalies and structure of Shakespeare's plays, who was Mr. Samson to say she was wrong?

This was Mr. Samson's second attempt to introduce *Othello*, the first being interrupted by DeSean's narcolepsy. Mr. Samson walked between the desks and found mostly blank pages in the journals from the Shakespeare lecture. A few had words that more or less appeared on the PowerPoint like "Globe Theeter" and "Othello the protagoner," but little underneath the topics. These students had to see something in writing, *and* the teacher needed to instruct them of its importance, *and* the teacher had to tell them to write it down because they would be tested on it. If these conditions were met, they'd write something which would likely not make sense the next day. The fifteen-minutes Mr. Samson spent the day before on the intricacies of the Elizabethan theater never existed for them. This day's Shakespeare PowerPoint continuation would most likely stick to the students as long as a 94-mph fastball stuck to a swinging bat. Still Mr. Samson kept clicking through slides. If he tried to fill their brains with knowledge, but there were padlocks on their skulls, should he toss a marble in the pail?

"The deal about Shakespeare is this: you think only English teachers can understand him, but all of you are more literate than his audiences; believe it or not, you have more education than Shakespeare himself. The plays weren't written for the educated elite, but for the masses."

Mr. Samson paused to let that insight sink in.

"Chloe, what do you think about that?'

"I'm looking for a pencil."

The rest of the class had hands in backpacks, on laps, in sweat shirts, or were chatting with each other, or striking a new mediation posture: head on folded hands resting on desk.

Undeterred, Samson said, "Shakespeare wrote in the vernacular of his time. What does 'vernacular' mean? Anyone?"

Mr. Samson wrote VERNACULAR on the board. "Take out your smart phones and find the definition."

Within ten seconds, six hands appeared.

"Chloe?"

"It's the native language of a people."

Cooper exclaimed, "Shakespeare was a savage!"

Blake ejaculated, "O, Romeo, O, Romeo, don't stop, O, Romeo, O!"

The class broke up.

"Cooper and Blake!"

Abby asked, "What does 'native language' mean?"

Mr. Samson turned to Chloe. "Chloe?"

She shrugged. "How should I know?"

"Everyday language," Mr. Samson said. "The language you speak to your friends."

"Like using 'like' and 'omg'?" Abby suggested.

"Not only that, but Shakespeare understood that a play needed a hook at the beginning to grab his audiences. That's why a lot of the plays start with sex jokes."

"That's what I was saying about Romeo!" Blake announced.

"Blake, you are absolutely correct. In the first scene of *Romeo and Juliet*; one of the characters exclaims, 'My naked weapon is out!'"

"Look, girls, my naked weapon is out!"

"Blake!"

"Sorry, sorry, I'll be good."

Every student was at the edge of their seat. Finally, Samson was talking about something that interested them. Mr. Samson could see Chloe's fingers.

"*Othello* starts with a few cracks about sex. You have the play in front of you. Five extra credit points for the first person who can find one. Go to Act One, Scene One. Look at Iago's speech after Brabantio comes in."

Thirty seconds later Blake yelled, "I got it! 'An old black ram is topping your white ewe!' Yeah, baby!"

"Where?" Esther demanded.

"Here!" Blake stood and jabbed his finger on the page. "And listen to this: 'your daughter and the Moor are now making the beast with two backs!'" Blake grunted and pantomimed thrusting. "I love Shakespeare!"

"Shakespeare! Shakespeare!" the class chanted. Mr. Samson was glad they were engaged, but they were getting out of hand; Samson needed to throw a little cold water on them, so he assigned parts and started reading the play aloud. Nothing like stumbling through Shakespeare to calm a class. Still they seemed moderately interested during Act I. It would be better if Shakespeare had more sex, but when they left the classroom, even Chloe was smiling.

Wednesday afternoons were reserved for staff development. This day's task was to analyze data from last year's SBAC tests and brainstorm ways to raise scores; it was an odd combination of simultaneously being slipped a triple dose of Ambien while having an icepick hammered into your skull.

Dewey had shed his start of the year enthusiasm. He was now solely focused on the administrator's chief task, raising test scores.

"Here is the disaggregated data on your prior and present students' SBAC tests from last year. Take ten minutes to look for trends we can address."

Mo was surprised that students who suffered from serial absenteeism and didn't put any effort into class saw an increase in their scores as often as hard workers. The opposite was also true. Some who put in the effort lost ground. And though last year, Mo's students overall averaged a loss of two points, the year before it was one point, three years back his students gained five, but his curriculum was essentially the same. Then there was Noah, one of his brightest students, who tested at Far Below Basic when he was a junior.

Dewey called everyone back. "Any trends?"

Lisa Rodriguez volunteered, "Our underperforming subgroups, Hispanic, African-American, and low socio-economic males, are not closing the gap."

A couple of nods and "uh-huhs" greeted this observation.

Dewey said, "Ideas on closing it?"

Truck said, "How about we take a busload of kids to the capital and tell our politicians what they can do with their No Child Left Behind, Race to the Top, the Common Core, and the next bullshit that will fix public education. You want to fix education? Throw money at us. Either pay now or pay later with more prisons. How about I pull a Gandhi, chain myself to a column on the Capital steps, and go on a hunger strike? Doc says I need to lose twenty pounds. Who wants to join me? Dewey? Trish?"

Mrs. Haman ignored Truck's invitation but offered a suggestion. "A 'best practice' strategy would be to start class doing practice questions as warm-ups."

Truck jumped out of his seat quicker than a Red Sox fan when Boston recorded the final out and won the 2004 World Series to break the 86-year-old Curse of the Bambino. "Look, Trish, no disrespect to your 'best practice,' but say I spend ten minutes every day "best practicing." I don't know the math, but it'd be more time bubbling than learning *Macbeth*."

Tom Hanson, a math teacher, raised his hand. "That'd be 30 hours per class, about 18% of total instructional time."

"I'm not saying *every* day," replied an exasperated Hammer. "And you don't need ten minutes; five is enough. And your characterization of the questions being only multiple-choice is incorrect. There are writing components as well. And don't forget that questions provide opportunities to learn content."

"Kool-Aid," said Truck.

"This is not a joke. If we fail to raise scores, there might not be anybody teaching anyone because the state has the prerogative to close us. Minimally, I can guarantee that teachers who have three years of negative improvement will be non-reelected rehires; it will not matter if you have a Teacher of the Year certificate hanging on your wall."

Mo had planned on keeping quiet. The Hammer and Dewey were just doing their jobs. There was nothing to be gained by going off on the tests. He'd nod his head and then do as he pleased. Pretend and ignore was the way to subvert authority. But The Hammer had clearly targeted him. He raised his hand.

Mrs. Haman took an exaggerated breath. "Mr. Samson?"

"The problem is that the education deciders don't understand Campbell's Law, you know, the more a test is used for social decision-making, the more it will be subject to corruption; the more we use tests to reward and punish schools and teachers, the more likely cheating will take place. The teacher walks up and down the aisles. He sees a student with a wrong answer on her last question. He stands there until she changes it. When she stumbles onto the correct one, he moves. How about where teachers collect the tests and hold pizza parties where administrators and teachers fix wrong answers? A year before she was indicted for cheating, the Atlanta superintendent won National Superintendent of the Year."

Mrs. Haman replied slowly as if Mo were not terribly bright. "Yes, Mr. Samson, we are all aware of cheating scandals. They are outliers and not the norm. The norm is that people are honest. What we are presently engaged in is looking for patterns in the test results that might help us prepare our students for the tests they must take and must do well on. You wouldn't happen to have found anything?"

"Yeah, I got something. A lot of results are random. Slackers raise their scores and good students drop theirs. Who else saw that?"

A quarter of the teachers raised their hands. The Hammer looked like she wanted to pound Mo. Dewey did not look happy.

"Mo," he said. "I hear you. Really. But you know as well as anyone that taken as a whole, the scores aren't random. In fact, some teachers had great success. Tom, you raised scores on all your sub-groups. What did you do?"

"Just regular curriculum. Oh, wait. I was out for three months for jury duty. Maybe that helped."

Tittering broke out, and The Hammer put up her hand to lay down the law. "You will start your classes with practice questions. Discussion over. Staff development is adjourned."

"I won't do it," Mo proclaimed.

"With all due respect, Mr. Samson, this directive is not optional. You will begin class with practice questions. If you do not, I will write you a notice of unprofessional conduct. If your insubordination continues, you will put yourself on a path to dismissal."

"Trish," Dewey began, "Perhaps..."

The Hammer ignored Dewey.

"I trust I make myself clear."

Mo surveyed his colleagues. They were wide-eyed; this was a deciding moment; the coach had just called for a low fastball on a full-count against a dangerous hitter with men on base. Mo signaled change-up.

"With all due respect, Mrs. Haman, education is not the filling of a pail, but the lighting of a fire."

"Excuse me?"

"William Butler Yeats, on education. Google it. Let's make a deal. I teach my way. If I don't raise scores, fire me. I won't fight it. You want me gone. Here's your chance." Mo took a page of data, crumpled it, held it high above his head, and released it. "The gauntlet is thrown."

Chapter 14

THEY MADE IT official with a memorandum of understanding. Mr. Samson could teach his own curriculum. If his scores did not rise, he would be fired and have no recourse through his union. He was intent on showing that one didn't need to teach to the test, that good teaching would yield high test scores. The only problem was that his experience did not support this theory.

As AP Lit settled into their seats, Mr. Samson asked, "After a semester of poems, I want you to write your own definition of poetry."

While the class wrote, he found an email from Maria: *Mo, why are you supplying Haman with the rope to hang you?* Mo grimaced. She didn't understand. He'd talk to her. Meanwhile, he had fires to light.

Olivia volunteered, "Poetry is emotion put into words."

"Good. Noah?"

"Concentrated language. A poem says in 20 lines what a novel takes 300 pages to say."

"Nice. Poonam?"

"Pass."

"Come on. I saw you scribbling."

Poonam shrugged to the class. "He asked for it." She rustled her paper, cleared her throat, and announced, "A poem is a bunch of random words designed to make students look like idiots when we don't understand what the heck the poet is saying. Why can't he just say what he means? I'd rather get my teeth cleaned than read Robert Frost."

Mr. Samson went to his desk, opened a drawer, and tossed Poonam an unopened package of dental floss.

"For the one today." A number of guffaws, and Mr. Samson thought only in teaching can such a lame joke be funny. God, he loved it.

"Seriously, Poonam, I appreciate your honesty." To the class, "We're going to read, 'Ode on the Death of a Favourite Cat' by Thomas Gray. The diction is flowery and archaic because it was written in 1768, so take out your highlighters and annotate the you-know-what out of it. This one is difficult to recite, so if I mess up, please set me straight. Got the floss?"

Sometimes Mr. Samson choose a person to recite to. It grounded difficult poems. Poonam had a length of floss between her two hands which looked like she would have preferred twisting around Mr. Samson's neck rather than moving between her teeth. Poonam's eyes were on the teacher; Mr. Samson's eyes were on her, but on their own accord they moved to Dell.

> 'TWAS on a lofty vase's side,
> Where China's gayest art had dy'd
> The azure flowers that blow;
> Demurest of the tabby kind,
> The pensive Selima reclin'd,
> Gaz'd on the lake below.
>
> Her conscious tail her joy declar'd;
> The fair round face, the snowy beard,
> The velvet of her paws,

Her coat, that with the tortoise vies,
Her ears of jet, and emerald eyes,
She saw, and purr'd applause.

Still had she gaz'd; but midst the tide
Two beauteous forms were seen to glide,
The Genii of the stream;
Their scaly armour's Tyrian hue,
Through richest purple, to the view,
Betray'd a golden gleam.

The hapless Nymph with wonder saw:
A whisker first, and then a claw,
With many an ardent wish,
She stretch'd, in vain, to reach the prize.
What female heart can gold despise?
What cat's averse to fish?

Presumptuous Maid! with looks intent
Again she stretch'd, again she bent,
Nor knew the gulph between;
(Malignant Fate sat by, and smil'd.)
The slippery verge her feet beguil'd;
She tumbled headlong in.

Eight times emerging from the flood,
She mew'd to every watery God,
Some speedy aid to send.
No Dolphin came, no Nereid stir'd:
Nor cruel Tom, nor Susan heard.
A favourite has no friend.

From hence, ye beauties, undeceiv'd,
Know, one false step is ne'er retriev'd,
And be with caution bold.
Not all that tempts your wandering eyes
And heedless hearts, is lawful prize;
Nor all, that glisters, gold.

For a nanosecond, the image of Hailey, his high school girlfriend, transposed over Dell's smiling face. It was that same smile Hailey flashed the moment before his team mobbed him after he singled in a game winning run.

Hudson yelled, "Pass the floss!"

A chorus of "Me too!" followed. Mr. Samson stood in front of a room of disgruntled teens.

"What don't you get?" Mr. Samson asked.

"Besides everything?" Poonam said.

"Give me specifics."

Olivia asked, "What does 'pensive Selima' means."

Dell answered, "Selima is the cat's name. 'Pensive' just means she's thinking about the fish."

"What's 'malignant'?" Javier asked.

Dell's hand shot up, but Mr. Samson asked Javier, "What's the Spanish word for 'evil?'"

"Mal," Javier said. "Oh, it's like evil fate smiled knowing the cat would fall in."

Olivia ventured, "Selima came up for air eight times and on the ninth time she drowned. Maybe that represents that cats have nine lives."

Students nodded and now seemed interested.

Noah spoke before being recognized. "Look at the last three lines. They're warning about mistaking glitter for gold. Everybody in this class and all the teachers at this school believe a college education is gold. We've been on the college track since we got out of diapers; do this, don't fail that, take this class, volunteer at the food pantry. We're like zombies..."

Noah stood up, forwarded his arms zombie-fashion, and monotoned, "must...get...to...Harvard."

The class was discombobulated. Noah continued. "My dad thought he hit the jackpot by getting into Yale law school. Now he defends companies against environmental lawsuits. He drives a Porsche, owns a vacation home in Tahoe, and is the unhappiest man I know. Javier read his poem last week about his illiterate dad who's proud to work in the fields because he feeds people and gives Javier the chance for a better life. Sorry, Mr. Samson, but the college prep track is bullshit."

Poonam jumped in, "It's not Mr. Samson's fault!"

Noah shot back. "That's not what I said. I said the system wants you to believe that college is gold, but it's not."

Poonam looked ready to bean Noah with the floss canister; her face was crimson. "Nobody made me take this class. It's my choice to take it and push myself, and yeah I don't really care about literature and poetry. I'm taking it for my college app..."

"That's what I'm saying," Noah interrupted.

"Well, that's not what I'm saying if you'd let me finish. Getting a college degree isn't glitter. It's gold. I want to have a nice house and a job and a family. You can call me superficial, but there's nothing wrong with the American Dream."

"The American Dream is glitter too," Noah answered. "A Porsche won't make you happy."

"Yeah, listening to Bob Marley is the way to nirvana."

Noah fixed Poonam with a hard stare. She mirrored his look. Mr. Samson was ecstatic that a 250-year old poem was catalyzing real emotions. Still, he took a step forward because it was possible that the antipathy between Poonam and Noah could end badly.

In a measured voice, Poonam said, "If the American Dream is glitter, I'll take it over working minimum wage or in the fields. No offense, Javier."

"Don't worry about it," said Javier. "I'm not working in the fields. I'm going to get me a fat slice of American Dream." He addressed Noah. "Maybe your Dad is bitter about the Porsche because they always breakdown. I'm going to get a Beemer."

The bell rang and Mr. Samson said, "Your homework is to write an ode, a poem to something. You can write an ode to your car, your horse, your TV, your best friend, your high school. Whatever. Just make it good. Noah, have a second?"

The students filed out. Before Mr. Samson said anything, Noah enthusiastically said, "That was a good discussion. I don't have them in too many classes."

"You bring up some good points," Mr. Samson replied. "Poonam has some strong points as well."

"Yeah, I kind of exaggerated my dad's bitterness. But I sure don't buy into the suburban house, wife, 2.3 kids, and all that."

"That's your choice. But you don't want to close any doors."

Noah looked quizzically at Mr. Samson.

"I know you're not interested in college right now, but your GPA isn't bad. If you ace your classes this year, you could get into a pretty decent school; you might want that option sometime later. Many of the great rabble rousers of the world went to college. Martin Luther King, Jr. had a doctorate in divinity."

"Malcolm X got educated in prison."

"But you get my point, right?"

"I hear you, but I just can't do it in classes I don't like."

"There are lots of things I don't like, but I do them."

"Isn't that just hypocrisy?"

"That's the problem Holden Caulfield had. He wanted to stay pure and not compromise his beliefs. He wanted to live in the Garden

110

of Eden forever. But we all have to eventually eat from the Tree of Knowledge. Maybe you can think of hypocrisy more like complexity."

"I'll think about it." Noah turned to leave.

"One more thing. How come you tested at Far Below Basic in English on last year's SBAC?"

Noah hesitated and then pulled out his phone and scrolled through its pictures. "Look at this."

Noah had taken a picture of his answer sheet from the prior year. The answers were in the form of an extended middle finger.

"I thought for sure they'd catch me, but no one said a word."

"Why'd you do it?"

"Why? You know why."

"The system is corrupt and the test stinks."

"You know Dr. Truck's poster, 'What if they gave a war and nobody came?' I want to make one that says, 'What if they gave a test and nobody took it.'"

"I love your passion. That must be why I teach, to suck it up through you guys. The thing is this: while I agree with you, mostly, and while the SBAC means nothing to you, it does mean a lot to the school and to the community."

Mr. Samson almost added that if Noah took the test seriously and scored Advanced, Mr. Samson would have a job next year, but begging a kid didn't feel right.

Noah left and Mr. Samson mumbled, "He'll rise to the occasion. As Juliet told Romeo, 'I know it, I.'"

As English 12 piled in, he remembered that Juliet had been wrong.

To his English 12 class, Mr. Samson said, "Let's pick up the play from where we left off. Iago, if you recall, is angry at Othello for two reasons. First, he made Cassio second-in-command when Iago

111

was clearly more qualified, at least in Iago's mind. Second, he thinks Othello has slept with his wife. So Iago wants to destroy Cassio and Othello by planting the handkerchief of Desdemona, Othello's wife, in Cassio's apartment in the hope that Othello's jealousy will catalyze his rage leading to Cassio's death and Othello's self-destruction. Is that clear?"

The only thing clear was that after the sexual imagery of *Othello* was used up, the class was done with the play. But even for the student whose aspiration was to get his high school diploma with a 1.34 GPA, the issues of revenge and jealousy, the central themes of *Othello,* had to speak to him, for there was not a person who did not at times feel a murderous rage for revenge. Even Kimi, whose extreme four-letter word was "heck," must have at some point wanted to gore someone's ox. Mr. Samson was convinced of this universal truth and wanted his students to recognize that element in themselves. Shakespeare was the genius who artfully exposed this human trait, but his diction was not the stuff of Twitter or YouTube, so 21st century students were unable to follow him. It was as if Shakespeare hit a hard line-drive into the outfield gap but was so old, he could only limp to first base. He needed a pinch runner to score.

Inspiration rained on Mr. Samson as he lay in bed the previous night. He made a modern day scenario for the students to act out, and then they'd personalize *Othello*'s themes. If that didn't work, at least there'd be a chance they might remember that the play they were studying was about jealousy and revenge.

"Who wants to act out a scene?" No one raised a hand. He took his open hand and whacked his forehead hard enough for the texters to look up. "Doh! When I want quiet in the class, it's a cacophony, but when I want volunteers, it's like being in the stands when the visiting pitcher strikes out the last batter and ends the game."

The class always took a minute to figure out Mr. Samson's baseball similes. Sometimes they needed Ryan Dowling's help.

Today they appeared not to have even heard him. They were flabbergasted (his word, not theirs) that a teacher would smack himself in the head.

"Five extra credit points for every actor. I need three." Blake raised his hand. Mr. Samson waited to see if others would volunteer. He needed actors, but with Blake on stage there was the possibility that campus security might be needed. "Ten points," he pleaded.

Blake now stood with his hand up and said, "Q, me, and Cooper. Let's see the script," Blake and his mates grabbed the paper from Mr. Samson's hand; he resigned himself to five minutes of chaos. Most dramatic renderings including boys devolved into World Wrestling Federation melees. And those were love scenes. This one had conflict.

The script read, *Ivan thinks he has been slighted by his friend Oscar. Ivan decides to get back at Oscar by telling him that Oscar's girlfriend is two-timing him with Oscar's best friend Carl. To prove his point, Ivan stole an earring from the girlfriend and put it in Carl's backpack.*

"We got this! Esther, I need one of your earrings."

Esther made a face but took out an earring and gave it to Blake. Cooper put on his backpack. Mr. Samson stood by the closed door to block anyone trying to enter.

"Yo, my man, Carl!" Blake said to Cooper. "What be happenin', bruh?" The two boys exchanged a six-step handshake.

"Sup, Ivan, my brother from another mother," Cooper replied and they did a second handshake that ended with a hug. During the hug, Blake slipped the earring into the backpack.

Blake said, "Hey, ain't you got a date with yo bit…uh, girlfriend?"

"Yeah, later," Cooper said and turned to go.

"Whoa, Dude! She don't want to see you with no faggity man purse. Leave it. I got you."

Cooper took it off his shoulders and tossed it at Blake's feet while struting off-stage.

"Careful!" yelled Esther.

For the first time all year, Blake didn't respond to an occasion to leap off-task. Instead he said, "That bastard! I should teach him a lesson."

"Who you talking about, bruh?" Q entered.

Blake feigned surprise and took an exaggerated jump back. The class broke up.

"Nobody, nobody, nobody."

"I know you, Ivan," said Q. "You're covering for Carl. You're a true bruh, and I respect that, but I saw him bounce."

"Carl, didn't bounce cuz he was avoiding you," Blake insisted. "He's your BFFL. You got some chaw?"

"Sorry."

"I think Carl has some in his backpack." Blake nudged it towards Q. "My hands are sticky. I've been…" he looked down at his pants. The class roared. Mr. Samson's heart stopped. "…eating chocolate." Blake shot Mr. Samson a wry grin. He turned to Q. "Could you?"

"No problem." Q opened the backpack. "What the hell!!" He pulled out Esther's earring.

"What's Carl doing with the earring I gave my woman?"

"I'm sure it's innocent and there is absolutely no way they're sleeping together. Bruh, you got any condoms? Carl bummed my last dozen."

"I'm gonna kill him!" Q yelled running off stage.

The class applauded.

"Nice," Esther said to Blake. "Earring, please."

With a gallant bow, Blake handed it to her.

"Shakespeare would have been proud," Mr. Samson said to the actors. He turned to the class. "Could such a thing ever happen at school?"

"You mean does anybody ever make stuff up to get back at someone?" Abby asked. "Not once...today."

Mr. Samson continued. "So why do we do it?"

Esther said, "Just like the play. For revenge and power."

There was the potential for a good discussion, but Leon decided five minutes was close enough to the bell to start packing up. The rest of the class followed suit. The students engaged in idle chatter for a few minutes; it was as if the skit never happened, except that Mr. Samson noted that Blake and Esther held a heated conversation that he couldn't catch.

Reading essays required full attention, but grading daily homework took zero effort. Mo would skim, and if the name was legible, he'd give it a check. But he was taken by surprise by Poonam's "Ode to a Revolutionary" in which she mentioned Noah in the same line as Gandhi and Martin Luther King. When he read Noah's "Bright Eyes" with "the cheerleader whose spirit sparkles brighter than her pom-poms," he just smiled. It was the stuff of romantic comedy. Mo cradled a cup of green tea as he sat in his reading chair with his feet on the coffee table. With "Dark Side of the Moon" playing in the background, he mused, "Perhaps my Poonam is out there somewhere: A rich, introverted, businesswoman, who listens to Lil Wayne. Maybe I should bag OkCupid and subscribe to the Wall Street Journal."

The previous Friday he had his first online date. His first impression of the woman as she entered the coffee shop was not positive since her online photo clearly came from a previous decade. Then she spent the entire time complaining about her "bastard ex." Mo needed to be more discriminating in whom he contacted. He brushed his teeth and took care of his ponytail. Maybe he should cut it. But what about Dell's ponytail challenge. That was fun. The type

115

of woman he was looking for needed to be smart, pretty, and fun—an adult version of Dell.

He logged onto OkCupid and found a woman who was a history grad student at UC Davis. She had to be smart, and her profile suggested she had a sense of humor, and if her picture was accurate, she was cute. He emailed her.

If Katherine knew what he was resorting to, she'd probably chuckle—or worse—shoot him a look of empathy. Katherine already moved in with a guy from work. Mo wondered if they had something going on before the divorce, and he resented that she was moving ahead with her life while he was warming the bench unable to get back into the game.

Chapter 15

THE ESSAY WAS perhaps the most despised academic assignment at Reagan High. Like most tyrants, the essay began with good intentions. It allowed students to delve deeply into a subject, exercise critical thinking facilities, and improve writing. Just what the teacher ordered. But mostly it made plain the students' superficiality of thought and their abysmal grasp of written communication. Exposed to the world's greatest authors, students were commanded, "Now your turn." Their essays were finger paintings in comparison to the Mona Lisas and Guernicas created by the canonical authors that they read. And with oceans of red ink, teachers let them know it. And they resented it.

Topics were uninspiring. Discuss the main theme of the story. What do the symbols represent? Compare and contrast *Book A* to *Book B*. By high school, students had been trained that an essay followed the completion of every novel. No wonder they anticipated upcoming novels with the enthusiasm of introducing their hard-drinking boyfriends to their Mormon parents. Teens didn't want to write about how jealousy inspired a murder by a fictional man who spoke in incomprehensible English. Now if Jackie could write an essay about how Carmen was jealous of her because Jackie's boyfriend treated Jackie with respect, while Carmen's was a jerk, and then Carmen destroyed Jackie's relationship with rumors, that might be different.

Like the majority of teachers, Mr. Samson sold the essay as castor oil rather than ice cream. "You have to learn how to write a proper five-paragraph essay because that is the expectation when you're in college." He never pitched it as the joy of writing for self-discovery or for entertainment. He never said, "Write an essay that makes me laugh." And he graded AP Lit essays as if the students were already in college. To earn an A from Samson was as difficult as hitting a dinger off a breaking knuckleball. Probably not gonna happen.

Homework was to write a thesis, the single sentence that would lay out the main idea of the *Othello* essay. Like English 12, AP Lit read *Othello*. AP Lit started the play three weeks after English 12 and finished a week earlier. AP Lit students read twelve works of literature during the year. English 12 read—well—were assigned three.

"Okay, who's brave enough to share their thesis?" Mr. Samson eyed the students rooting through their backpacks to avoid eye contact.

"Poonam?"

"I knew you'd pick me!"

"The malignant hand of fate has once again targeted you."

"It's bad."

"Quit stalling. Let's hear it."

"Othello killed Desdemona because he thought she was having an affair."

Mr. Samson didn't believe in false praise. His first Little League team won 2, lost 14, yet they received trophies. Even the six-year-old knew that was ridiculous. However, the teen ego which presented itself as granite was only a thin veneer covering sandstone, ready to crumble with the whiff of a criticism. This thesis was worse than his team.

"It could be a little stronger. We know that Othello killed Desdemona because he thought she was having an affair, so you don't need an essay to prove it. The thesis has to be an opinion you can prove."

"I told you it was bad."

"It'll get better. Who else? Hudson?"

"*Othello* was the best tragedy Shakespeare wrote."

"Uh…"

"It's my opinion. You told us a thesis has to be an opinion."

"An opinion you can *prove*. I think rap sucks. That's an opinion. But I can't prove it, so it can't be a thesis."

"I can prove rap sucks," countered Hudson.

"Funny, but seriously, your thesis doesn't work." He turned to the rest of the class. "You need to be able to write a solid thesis. You won't pass the AP test unless you can write one, actually three."

"Tell us again how the test is a brutal, three-hour marathon," said Violet. She deepened her voice as if she were Mr. Samson. "Hour One: Read weird poetry and unintelligible prose, then answer 60 questions tough enough to trip English doctoral candidates. Then two hours to read more poetry and prose that last interested someone in the 17th century and write three perfect essays."

Mr. Samson's strategy of fear as motivator had turned to mockery. He laughed with the rest of the students but then thought back on his challenge with The Hammer that he would not teach to the SBAC. Shouldn't this apply to the AP test as well? He needed more time to process this, but the class was waiting, so he brought in his closer to save the game.

"Dell, your thesis please."

Dell read, "While many critics claim Othello's tragic flaw is his jealousy, his gullibility is equally devastating, for he never questions the falsehoods that Iago feeds him."

"How would you prove that?" Mr. Samson asked.

119

"Iago presents circumstantial evidence of Cassio and Desdemona having an affair because Cassio has Desdemona's handkerchief. Othello accepts Iago's version and never questions Cassio where he got the handkerchief. Had he asked, he would have found that Iago was lying."

"That's a strong, provable thesis," Mr. Samson said. "And the beauty is this is an issue worthwhile to look at today. Dell isn't just analyzing something from 400 years ago that has no relevance. Think about how all of us are told certain things to be true about various people, but we often never question the validity. You might even reference a contemporary situation as part of the essay. Well done, Dell."

Poonam said, "That's Dell. A regular human can't write like that."

"Why not?"

"Because she was born that way."

"Dell," asked Mr. Samson, "is that right? Did you come out of the womb already knowing when 'its' gets an apostrophe?"

"And when to use 'whom' versus 'who.'"

"How *did* you get so smart?" Poonam asked.

Every head in class swiveled towards Dell. She was of them yet not of them. She was a fellow student but had ability beyond them. Perhaps her magic wasn't something far off in the stars but something close and attainable.

"When I was in grade school my father made me redo every assignment until it was perfect. I rewrote everything. In third grade I rewrote my fable about how the howler monkey got his howl like ten times…"

"Oh my god!" said Poonam. "Last year, my sisters told me Mrs. Garcia still used that as an example."

"Poonam," said Mr. Samson, "You're a cheerleader. How long did it take to perfect that move where the cheerleaders throw Kimi up in the air and she does the splits before you catch her? Like 30 minutes?"

"Are you crazy! We practice two hours a day and a Toe Touch Basket Toss takes weeks!"

"How long did it take you to write your thesis statement?"

Poonam was silent.

"The secret to everything is practice and reworking. Now break into pairs and go over each other's thesis. If yours isn't good, rewrite. When it's good, start on your intro paragraph."

As the students got to work, Mr. Samson reflected on Dell's fastidious father who insisted on perfection. Could he be a fastidious teacher? He took out a calculator. Of his 180 students, at least 170 needed serious writing help. To go over an essay with the same detail as a tiger dad would require 30 minutes. 30 times 170 came to 85 hours. One essay per month would equal an extra 21 hours per week on top of the 50 hours he already put in. He *could* do it, but Mr. Samson knew he wasn't going to be the tiger teacher that people wrote books about. He wanted to make his students better writers, but he wasn't going to sacrifice his life to make it happen. He helped students who wanted to improve. If they didn't care, he didn't care. Was he giving up on them? Yes. And he felt somewhat badly about it, but to think that a teacher could magically turn a student around without the student wanting it to happen…he didn't think it was possible, and then he got an idea. The week before, each student took a significant passage and illustrated it. Mr. Samson was struck by their artistry and bemoaned the fact that neither the AP exam nor the SBAC rewarded understanding obtained through non-analytical means. If the biblical story of Creation were the text and young Mike Angelo submitted drawings of a fresco he proposed to paint on a ceiling of a chapel, he would not get college credit.

"Violet's right. I worry you too much about the AP test, so here's an alternative prompt: Write about anything in Othello as long as you can justify it's somehow connected to the plot, characters, or theme of the play. You can do an essay, a short story, a comedy sketch. If you rather do a piece of visual art or write a song that would be equally great. It just has to be something you want to do."

Chapter 16

A S HE WAITED for English 12 students to enter, Mr. Samson soliloquized, "Why bother teaching them Shakespeare? His syntax is so convoluted, that what the Ol' Bard is talking about no idea at times I have. Verily, his language is exquisite, and yea his insight into the human condition is profound, but the reason we teach him is because that's what we were taught; not a particularly justified motive."

For homework, students translated twenty lines of Shakespeare into modern English. Mr. Samson asked Emma to read hers. She declined, so Mr. Samson offered five extra credit points. Still she declined, so he sweetened the bribe: she could pass on the next pop quiz. She agreed and came to the line, "If I was the Moor, I would not be Iago."

"Who's the Moor?" Mr. Samson interrupted.

"I don't know."

"It's Othello."

"Oh, that makes sense."

"Good. So explain the importance of Othello being a Moor."

"I don't know what a Moor is."

"You didn't look it up?"

Emma looked blankly at Mr. Samson.

"The fact that Othello is a Moor is the key to the whole play. You can't translate something and not look up the most basic word."

Mr. Samson projected Google on the classroom screen, typed in "Moor," read the definition, and said, "Othello is black. The fact that he is a successful black man in an all-white world is key."

Emma refused to read any more. Later, when Mr. Samson made his way around the classroom, she stiffened. It was then that Mr. Samson realized what a jerk he'd been to a student who was one of five who did their homework. The problem was that in the heat of multitasking to both catalyze learning and maintain order, Mr. Samson neglected the fragility of the teen in front of him. He felt lousy and made a mental note to act extra nice to Emma; maybe that would regain her trust though he doubted it.

He planned an art project for the day's activity. Students would gather in groups and trace the outline of one student on an 8-foot sheet of butcher paper. They would choose a character from the play, find passages to illustrate the character's traits, and make a symbolic picture of the character based on the traits.

"For example," he said, "Iago claims, 'I am not what I am,' an allusion to the Hebrew God who told Moses his name was, 'I am what I am.' One might draw a symbolic representation of the devil to go with that quote. Maybe give Iago a tail and horns."

No matter how well explained and no matter how well the supplies were prepared, ten minutes of chaos erupted whenever students were given the opportunity to work together.

The first group to get going had Blake tracing Esther.

"Who are you doing?"

"Emilia," said Esther. "She's got a good philosophy. If men cheat on you, do it to them twice as much."

"Quit fidgeting," commanded Blake. "Samson, you're distracting the model."

Mr. Samson checked the other groups and returned to Blake and Esther's group. They conversed on how Emilia spoke about women's equality 300 years before Susan Anthony. Suddenly, the tension of the class rose, and Leon Pruzinsky threatened, "Never look at my girlfriend, douchebag!"

Leon was staring down Jesús Jimenez, a quiet kid whom Mr. Samson had mistakenly marked absent a couple times that semester. Jesús took a step back and stuttered, "I-I wasn't looking."

"Bullshit! You were checking out Chloe's butt!" Chloe had been face down on the butcher paper wearing exceptionally tight jeans.

Leon continued. "That was your last look!" Mr. Samson crashed through a pair of desks, accidentally bowled DeSean over, but before he reached him, Leon delivered Jesús a hard blow to his jaw, knocking him to the ground. Leon dove on the prostrate boy, but Mr. Samson grabbed his cocked arm and jerked him to his feet so hard, he dislocated Leon's shoulder.

"Motherfuck!" Leon yelled as he turned to see his assailant who had not relaxed his grip. "Let go!"

Mr. Samson roughly released Leon and went to Jesús who was being helped up by his friend Fabio. His jaw appeared broken.

"You okay?" Mr. Samson asked Jesús. Tears rolled down his face, but he did not cry. "Fabio, help him to the office."

"That's it for you, Samson!" Leon spat through his grimace. "They're going to fire your sorry ass."

"Shut up, Leon," Mr. Samson commanded.

"It is unacceptable to speak to a student in that manner," a new voice called; standing in the doorway was The Hammer. "What is going on here?"

"Leon busted Jesús' jaw, and Samson hammered Leon," Blake gleefully volunteered.

The Hammer turned on Mr. Samson. "You struck a student?"

"I pulled him off Jesús."

"Right," Leon said. "He dislocated my arm."

"Can you make it to the office?" The Hammer asked.

"Yeah."

"I'll help him." Chloe put her arm around Leon's waist and they walked out the door.

The Hammer took out her walkie-talkie. "I need a sub in room N103."

"What?"

"You are to wait for me in the office."

Kimi, the secretary of Students for Christ said, "I saw it. Jesús wasn't doing anything, and Leon hit him, and Mr. Samson pulled him off."

"Samson's a beast!" Blake yelled which Cooper echoed in agreement.

"The office," The Hammer commanded Mr. Samson.

At the end of school, Dewey, Mo, and The Hammer gathered in Dewey's office.

Dewey held the incident report and said, "The ER confirmed Jesús' broken jaw. After Ms. Johnson popped Leon's arm back into his shoulder, I sent him home. His unprovoked attack calls for an expulsion hearing. I'll have Susan schedule one. Unless someone has anything to add, I think that's it."

The Hammer said, "A teacher injured a student. This calls for a formal investigation. I am not convinced that Mr. Samson acted without malice."

"Trish, we have a class of witnesses who all say that Mo stopped Leon from doing more harm to Jesús. Mo probably kept him from getting a felony."

Dewey stood up signaling that the meeting was over. Mo stood as well. The Hammer remained seated.

"Is it just me, or are we saying that Mr. Samson's use of force, unprecedented in this school district and blatantly breaking Ed. Code, is acceptable? Minimally it needs to be reported and investigated."

Dewey sat back down and lifted the incident report. "Here's the report I'm submitting to the superintendent. They might have some questions, and maybe do an investigation on their own, but as for what we can do here, I think we're done."

"Mr. Samson is an adult who works out daily with weights. He pulled Leon's arm from its socket. There was no need to use such force to subdue a teenager."

Dewey said, "Trish, Leon trains in mixed martial arts. He was sitting astride Jesús and was enraged. Leon could have killed him. For real. Then Leon's looking at second degree murder. Mo did what any of us would have tried to do. Leon should be grateful he escaped with a dislocated shoulder."

The Hammer remained unmoved.

"It's my call, Trish. Let's call it a day."

Since when had Dewey ever taken his side over The Hammer's? Mo started out the door before giving Dewey a chance to rethink the situation. The Hammer shot Mo a look similar to the one Leon had earlier given Jesús.

"How's Bible Dude?" Maria asked when they sat down at Tapas World on Friday afternoon.

"Bible Dude?"

"That's what they're calling you."

"You're kidding."

"Maybe it's time to cut that ponytail."

"There are two things I don't get. One, how come Leon only got a five-day suspension? And two, why didn't Dewey let The Hammer go after me?"

Maria smiled. "Number one is easy. Guess who Leon's aunt is?"

127

"No idea. Who?"

Maria sang, "If I had a hammer, I'd hammer in the mor-or-ning."

"Haman?"

"The Hammer's sister is...drum roll please...Leon's mother."

"That little bastard should be expelled. Connections are such bullshit. So what about number two? I've never seen Dewey shut down The Hammer like that. I don't get it."

Maria blushed.

Mo wagged his finger at her. "Maybe if the two of you get married, I won't get fired when my test scores suck."

"So now you approve." She shook her head. "It'll never happen. We hang out, but we're not a couple. What about you? Last I heard you were having some luck with OkCupid, right?"

"Been on some dates. Even had two with this grad student."

"Robbing the cradle, are we?"

"Ha-ha. But on the second date, I took her to La Trattoria and she belittled the waitress because the lamb wasn't pink enough and when the check came, she tried to get me to stiff her."

"You're kidding."

"I've had a couple of others, but nothing really."

"You have to kiss a lot of frogs first, right?"

"I guess, but the whole thing's discouraging."

"Maybe you're not ready to be in a relationship yet," Maria suggested. "It really hasn't been that long since you and Katherine split."

"Maybe, but I do have a date tomorrow night."

"Someone from OkCupid?"

"Someone from my second period class."

Maria's face blanched. Mo laughed.

"Mo, that is so not funny."

Chapter 17

THE BOYS ENVIED Leon's 1963 El Camino. When his uncle passed, Leon paid his respects with the rest of the family, waited two days following the funeral, and asked his Aunt Patricia if he could have the rusted hulk taking up space in her garage. He spent two summers and hundreds of hours stripping the car to its elemental parts, cleaning, repairing, and replacing them. He painted the car cherry red as if to dare police. On the tailgate was calligraphed in black script: *Jackson Haman 1977-2010.*

Leon picked up Chloe. She climbed in, scooted over on the bench seat, and Leon draped his arm around her.

"You have your essay, right?" Chloe asked.

"I got his essay, and if he ever touches me, I'm going to teach that prick something."

Chloe slid out of Leon's arm and stared at him.

"Don't do anything dumb. He can get you expelled."

"Don't worry." Leon brought his girlfriend back into his embrace. "If anyone does something stupid, it'll be him. I'm watching. Everyone is."

Though Leon arrived later than most students, he pulled into the shaded parking spot closest to the school entrance. The first day he drove the El Camino, he arrived early, parked in the spot, and as admirers gathered around to ogle, Ryan Dowling said, "Damn, that is one fine bitch. It belongs right there, like in a magazine." Ryan's proclamations were less violated than any Reagan High regulation.

Leon's first class was art. The previous year, his cyborg sculpture took first prize at the county fair. Now he was making cyborg mugs and selling them to students who used them as beer steins at keggers. Drinking from a Leon Cyborg, imbued the partier with a certain amount of status. Earlier in the year, a sophomore girl traded a blow job for an LC.

Friends welcomed Leon back and talked shit about Samson and the "Dweeb" Jesús. This morning, Leon started an LC which featured a Native American with a pony tail rapped around the mug. There were X's over the eyes.

"How much you charging?" De Sean asked.

"Not for sale."

After art, Leon started for English 12. The bastard Samson would fail him for the grading period if he didn't have his essay, and then Leon couldn't play football. The class hadn't finished reading *Othello* before his suspension. Chloe couldn't help because she, like everyone else, barely got that *Othello* was a play. While at home, Leon watched the movie and noted how Iago manipulated all the characters to bring down Othello. Leon would find Samson's flaw and bring him down. Leon found an essay online and rewrote it in his own words to avoid plagiarism. He marched over to Samson's desk.

"My essay."

Samson pointed to a stack on the corner of the desk. Leon placed his on the top and straightened the pile. "I've done a lot of thinking about what I did and realize I was wrong. I apologized to Jesús, and now I'd like to apologize to you."

Samson's face froze like he was having a stroke.

Leon put out his hand. "I don't blame you for what you did."

Samson shook his hand. "Welcome back."

The bell rang and Samson said, "Now that we've finished *Othello*, you'll have the opportunity to read a book of your choice."

"Finally," said Chloe. "Your books are boring. I'm going to read *The Hunger Games*."

"You'll have a choice of ten awesome, classic novels."

Chloe texted Leon: *o boy!*

Samson picked up a book. "For those who like "Bohemian Rhapsody," you might enjoy this little number: *The Stranger*. It deals with existentialism, the philosophy which claims that there is no God and therefore no outside power to give meaning to life. In the words of Freddy Mercury, 'Nothing really matters at all.' Without a doubt, he read *The Stranger* and distilled it into a five-minute song."

Chloe texted: *trying 2B cool like I know Queen*

"Now this novel..." and Samson summarized nine more books. Leon picked *The Stranger* and while most people pretended to read, he read. It was funny. His grandpa on his dad's side was a famous Texas evangelical preacher, but Leon didn't believe and thought morals were for fags and pussies. He liked *The Stranger*'s protagonist because he didn't live by society's rules. He respected that. Leon's core value was strength. People either had it or didn't. He had it. His aunt was strong. One week after his uncle dropped dead in the weight room, she was back at work. During his suspension, Leon and his aunt talked, and he learned that she hated Samson as much as he did. She told Leon to keep his eyes open. She didn't need to worry. Samson couldn't take a piss without him knowing; Leon would do anything to get that bastard canned.

Ten minutes into his reading, Blake tweeted: *penis game*. Leon smiled, but he couldn't participate. He was going to be a fucking model student. That was the secret of Iago. That was how he would destroy Samson.

Blake whispered, "Penis." Lots of chuckles. Samson looked up. Leon read his face: *Why can't those idiot kids quit fucking around and read?*

It was quiet for a minute and then DeSean whispered slightly louder, "Penis." More chuckles. Samson looked like someone shoved an enema up his rectum.

A couple of more minutes and then Cooper said, "Penis," at the volume of regular speech while coughing. Everyone cracked up, but Samson was clueless. What a dweeb. Clearly, Cooper was the winner because Samson would figure it out if someone tried to top him. The rules of The Penis Game stated that each player had to say "Penis" louder than the last person. The loudest person who doesn't get caught wins.

"Get reading!" Samson yelled and started patrolling the class. He was pissed. Oh, are we disturbing *your* reading? Leon muttered.

DeSean yelled "Penis!" and Samson rushed over to confront him. DeSean didn't give a shit. He held out his open palm and smiled, "C'mon, Samson, wanna arm wrestle!"

The entire class went berserk. Samson tried being cool.

"DeSean, you are supposed to be reading a book." *Lord of the Flies* sat on his desk.

"I never read a whole book in my life."

"You're kidding?" Samson replied.

DeSean raised his eyebrows and smiled. Blake said, "DeSean got stuck on *The Cat in the Hat*, right?"

"I saw the movie, so I got the story."

Samson was a deer in the headlights. Fucking clueless. He stared at the clock like it was going to tell him something, then he said, "Okay, read until the end of the paragraph that you're on. Put a bookmark in, and do not dog ear the page! Progress report grades are coming out this week, so if you want to know your grade, line up at the desk."

DeSean was first in line. Samson scanned his computer and said, "Sorry, DeSean, you've got a D."

"Sorry?" DeSean pumped his arms high and hollered, "I passed!"

Samson shook his head; Leon was gleeful. "This is going to be fucking cake."

Chapter 18

AT THE END of the day, Mo slid open his bottom desk drawer to pick out a single Hershey Kiss. His habit was to eat about five but one at a time as if to say he had the willpower to stop at one. When one proved not to sate him, he'd open the drawer for number two. Same with numbers three, four, and five. By five, stomach discomfort usually outweighed taste, and he stopped.

He was on number two when Dell walked in. Though there was no reason to be embarrassed by eating chocolate in front of a student, he shoved the wrappers in the drawer.

"Hi, Mr. Samson. You're not busy?"

"Hey, Dell. Come in. I read your *Othello* assignment. It was great."

"Really?"

"Only you and Noah took me up on the alternative. The use of leaked emails from the White House where you equated Othello's gullibility toward Iago's lies to the United States' gullibility toward the Bush Administration's lies about Saddam Hussein's weapons of mass destruction was inspired. How did you come up with that?"

"We read about the start of the Iraq War in History last year. The main difference was Bush and Cheney didn't get ruined like Iago."

"Better not post this online or the NSA will start monitoring your calls."

"It can be our secret."

"It's not proper for a teacher and a student to have secrets."

Dell flipped her hand as if she were shooing a fly. "Proper's boring, don't you think?"

"So what's up?" he asked.

"I have a big favor to ask."

Mr. Samson closed his eyes and pressed his index and middle fingers into both of his temples. "One letter of recommendation for Delphenia Westergard." He opened his eyes and lowered his hands. "Glad to."

A moment of shock crossed Dell's face and then she smiled. "I guess students are pretty predictable."

"No more predictable than teachers. Here. I'll write the question I'm going to ask you on this piece of paper."

Blocking the paper with his hand, he scribbled a few words.

"Okay. What's my question?"

"Uh, what college do I want to go to?"

Mr. Samson pushed the paper to Dell. She read, "Where you applying?" Dell laughed. "I guess we're not so different."

"I guess not. So where you applying?"

"You know, the Ivies, Stanford, Berkeley."

"I'm sure you'll have your pick."

"Thanks, but the competition is—well—you know."

"I know, but you're an elite student with an excellent college essay."

"Colleges like people with passion. I'm into the equality of sexes and all that, but it's not a full passion. I want to have passion like you have for literature. It's inspiring to know a person with real passion."

Mo felt warm in the face. He said, "I have to get to a meeting. If you can bring me your resume, I'll get on that letter."

"Oh, right, sorry, I didn't mean to take so much time."

"No, no, no. You're always welcome to come in and chat." Mo reached behind his chair for his briefcase. He felt her eyes linger on him for a few moments, then she got up to leave.

"I really like talking with you. Bye."

Five minutes later as he got up to leave for the meeting, he swept a dozen chocolate wrappers from his desk.

According to education experts, the best place for a student to sit is in the "Power T" which is made up of the entire front row and the middle seats of the other rows. Mo took his usual spot for staff development, the last row, farthest table from the front and center of the multipurpose room. Other teachers filed in; few entered the Power T; most sat by their friends and commenced to gossip. Truck took the seat next to Mo and threw a handful of toothpicks on the table.

"For prying our eyes open. If this b.s. is more inane than usual, we can shove the leftovers under our fingernails; it'll be harder to fall asleep then."

Mo laughed. Vice-Principal Haman standing in front of the room glared at the two. She held up her hand as a signal for silence in the same manner as a third-grade teacher which she was before getting her administrative credential. The 70 teachers ignored her in the same manner as their students ignored them at the tardy bell.

"If you can hear me, clap twice," The Hammer commanded. Jennifer Hamilton, the untenured first year art teacher, clapped. Everyone else continued to ignore The Hammer, so she raised her voice and launched into staff development.

"I sent you all an email last week to come to staff development having read Chapter Five in *Teach Like a Master* and bringing a poster illustrating what you learned."

Not even Jennifer had one. Mo had scanned the chapter. It contained advice such as the best way to escort a class coming in from recess. Clearly, The Hammer had read it as an elementary school teacher and assumed it would translate into high school.

For a moment The Hammer was at a loss. Dewey stepped in to help her save face. "Staff have been working on progress reports, so they may not have had time to make posters. How about someone sharing one thing you learned from the chapter." He searched for a friendly face and called on Jennifer.

"The book talks about being consistent with your students. For example, don't make a threat unless you follow through."

"Thank you, Jennifer," said The Hammer reasserting control. "Consistency is so important. Anyone else?" No one volunteered, so she played the teacher trick of picking someone off-task for a gotcha. Truck was surfing his phone checking BMW motorcycles.

"Mr. McGuire?"

Truck kept surfing.

"Mr. McGuire?"

Truck lifted his head. "It's Dr. McGuire."

"Dr. McGuire, can you please share with us one idea you learned from the chapter?"

"I learned if I don't read this crap, my entire day won't be ruined."

As a soon-to-be retiree, Truck no longer played the staff development game. Mo knew that if The Hammer had one iota more sense than a baseball, she would let Truck's comment pass and never call on him until the toast at his retirement party.

Instead, The Hammer took a step forward, indicating she was ready to do battle; Dewey quickly redirected, "Besides not making false threats, how else can we be more consistent?"

A short conversation followed. Dewey wrote six ideas on the board. Mo was willing to bet his future pension that no one would be any more consistent in his teaching based on these suggestions. That was the essence of staff development. A suggestion given or a new strategy taught, it'd be implemented by a third of the staff for a week, then teachers would revert to their defaults, and at the next staff development a new strategy imparted. Repeat until United States' test scores rival Finland's and South Korea's.

Mo hoped they would be excused early, so he could grade the *Othello* essays. But The Hammer passed out copies of an article from the National Education Association magazine titled, "Collaborative Schools." Mo read it last month when he, like every teacher in the nation, received the magazine in the mail.

"We'll jigsaw this article," The Hammer commanded.

Jigsaw was a technique to read difficult texts. A text was divided into a number of short parts and different students were assigned to read a part in order to prevent students from being overwhelmed by the entirety of the text. The students would then explain their parts while the others took notes. Mo was confused because this two-page article was written at a 6th grade level. It would take five minutes for David Rooney to read, and there was consensus that the P.E. teacher had suffered more than his share of concussions during his football career.

Though the jigsaw was patronizing, the article was spot on; its thesis: schools which allowed teachers to collaborate among themselves on creating curriculum and were not told what or how to teach by administrators were stronger schools. Mo was surprised that The Hammer saw this as good.

"Hey, Trish, why don't we take staff development time for the rest of the month to collaborate on curriculum the way they describe it in the article?"

The Hammer explained slowly, "Mr. Samson, we already have a curriculum. We read the article not for creating a curriculum but for fostering a collaborative staff environment. I am hopeful that we can. I hope that is clear."

The Hammer paused and Mo's cell phone vibrated. Truck texted: *Let's collaborate—everyone pitch in $20 & buy Trish a one-way ticket to Duluth.*

She added, "Don't forget to start classes with sample questions from the SBAC. Further, send me a list of five students that you are going to pay special attention to in order to insure that they achieve substantial growth this year. Be ready to discuss intervention strategies for these students by next meeting. That's all. You are dismissed. Have a good day."

Mo texted his dentist to schedule a teeth cleaning the following Wednesday.

At home, Mo continued to slog through the pile of *Othello* essays. 81of 129 students turned them in. Most of the rest would slowly dribble in until the last week of the semester when a dozen would show up. In theory, he did not accept late work. "Would you ever tell your boss, 'I didn't get to mop up the 20 jars of Ragu that fell off the display, but don't worry, I'll have it done next week, next month at the latest.'?" But if Blake Thomas came running in twenty minutes after the dismissal bell on the final day of the semester with three late essays in hand, Mo would say, "Put them on the pile."

For the on-time essays, Mo would comment on them depending on the student. As a first year teacher, Mo attacked every essay as if he were an editor at the *New York Times* readying a front page article. By the time he finished, the essay was a Rube Goldberg diagram with arrows, numbers, circles, red ink, exclamation points, and question marks interspersed with comments. Sometimes he wrote more words than the student did. He would typically stay up until 2:00 a.m. His job was to turn semi-literate teens into coherent writers. While most students fixed spelling mistakes and changed "there" to "their," the majority of them ignored comments like, "Delve deeper into this." or "This paragraph doesn't support thesis."

Over time, Mo read essays not as a copy editor but as a coach, giving them one or two pointers to work on. And though he no longer needed the extra innings beyond midnight, 81 essays took time. He could handle no more than 20 per sitting. His strategy was to read a strong student's first and set the bar. Four horrendous essays in row induced a light coma, so Mo interspersed readable students throughout the pile. He thought about marketing a surefire, non-addictive insomnia cure: a packet containing a red pen and three high school essays on *Hamlet*.

This was the third night reading *Othello* essays, and Mo began with Leon's. He wanted to be wide awake and find every dangling modifier and sentence fragment. Leon's act of contrition was an act. He'd love to fail him. He knew he should act the adult, but his dislike for bullies like Leon verged on primal. Maybe he taught high school because he was still working out his teenage emotional garbage. The Hammer was likely right. He probably could have subdued Leon with less force. But Leon's essay was solid, and while Mo would have bet it was plagiarized, Leon covered his tracks. Mo gave him a B.

Mo had given up coffee except when grading essays. He needed a pot of it to jolt him through DeSean's: *The essay that I want to tell you about is about a man whose name is the same one of the play by Shakespear called Othello who was an african-american living on an island in Italy by the name of Venice though the "action" of the play was taking place on an island which for the most part was pretty much nearby.*

The last essay was Esther's. It was plagiaristically good. The first tip-off was proper use of commas and semi-colons. Though an indictment against the value of public education, a student correctly punctuating an essay was a red flag. Finding plagiarism was bittersweet for Mo. Bitter because he hated students cheating, and he'd have to contact the parents and maybe bring Dewey in. But there was a perverse sweetness in discovering copied work.

Mo pasted one of Esther's sentences into Google and came up with nothing. He put in another, another miss. Mo tried a third time. Three whiffs was a strike out, and he'd give the student the benefit of the doubt. Mo googled: *In this play we witness the demise of a paragon of a wife and a valiant Moor,* and there it was on 123helpme.com.

Had this been Leon, Mo would have done a home run dance, but it was Esther; he felt kind of dirty because he liked Esther's energy; however, this essay could prevent her from graduating.

Chapter 19

M R. SAMSON DECLARED, "According to Nobel Prize winning author Ernest Hemingway, 'All modern American literature comes from one book by Mark Twain called *Huckleberry Finn*. There was nothing before. There has been nothing as good since.' Hemingway said that in 1935. He still might be right."

Mr. Samson always read the start of a novel aloud, so the students could dial in to the voice of the narrator before reading it on their own. Many students didn't like books because they didn't know how the book was supposed to sound.

As if he were a poor, unschooled, southern kid, Mr. Samson began:

You don't know about me without you have read a book by the name of *The Adventures of Tom Sawyer;* but that ain't no matter. That book was made by Mr. Mark Twain, and he told the truth, mainly. There was things which he stretched, but mainly he told the truth. That is nothing. I never seen anybody but lied one time or another, without it was Aunt Polly, or the widow, or maybe Mary. Aunt Polly -- Tom's Aunt Polly, she is -- and Mary, and the Widow Douglas is all told about in that book, which is mostly a true book, with some stretchers, as I said before.

Now the way that the book winds up is this: Tom and me found the money that the robbers hid in the cave, and it made us rich. We got six thousand dollars apiece -- all gold. It was an awful sight of money when it was piled up. Well, Judge Thatcher he took it and put it out at interest, and it fetched us a dollar a day apiece all the year round -- more than a body could tell what to do with. The Widow Douglas she took me for her son, and allowed she would sivilize me; but it was rough living in the house all the time, considering how dismal regular and decent the widow was in all her ways; and so when I couldn't stand it no longer I lit out. I got into my old rags and my sugar-hogshead again, and was free and satisfied. But Tom Sawyer he hunted me up and said he was going to start a band of robbers, and I might join if I would go back to the widow and be respectable. So I went back.

Mr. Samson stopped and looked up hoping to see a sea of smiling faces.

Poonam guffawed. "Are you serious? The best American book ever? Every day, you're all 'be clear and use good grammar,' and here's this *great* book with lines like 'There was things which he stretched.' Hello, subject-verb agreement. There were things, Mr. Twain. There were things."

Dell said, "The thing about *Huck* is that it was written in the vernacular of an uneducated kid. Was it the first American novel to be written in the vernacular?"

"You're doing great, professor," said Mr. Samson. "Continue."

Dell blushed. "Lots of people banned the book when it came out because they thought that Huck set a bad example for kids. The irony is that he's the most moral character in the…"

143

"Whoa," interrupted Mr. Samson. "Let's not give it away."

Mr. Samson redirected Dell's thread. "The book is a satire against what Mr. Twain thought were the hypocrisies inherent in civilization, religion, and racism. It's filled with irony heaped upon irony. Who can point one out?"

Noah said, "Tom Sawyer invites Huck to be part of his gang of robbers but only if he goes back to the widow and acts respectable."

"That's stupid," Poonam said. Mr. Samson was going to explain more, but Poonam flicked her wrist and said, "Read."

Mr. Samson continued:

> Her sister, Miss Watson, a tolerable slim old maid, with goggles on, had just come to live with her, and took a set at me now with a spelling-book. She worked me middling hard for about an hour, and then the widow made her ease up. I couldn't stood it much longer. Then for an hour it was deadly dull, and I was fidgety. Miss Watson would say, "Don't put your feet up there, Huckleberry;" and "Don't scrunch up like that, Huckleberry -- set up straight;" and pretty soon she would say, "Don't gap and stretch like that, Huckleberry -- why don't you try to behave?" Then she told me all about the bad place, and I said I wished I was there. She got mad then, but I didn't mean no harm. All I wanted was to go somewheres; all I wanted was a change, I warn't particular. She said it was wicked to say what I said; said she wouldn't say it for the whole world; she was going to live so as to go to the good place. Well, I couldn't see no advantage in going where she was going, so I made up my mind I wouldn't try for it. But I never said so, because it would only make trouble, and wouldn't do no good.

144

Now she had got a start, and she went on and told me all about the good place. She said all a body would have to do there was to go around all day long with a harp and sing, forever and ever. So I didn't think much of it. But I never said so. I asked her if she reckoned Tom Sawyer would go there, and she said not by a considerable sight. I was glad about that, because I wanted him and me to be together.

The students laughed in all the right places, and even Poonam couldn't suppress a smile. Mr. Samson knew the book was successfully launched. There was hope for this generation.

At the end of class, Dell walked over to Mr. Samson like she was bowlegged and had her thumbs tucked behind imaginary suspenders.

"Mr. Samson," she drawled. "I jist wants to thank ye for givin' me that good ol' recommending letter I can send to them fancy-pants colleges and places. It was writ real good with them big words put in the right places. You is a cracker-jack writer and I does 'preciate it awful good. You ever got a favor you wants me to do, say the word."

"How about hacking into California's teacher retirement fund and adding two digits to my account balance?"

The first student of the next class walked in. Dell added, "Really, that was a great letter. Thanks." And she raced out the room.

Though Mr. Samson loved literature, the juggernaut of education during the first part of the 21st century had been inexorably turning towards non-fiction. To succeed in an information-heavy world, students needed to be able to critically read articles, workplace documents, and websites. Mr. Samson knew an English teacher was more than a classicist stowed away in an ivory tower dispensing wisdom garnered from the pantheon of dead, mostly white, mostly male authors. He was a part of the world and was interested in having students grapple with the issues of the day. He brought in articles on runaway health costs, sex trafficking, and animal rights. The class had just finished an article from *Time* magazine which showed the latest research on animal behavior blurred the line between humans and non-human animals.

"This is ridiculous," fumed Q. "A crow takes a piece of wire and bends it into a hook. Now they're 'tool makers'? Even if it had opposable thumbs, which it doesn't, a crow is never going to build a car. Why are we reading this?"

Chloe said, "What about the elephants who mourn when one of them dies? It's like they have souls or something."

Q was unperturbed. "The death messed up their pecking order, and they can't leave until they figure out a new one or something like that. I don't know, but you can't say because they stand around they're mourning."

This was the happiest Mr. Samson had ever seen Q.

"Explain how Koko the gorilla speaks sign language," Esther took up Chloe's argument.

"A gorilla signing, 'Koko wants to play with doll,' is not learning calculus. We are totally different from every other animal."

Mr. Samson addressed Q, "You say humans are great learners compared to other animals. Then how come your third grade teachers taught the comma rules, and every year, including this one, you guys need to be taught the rules again?"

"What are condom tools?" Blake asked innocently, and the class broke up including Mr. Samson, who rolled his eyes instead of sending him outside. But the conversation was clearly over, so it was time to shift gears. For a week, Mr. Samson had used the last 20 minutes of class for students to read their books. The first couple of days, many of the students pretend read and texted until Mr. Samson came by to check on them. But slowly, as they noticed people like Leon and Esther reading, they picked up their books and read for real.

146

The satisfaction that he got from watching them read was sublime. He mused that even in a day of ubiquitous internet entertainment and incessant texting, it was possible that a good book could hold a student's attention if given the time and space. With all the workshops on lesson planning and all the hours knocking his head to come up with curriculum that captured the students' attention, his most successful lessons were often, "Take out your book and read." Though they wouldn't admit it, books provided teens a respite from the yoke of being perpetually wired.

While Mr. Samson did a quick lap around the classroom before settling into his own book, he noticed that DeSean's copy of *Lord of the Flies* was open to page 32 and his eyes were moving across the page. Mr. Samson vowed that if DeSean actually finished the book and said, "You know, Mr. Samson, these kids sound kind of like us," he'd give DeSean an A in the class.

He walked by Chloe. Though she wanted to read *The Hunger Games*, she was well into *The Handmaid's Tale*, a novel about a dystopian North America where fundamentalist Christians subjugate women. He saw that her handbag had an illustration of two pandas in a bamboo forest. Perhaps the bag symbolized her love of animals and gave her the strength to take on Q earlier. Something about the pandas caught his eye. He looked again. They were making the beast with two backs.

Esther popped into the classroom while Mr. Samson was eating lunch.

"You wanted to see me?"

"Your *Othello* essay. Is there something you want to tell me?"

"No."

"Does 123helpme.com ring a bell?"

"No."

Mr. Samson sighed. He handed Esther her essay. "Plagiarism" was written across the top.

"This is my work. I wrote this."

"I could fail you and you won't graduate. Is that what you want?"

Esther stared at the paper and then, "You rushed through the play. It was really confusing, so—yeah—I looked at a website for ideas. Everyone did, but almost all of the writing is mine. That's the truth."

"So you're going to take a fail and not graduate. Thanks for coming in." Mr. Samson turned to his computer. Esther crossed her arms and fumed.

"What do you want me to do?"

"Hang on a second," Mr. Samson deleted an email about a Common Core workshop and turned back to Esther. Though he wasn't supposed to notice, he couldn't help himself. Esther was stunning. Since he was in conversation with her, he had an excuse to look. He asked himself, "Am I a perv?" but what he said aloud was, "You need to come clean, and then I'll tell you."

"Yeah, okay, I did it," Esther admitted.

"Why?"

"Because I work twenty hours a week, my boyfriend lives 30 miles away, and really, I couldn't care less about *Othello*. So what do you want me to do?"

Esther's face remained tight, her jaw clenched.

"Thank you for your honesty. Admitting one's mistake is…"

"Look, Mr. Samson," Esther interrupted. 'Do you want me to rewrite it? I'd like to get some lunch."

"Yes, but you need to write it here in the classroom. You can do it on an off-period, at lunch, or after school. You have until next Friday. That's it. See you tomorrow."

As Esther stormed out of the room, Mr. Samson recalled that the week before, he put his grocery bag on the ground next to his car. As he opened his trunk, a woman drove over the bag. She apologized profusely and told him to call her, let her know the amount of groceries she destroyed, and she'd send a check. When he called the next day, she blamed him for putting his bag in "my car's right of way" and refused to pay. Why couldn't people take responsibility? Didn't they know that doing the right thing would make them feel better about themselves?

Mo sank into the couch in Maria's office as she finished a phone conversation with a parent about her suspended son. She hung up the phone and said, "It should be a law that potential parents take a class on parenting."

Mo said, "How about women and men whose IQs are under 90 get sterilized after their first baby, sort of like taking a page from China's book."

"Serious?"

"You got to admit that idiocracy thing is dumbing down America. Too many intelligent people not having kids and too many idiots breeding like—well—take the Norwells. Three drop-outs out of four kids. The fourth's GPA hovered around 1.0. Shouldn't mom get her tubes tied?"

"You're advocating eugenics?"

"No, of course not. It's just that—oh—nevermind." This conversation was going wrong. "What about Dell Westergard? Where do you figure she'll wind up? Harvard? Stanford?"

"By the way, the woman I was just speaking to is a vice-president at Aerojet; she gave her kid a new Mustang for his birthday. He was found in the parking lot smoking a bong in same said car at lunch. Not terribly bright. The question is: should Dr. Sinclair with an

IQ higher than both of ours be sterilized, so we don't have to deal with another Q?"

Mo felt chastened; Maria continued, "Dell's got the grades, test scores, plays in the Sacramento Junior Symphony, and you said she wrote an excellent admissions essay. She'll get into an elite school, but I don't know. She might seem more mature and well-read than 99% of the staff, but compared to the non-academic teenager, I wonder if she's not more fragile underneath. Keeping the façade of perfect student is tough. She could crack at a high-pressure university."

Mo nodded, amazed at Maria's ability to succinctly sum up the essential issue of a student, and even happier that Maria's accurate portrayal tied the random, inappropriate feelings he'd been having about Dell into a bundle of kindling that he could now burn. Besides, the OkCupid thing was going pretty well. He was dating an elementary school teacher from Yuba City. She was very nice and the physical chemistry was excellent. She was, however, a weekly churchgoer, but Mo wasn't ready to get married, so it wasn't a deal breaker.

Mo wasn't ready to leave, so he said, "And then there's Blake Thomas who has the self-control of a toddler before naptime minus the cuteness."

Maria laughed. "If you wanted to sterilize him, I wouldn't stand in the way."

Chapter 20

IT WAS GAME DAY, the second round of the playoffs. If the Reagan High Cowboys beat their archrival, the Carter High Diplomats, they would go to the championship game. If not, it would be the end of Poonam's ten years as a cheerleader. She didn't want to think about that as she lay in bed following the 5:30 alarm. She had a few more minutes to relax before the second alarm at 5:45. As she lay there she remembered that she didn't get to Samson's homework.

"Crap," she said and threw off the quilt. "Who else gives homework the day before a playoff?" Samson only picked on her when she wasn't prepared. It was too early to call Dell, so she turned on the computer.

"Saraswati, bless you for SparkNotes." Her Facebook homepage opened and she quickly checked for any pre-game emergencies. Luckily, nothing.

They were assigned chapters 17-18 in *Huck Finn*. Samson mentioned an aristocracy, a feud, and lots of irony. Poonam never had a teacher so obsessed with irony. It wasn't even that funny. The assignment was to find and explain an irony. She discovered that two families had a feud where they killed each other on sight. Then on Sunday both families went to church, sat together with their guns between their legs, and nodded their heads as they listened to a sermon on brotherly love.

"Booyah! I got your irony, Samson!"

Poonam took the day's first shower; she'd take another prior to the game. She blow-dried and brushed her hair. She had ironed her orange and black cheerleading outfit the preceding night. She checked herself in her full-length mirror, plucked a couple of stray eyebrow hairs, then put on eyeliner, thickened her eyelashes, rouged her cheeks, and did a double-check for last minute zits. She carefully applied gloss on her lips to give them a shimmery, wet appearance. She brushed her hair a second time and added the black and orange ribbon that she tied into a bow.

Poonam was glad to be a girl, glad to be a cheerleader, but whenever she thought of how easy guys have it in the morning, she got jealous. "Roll out of bed, optional shower, slap on deodorant, throw on a t-shirt, and pick up a pair of Levis from the floor," she addressed the mirror. "We should be like birds where the guys are the ones who get dressed up." Though she really liked her new boyfriend, she wished he would take more interest in his presentation.

"Hey, guys!" she called as she skipped down the stairs. Sitting around the kitchen table were her father, mother, and nine-year-old twin sisters.

Her father put down the paper, picked up his coffee, and playfully said, "Ah, the princess has arrived."

"Dad," she complained and then to her mother, "Well?" She turned around to give her mother the entire view.

"Nice. How about some breakfast? You're going to need energy for the big game."

Poonam poured a large dollop of yogurt in a bowl, tossed in a handful of granola, and cut in a banana.

"Juice?" her mother asked. Poonam nodded and her mom poured her a glass. "Want me to pack some leftover samosas for lunch?"

"Mom, it's game day. Culinary class makes us lunch."

"Oh, I forgot. And don't you forget tomorrow night is Uncle Rajiv's birthday dinner."

Poonam had already made plans with Noah, but she couldn't ditch Uncle Rajiv; being Indian meant family always came first. That wasn't the thing that really bugged her. The thing that really bugged her was how racist her "modern" Indian parents were about non-Indian boys. Didn't they realize this wasn't India? Anyway, she wasn't going to marry the boys she dated in high school.

"I know. Hey, is it alright if I invite Noah?"

Poonam's father took a gulp from his coffee and said, "You're seeing a lot of him."

Poonam did not like her father's tone at all.

"Yeah. You're okay with that, right?" Poonam looked from her father to her mother who was looking at her father.

"Well," her father paused and Poonam involuntarily held her breath, "your mother and I have been wondering…it's not that he's not Indian…he's not planning on going to college is he? And…we've heard that he—uh—smokes marijuana."

"It's just a rumor, dear," her mother amended.

Poonam made no effort to contain her rage. "Oh my god! I knew you hated him! He's like the smartest boy in school! You are so superficial! Maybe you should ship me off to India, so I can marry some 50-year-old businessman who reeks of garam masala!"

"Poonam, that's not fair…" her mother said.

"Would you rather I go out with Ryan, Mr. All-Star Jock?"

"He's a nice boy," her mother said.

"Well, FYI, that 'nice boy' drinks a six-pack, *minimum*, after the games. Noah doesn't drink and he definitely doesn't smoke. He just really, really respects Reggae music. I can't believe I'm related to you guys! Good-bye!"

Poonam left the table, her breakfast untouched. Her father said, "Poonam, I'm sorry, really. Sit. Please. You have to eat."

"I'm not hungry." She had her backpack in hand.

"Your father said he's sorry, and he is," Poonam's mother said. "We'd be honored to have Noah join us. Will he eat tandoori chicken?"

"I guess."

"Okay, then it's settled. If you're not hungry, then at least take a banana with you."

Poonam broke off a banana and marched out the door. As she sat in her car, she thought about texting Dell, but lately they were kind of drifting apart. She doubted Dell would understand anyway. For months, Dell had been obsessing about getting into the best college in the universe. The funny thing was that while Dell was the most book-smart person in school, when it came to things like relationships, she could be pretty immature. Poonam put her phone down and told herself that they'd be close again.

"Hey," Noah said as he walked up to Poonam's locker.

"Hey."

Noah was dressed in a shirt and tie like all the football players. He was very handsome with those long dreads, and his face had mostly cleared of acne after he started using the cream she gave him.

"You look great," Noah said. Then he made a face. "Something's bugging you. My tie doesn't match my eyes?"

"It's amazing how fast parents can ruin your day."

"What's up?"

"It's nothing, something stupid...Hey, my mom wants to invite you to dinner tomorrow night: Tandoori chicken—you know—Indian style."

Noah stared at Poonam for a few seconds. "Let's see. Parental units mad that daughter is dating boy with questionable morals and no future prospects as evidenced by stoner hair. Doesn't mention ethnicity, but it's implied she should date a nice Indian boy. Big scene. Resolution: Tandoori feast. Close?"

Poonam couldn't believe how insightful Noah was. She laughed, hugged Noah, and said, "You are such a freak. Let's go hear Samson go on, yet again, how awesomely great ol' Mark Twain is."

The two of them walked hand-in-hand down the corridor to Samson's class. Poonam had moved next to Noah in the back of class leaving Dell by herself in the front. The prompt on the board read: *What irony did you find in last night's reading? What satirical point is Twain making? Do you agree with him?*

I so got this one, Poonam told herself and wrote: *It was ironic that these two clans hated and even shot each other over a feud, but when they got to church everyone just sat there holding their guns and yelling "Amen!" to the minister's sermon about love your neighbor as yourself. It's ironic cuz they all like the sermon on loving your neighbor, but they try to kill each other when they go outside. Twain is saying people who are religious are hypocrites. I totally disagree. The people at my temple are great. We do lots of things for the community. Mark only looks at the bad stuff and never the good. People are a lot better than he thinks.*

Samson had people trade their journals and talk about the ironies. Noah's was about how the two most civilized families in the area were actually barbarians. According to Noah, Twain's point was about the corrupting influence of civilization. That was why he made the hero a "feral boy."

Noah was smarter than SparkNotes, and Poonam had a quick daydream about Noah becoming a professor. Before she figured out her place in the scenario, Samson called the class together.

Samson called on Olivia. She and Poonam used to be friends, but she tried too hard to look All-American with a wardrobe strictly Hollister and A&F. And she only listened to Justin Bieber, Taylor Swift, and Christian Rock. Noah had turned Poonam on to a lot of old-time music that was surprisingly good: Bob Marley, Jimi Hendrix, and The Clash. When Olivia and Poonam were friends, she brought Poonam to her church a couple of times. Poonam thought it was cool how into their religion all the people were, way more than the people at her Hindu temple, but after a while, Olivia's praising Jesus all the time kind of got on Poonam's nerves.

Olivia said, "The Shepherdsons and Grangerfords weren't real Christians. Real Christians would never act like that. Christians forgive and forget, so they could never be in a feud."

Poonam didn't really agree, but she had to admit Olivia had a good point.

Noah rustled in his seat and then said, "I don't buy the real Christian, fake Christian thing. You're a real Christian when you're nice, but when you're not, you're not a real Christian? I bet the Shepherdsons and Grangerfords, believed they were real Christians, so wouldn't that make them Christians, or does someone else get to define what a real Christian is? And what if the Shepherdson who killed Buck went to his priest, said he was sorry, and asked Jesus for forgiveness? Would he be a real Christian then? Forgive and forget. Is that it? Turn the other cheek when Hitler gasses your family? What if Hitler asked for forgiveness for the million children he murdered? Would he have been a good Christian then? Twain is pointing out the hypocrisy of religion in…"

Olivia's eyes watered; she was outmatched by Noah, and Noah was just warming up, so Poonam scribbled: *CHILL!!!!* across an entire page of her journal and shoved it in front of Noah. Noah stopped and stared at Poonam.

Noah had upset the order of the class. He had not been content with throwing a stone at Olivia's sacred cow. He ground it into hamburger, grilled it, stuck it on a bun, and devoured it. For the sake of Olivia, Samson should step in. That was the role of the teacher. But he said nothing. Clearly, Samson agreed with Noah; he let Noah be his henchman and was going to let this stand. They were probably right, but what about Olivia? All eyes turned to Olivia; her shoulders heaved. An awkwardness enveloped the classroom. If it wasn't about a poem or book, it was as if feelings didn't exist to Samson. He walked to his desk totally clueless that one of students was having a full on crisis. Noah knew he went too far but sat like Buddha, unable to take it back or say anything to act as balm.

Poonam stood up having no idea what she would say.

"Yes, Poonam?" Samson turned to her.

Poonam caught Olivia's eye across the room and addressed only her. "No one, not Mark Twain, not Noah Chu, not Mr. Samson, not our priests, not even our parents, can ever tell us what is right or wrong. Our sense of right and wrong begins with God. Our relationship with God comes from the love in our hearts. That is the essence of a real Christian; it is the essence of a real Hindu, of every good person. You're totally right about those families. They weren't real Christians, they were terrible people because they didn't have love in their hearts. And even if you don't believe in God..." she looked at Noah, "the important thing is to be a good person. It doesn't matter if you go to church every day or are an atheist; the only thing that matters is being a good person."

As she stood there shaking, Poonam wondered if she had made a complete idiot of herself. For a moment there was silence; then she could hear breathing resume around her, and the air lightened. Olivia smiled at Poonam and she smiled back. Poonam sat down and Noah squeezed her sweaty hand.

Chapter 21

MR. SAMSON HAD lived long enough to realize that age had little or no impact on a person's wisdom. He knew an 83-year-old philosophy professor emeritus who was petty and immature, and one class period prior, an adolescent cheerleader taught him a profound lesson about love. He was reminded of a story his Jewish grandfather told him about a young rabbi pontificating a point of law in the company of his elders. The most revered rabbi cautioned the young man, "It is better for youth to watch and learn, for wisdom is like fine wine that improves with age." The young rabbi replied, "Maybe wisdom is more like bread: best when fresh from the oven."

Mr. Samson had much to learn from his students; it was an error to think education as a one-way street.

His plan for English 12 was to do a poem in honor of the football game. He passed out John Updike's "Ex-Basketball Player."

"I know this is a different sport, but the sentiments are similar."

Ryan Dowling, the all-star athlete, was the reason for the poem. Mr. Samson conjured up the poem and began:

"Ex-Basketball Player" by John Updike

Pearl Avenue runs past the high-school lot,
Bends with the trolley tracks, and stops, cut off
Before it has a chance to go two blocks,
At Colonel McComsky Plaza. Berth's Garage
Is on the corner facing west, and there,
Most days, you'll find Flick Webb, who helps Berth out.

Flick stands tall among the idiot pumps—
Five on a side, the old bubble-head style,
Their rubber elbows hanging loose and low.
One's nostrils are two S's, and his eyes
An E and O. And one is squat, without
A head at all—more of a football type.

Once Flick played for the high-school team, the Wizards.
He was good: in fact, the best. In '46
He bucketed three hundred ninety points,
A county record still. The ball loved Flick.
I saw him rack up thirty-eight or forty
In one home game. His hands were like wild birds.

He never learned a trade, he just sells gas,
Checks oil, and changes flats. Once in a while,
As a gag, he dribbles an inner tube,
But most of us remember anyway.
His hands are fine and nervous on the lug wrench.
It makes no difference to the lug wrench, though.

Off work, he hangs around Mae's Luncheonette.
Grease-gray and kind of coiled, he plays pinball,
Smokes those thin cigars, nurses lemon phosphates.

159

Flick seldom says a word to Mae, just nods
Beyond her face toward bright applauding tiers
Of Necco Wafers, Nibs, and Juju Beads.

Ryan Dowling looked interested.

"Okay, Mr. Dowling, I believe you, like Flick Webb, are an accomplished athlete. Can you shine any light on the poem? Take your time, don't mind me."

Mr. Samson turned to the white board and drew five rectangles in a row, long sides vertical. He placed circles atop four of them, so they looked like heads on torsos. Near the top of each rectangle he added gas pump hoses, one on each side; they resembled arms.

"Has anyone ever heard of the company Esso?"

Q said, "It's the oil company Standard Oil. S.O. Esso."

"Very good, Q," and Mr. Samson drew an E and an O on one of the circles in the place where the eyes would be, and he put the two S's underneath where the nostrils would be.

"Ryan, what do you see?"

"A basketball team?"

"Excellent. Continue. What's the poem saying about Flick Webb?"

"He was a good basketball player."

"That he was. Emphasis on *was*. Now what is he? What's the poet saying?"

"I don't know."

"Do you need someone to pass you an assist?"

"Yeah, sure, someone give me the ball, so I can dunk one over Samson. Q?"

Q shrugged his shoulders. Esther raised her hand. Ryan cocked his head, "You play ball?"

"No, but I get it. Samson gave you a hint. *Was*. He *was* great. Now look at his team. Five gas pumps. Get it? That's his team. He pumps gas. Why? Because he thought he was the shit. He was the big stud, but after you graduate high school, no one cares how many points you scored or touchdowns you made. No one cares if you can dunk a ball when you get into the real world."

"Damn, girl," Ryan said. "Impressive."

Mr. Samson added, "I've seen the truth of this poem. At my ten-year high school reunion, many of the jocks were out of shape and doing nothing with their lives besides drinking beer."

"Unlike you who have turned into a very big deal English teacher," Blake mocked.

"That's right, Blake. I became a teacher. Sports were important for me too, but they aren't everything. That's the point. I hope you guys have a great game tonight. But whatever happens, life moves on. Don't be Flick Webb."

Mr. Samson was chewing on the first half of his peanut butter, jelly, and banana sandwich when Dell appeared in the doorway.

"Busy?"

He waved her in.

"What's up?" he asked.

Dell walked over to Mr. Samson's desk, pointed to the empty chair beside it. "May I?"

Mr. Samson signaled with his hand, took out a bag of Kisses from the drawer, and offered it to Dell who took one.

"It's nothing really. It's just that—well—Poonam is my best friend, but these days we barely talk. When we do it's Noah, Noah, Noah. I'm happy for her, but I've got things on my mind too."

Dell paused and gave Mr. Samson a significant look. He was so much more at home with conversations on Twain and Yeats.

"It's my mom. Remember how I told you she's having a hard time dealing with—you know—my dad thing. Now she's using me as a therapist. I told her maybe she should see a real therapist. She's always been this rock in my life. She's always been there for me, encouraged me, helped me, everything."

"And now," Mr. Samson ventured, "she's redefining the relationship?"

"Exactly! I knew you'd understand. What do you think I should do?"

"I think you should talk to Ms. Mendoza. She's much better at giving advice. I'm good with questions about Twain."

"Ms. Mendoza is nice and everything, but I don't feel comfortable talking to her. I feel like she judges me."

"No. We've spoken about you. She thinks you're an amazing student and has great respect for you."

"I'm sure that's true, but I can't talk to her."

"There are other counselors."

"I don't know them; it would be awkward."

"Are you asking *me* to talk to your mother?"

"That would be so great! She'd listen to you! She thinks you're the best!"

Mr. Samson realized he shouldn't have said anything and wondered how he'd extricate himself from what his big mouth got him into. He'd simply put off the conversation until everything blew over. After all, Dell was a teen; one day her mother would drive her crazy, and the next day they'd be best buddies.

"Why don't I have her invite you for dinner? She's been wanting to do that since you wrote that awesome letter of recommendation."

"Uh..."

"Brunch?"

"Uh...okay."

Dell jumped up and hugged him in his seat as Esther stepped into the classroom.

"I'm not interrupting anything?" she asked from the doorway. Mr. Samson stood up and Dell's arms went flying to her side. She turned extremely red, the color Mr. Samson imagined his face to also be.

"No, no," assured Mr. Samson. "Dell was just thanking me for a letter of recommendation. She's applying to Stanford. And Harvard, right?"

"Brown, too," Dell agreed. "I have to go get lunch. See you later." Dell bolted from the classroom.

"Don't worry, Mr. Samson," said Esther. "I didn't see anything."

"See what?"

"Nothing. No student arms wrapped around her teacher. No embarrassed looks. Nothing."

Mr. Samson was mortified. "You know today is the last day for your *Othello* essay."

"That's what I came to talk about. Can I do it next week? The time kind of snuck up on me."

"I gave you a week and a half. Most teachers would have given you a zero and …"

"I promise I'll do it on Monday. Okay?"

He didn't want to fail her.

"It'll be a full grade lower."

"That's fine. Thanks," and she left the classroom. His hand went to the bag of Kisses. He took one out, unwrapped it, and threw it into the trash; he was already nauseous.

Chapter 22

IT WAS ACCEPTED wisdom that from conception, Ryan Dowling would be an exceptional athlete. His mother was a swimming gold-medalist at the Junior Olympics, and his father was a stand-out baseball player who was drafted out of high school by the San Francisco Giants. A powerful hitter and nimble third baseman, he batted .323 in his first 20 games for the Giants Double-A affiliate, when he chased after a foul ball. He called for it, but the shortstop did not heed him. The two players collided heads, and while the shortstop suffered a concussion, Jeff Dowling was left a paraplegic.

Despite his disability, Coach Dowling was in his tenth season as Cowboy baseball head coach. Ryan was the current star. The Oakland A's were talking to him. He was also being courted by the UCLA and Oregon State football programs. He hadn't made up his mind. Baseball was a surer bet. The A's would likely offer a signing bonus close to a million dollars. Even though baseball disabled his father, Ryan knew the chances for career ending and catastrophic injuries were far greater playing quarterback than playing centerfield. But what sport could compare with football?

Baseball had been America's sport in the 20th century, but now football was undisputed champion. War veterans assured Ryan that the only comparable adrenaline rush of combat was football. Besides the man-o-man combat central to every play, football was the ultimate team sport. A group of young men training together created a band of inseparable brothers. For a dozen Friday nights in fall, they'd pit themselves against another band of brothers. For Ryan, victory was better than sex. Let those fearful of concussions and injury stay home. They would never be real men.

The Cowboys were solid, but the Diplomats were talented and had delivered the Cowboys their only defeat earlier in the year. This game was payback.

The football players and cheerleaders were lunching on tri-tip sandwiches. This was the unofficial start of the pre-game warm-up.

Defensive cornerback Blake Thomas ripped an exceptionally large bite from his sandwich as if he were a savage huddled over his first meal in a week. With a barbeque sauce goatee, he shouted, "Yo, Cowboys! Ready to blast the gay Diplomats!"

While others responded with war cries, Ryan said, "Easy Cowboys. Six hours to kick-off. Let's not shoot our wad early."

And Blake went back to his tri-tip.

Ryan had people's attention so he continued, "What was Samson's idea with that poem today?"

"What's his idea any day?" said strong safety Leon. "The guy's a fucking douche."

"Get over it, Leon," said Noah. "He's a good teacher."

"Who the fuck asked you? Why don't you go back to China and make me a new phone."

"I'm Vietnamese; didn't they teach you the difference in white trash school?"

"Hey, what the fuck," said Ryan. "We're against Carter, not each other." The boys were placated. Ryan continued, "That poem kinda weirded me out, like he picked it just for me."

"Samson always picks on me," said Poonam. "I wouldn't worry about it. What's the poem?"

Ryan reached into his backpack and handed the neatly folded "Ex-Basketball Player" to Poonam. She and Noah bent their heads together to read it.

"Yeah, he's like that. He picks poems for different people. It's cool, but—yeah—weird. It's like he's warning not to put all your eggs in the sports basket. Maybe it's good advice."

Leon scoffed. "The A's are going to put a million fucking eggs in Ryan's basket. Samson drives a car uglier than DeSean's; he doesn't know shit."

Ryan nodded at Noah and carefully put the poem away.

The afternoon prior to a home game was always the same for Ryan. He sequestered himself in his bedroom, turned his phone off, lay on his bed with headphones on, and entered a state of relaxation where he let his body melt into his bed. It was when he reached his deepest state, he would visualize how he saw his performance. Looking over the defense at the line of scrimmage, setting up strong in the pocket, throwing spirals to his streaking receivers. His dad taught him that if you can visualize what you want to do, then doing it for real comes. Unlike Blake, he respected the Diplomats.

The night before, Ryan and his dad went to Chavez Park, sat on their bench, and talked strategy, like they did before every game. At the end, his dad said, "Assume the Diplomats worked just as hard as you. Assume they have as much talent as the Cowboys. Assume they want it bad. Assume they'll stand a little taller in school on Monday, if they take out the big Cowboy." He placed the palm of his hand on Ryan's chest. "The secret of all sports, the secret of success in everything, is here. The strength of your heart is where you beat your opponent. They want it. You've got to want it more."

Chapter 23

MARIA AND MO were bundled in jackets standing in the bleachers prior to kick-off.

"Would you look at the body of that physical specimen," Mo said.

"Who?" Maria asked. "Ryan Dowling?"

"That guy." Mo pointed out Dewey striding up and down the field, talking to coaches and playing the high school principal. She smiled. "He doesn't have that bad of a body."

"My boyfriend doesn't have that bad of a body," Mo teased.

Maria looked up to the sky. "God, is there any teacher—no—human being more immature than Mo Samson?"

Mo was in a good mood. He had a weekend with no essays to grade and a promising date Saturday night.

The bleachers were packed with students, parents, and a good portion of Dos Robles. If the mayor mismanaged the budget and gave the town junk bond status, he could be forgiven, but if the football coach did not have a winning season, he'd have to look for a new job.

"I'm cold," said Maria. "Let's get something hot to drink."

They made their way over the metallic benches and through the throngs of people yelling greetings to both of them.

"That's the thing about being a teacher," said Mo. "In what other profession can you bitch out a class in the afternoon and still be a minor celebrity in the evening?"

The "Snack Shack" resembled a World War II concrete bunker. Inside were a nacho cheese machine, popcorn popper, hot dog warmer, sno-cone ice machine, twenty boxes of pizza, and tiers of candy. Profits went to the senior class trip, so staffing the concessions was a group of seniors, a few parents, and the teachers who were senior class advisors, one of them Truck.

Mo said, "I thought they gave you a dispensation for being so old."

"My last snack shack duty. I don't know how I'm going to survive without someone yelling, 'I tol' you no peppers on dem nachos!' Maybe I'll come back and volunteer."

"You're a wheel within a wheel, my friend. You're all sarcastic, 'I'll come back,' as if after this year it'll be the last we see of you. But I know you. Next year you'll be sitting on the 50 yard line, one hand on your nachos, and the other fluttering your Cowboy banner. You'll be in a state of nirvana wearing your 20-year-old staff t-shirt until you overhear some freshman girls giggle, 'Who's the old dude spilling nacho cheese on his shirt?'"

Truck grinned. "Old teachers never leave. We stick around for a couple of years as subs until they stop calling us. Then we hang ourselves."

Maria made a face. "You're both so morbid. I thought you and Nina were going to travel?"

Truck handed them hot chocolates. "Of course we are. Hey, you're holding up the line; I've got Skittles to sell. Go watch the Cowboys make war on the Diplomats. God, it was so much better when they were the Carter High Redskins."

On their way back to their seats, a pretty woman, possibly the former Miss Sweden, wearing a yellow, puffer jacket unzipped to reveal a revealing top, stopped Mo and introduced herself as Gretchen Westergard. She'd been meaning to call and thank him for the "much-too-generous recommendation letter." Dell stood slightly behind her, embarrassed by her mother's enthusiasm.

"You must come over, so we can thank you properly," said Gretchen. "How does Sunday brunch sound?"

Mo couldn't think of an excuse, so he assented.

"10:00?" Mrs. Westergard scribbled an address on a piece of paper and handed it to Mo.

They got to their seats and Maria teased, "Any moral qualms about dating the hot mother of a student?"

"You thought she was pretty? C'mon, let's watch football," and the two of them took their seats as the team captains gathered for the coin-toss.

The normally perfunctory ceremony was emotionally charged as Ryan Dowling's co-captains: fullback Manny Ramirez and middle linebacker DeSean Williams pumped their arms in the air when they won the right to receive the kick-off. Ryan looked on as Achilles must have viewed his troops before a battle; the self-possessed look atop his own soon to be released mayhem.

The teams lined up for the kick-off. Noah Chu and sophomore tailback, Isaiah Williams, DeSean's speedy younger brother, stood at the five-yard line. Noah took the kick at the seven-yard line and galloped up the right side for ten steps before cutting left away from a tackler. In his enthusiasm to make a quick tackle and establish dominance on the opening kick-off, the Diplomat end who was supposed to guard the far sideline, moved in too soon. Noah darted for the opening and a vicious block by Isaiah launched Noah up the left sideline. He passed the 30, 40, and crossed midfield. Two Diplomats were in pursuit. The first caught him at the Diplomat 40 and made an illegal grab on Noah's facemask, and Noah went down like an outfielder running full speed into the fence. The crowd stood as one to protest. To add further insult, the second Diplomat made an undiplomatic late hit burying his helmet into Noah's knee. Noah screamed and both teams poured onto the field.

Eight seconds into the game and there was a melee. Mo vaulted over the bleacher walls and ran straight into the middle. He did not discriminate. Whenever he came to a pair of players, he grabbed the nearest by the shoulder pads, ripped him off the other, and unceremoniously tossed him aside. He broke up five fights and grabbed Leon who appeared to have already knocked his opponent's helmet off and was going in for the kill. Mo threw him from the fight as if he were a rag doll. By this time, the coaches, refs, both principals, and some of the cooler-headed players had regained order. Dewey nodded at Mo and with a lift of his eyes to the bleachers, suggesting Mo's services were no longer required.

The refs assessed penalties for the facemask and late hit. The late hit player was ejected. Leon and Blake who led the Cowboys into the fight were ejected as were two other Diplomats. Noah was sent off in an ambulance.

Play resumed with the ball on the Diplomat 22-yard line. On first down, Ryan threw a touchdown to Isaiah. By the end of the night, Ryan had thrown for 327 yards and five-touchdowns. The Cowboys slaughtered the Diplomats 49-17.

As Mo and Maria walked to the faculty parking lot, students congratulated "Bible Dude."

Maria said, "I have to say, watching you pick up extremely in-shape young men covered in helmets and pads as if they were toddlers was a little scary. I don't know about the other 3,000 fans, but to me, you were the show."

Mo was silent. Everything went too fast. He had been out of control. He wished he were calmer, like Ryan Dowling who sensibly reacted by keeping the non-combatant Cowboys from going after the Diplomats. Mo beat himself up for the audacity to think he could

170

teach Ryan something with a poem. Ryan was in no danger of becoming Flick Webb from "Ex-Basketball Player." He had his act together way more than Mo had. Maybe that's why Mo needed poetry. Ryan didn't.

They got to Maria's car. "Were you scared?"

"It's like I become a Mr. Hyde. I see something and react. I don't think about it. I've always been like that. In 4th grade I was walking with my friend Phil Rosen at recess when John Kramer yells, 'Hey, Phil!' and pegs Phil with a four-square ball right in the face. 'That's for giving me the wrong answer on the quiz.' Phil was way smaller than John, so I grabbed John by his shirt and punched him in the face."

Mo looked at his feet.

"Being tough isn't the character trait I'm most proud of."

"You're a good man, Mo Samson. One day some lucky woman is going to appreciate you. And you have two dates this weekend. OkCupid tomorrow and Sunday brunch. God, how awkward will that be?"

"It'll be easy. I'll walk in the house, look mom in the eye and say, 'Good morning, Mrs. Westergard, you have lovely breasts, I mean a great daughter.'"

"Ha-ha. Have fun Saturday night and watch yourself Sunday brunch. If you wind up in the ER from getting conked on the head with a frying pan, call me."

Chapter 24

M R. SAMSON STOOD on Dell's porch, finger poised over bell. The previous night's date was pretty, vivacious, held a stable job, and was clearly interested. They ate sushi, played pool, then went to Rick's Dessert Diner where they talked and split a slice of cherry pie. He had fun, but as he drove home, he felt a light nausea, a discomfiture of spirit. His date wasn't humorous, was apolitical, and didn't like the outdoors. Of course, he didn't expect a woman to be everything; he certainly wasn't perfect. The problem wasn't in the interests they didn't share; they were an excuse. The problem was he felt no connection.

A teenage memory came over him. His Jewish grandfather subsidized each grandchild to spend a high school semester in Israel. His father forced him to go, and much to the boy's surprise, he liked it, especially the study of Bible stories. He didn't become religious and wasn't interested in moving to Israel, but he found wisdom in Genesis. When God made Eve from Adam's rib, God described her as a "helper in opposition to him." A rabbi explained, "A woman helps a man discover his true self by challenging his views of himself and the world. And vice versa."

That was what was missing. It was what was missing with Katherine. He had been overwhelmed by Katherine's beauty and self-assuredness, yet she was not his helper in opposition. And vice versa.

The door opened. Mr. Samson was greeted by a smiling Mrs. Westergard wearing white yoga pants and a lavender top that hugged her torso and showed off her slender but well-defined arms. A rose tattoo wound around an upper arm.

"Were you going to stand in the cold all morning? Come in and get pancakes while they're hot!"

She waved him into a living room that resembled an upscale Scandinavian Designs showroom with its floor to ceiling windows against a hardwood floor. Interspersed between primary colored throw rugs were overstuffed chairs, a leather couch, and a well-ordered stack of art books atop a maple coffee table. Mo felt an urge to take off his shoes and settle into a chair with the Picasso book. What if Maria's joke was prescient and by some crazed turn of fate Dell's gorgeous mother was his "helper"? Awkward.

The table was set with blue trimmed dishes, a crystal vase holding purple irises, and a pitcher of fresh orange juice. Dell stood by the stove adding to a stack of Swedish pancakes.

"Coffee?"

"Tea would be great, thank you, Mrs. Westergard."

"Gretchen, please," she said and holding up a bottle of Prosecco asked if he would like a mimosa.

"No, thank you."

"I do occasionally enjoy a splash to liven up the orange juice." Gretchen carefully poured a thimbleful into her drink.

Dell brought over the pancakes which were smaller, thinner, and paler than their American counterparts. As they ate, the three tried to see pancakes as symbolic of the respective cultures, but besides the obvious comment about American obesity related to American-sized portions, there was little symbolism.

There was a moment of awkwardness, and then Gretchen gushed, "I couldn't believe my eyes watching you stop all those football players fighting."

173

Mr. Samson gave a tight smile.

"Dell tells me that all the social media has been about the Bible Dude and..."

"Mom, you're kind of embarrassing him," Dell cut in.

"It's okay. Bible Dude not sensitive. He feel more at home tossing bodies in air."

Dell laughed. Gretchen poured herself a two-thimble second mimosa.

"Actually, have you seen Facebook?" Dell asked.

"I banned myself from Facebook."

Dell turned red. "Oh, sorry, I..."

"No worries."

Dell said, "Maybe I'll go upstairs. I need to finish some calculus. You and my mom can talk."

This was his cue. Mr. Samson hadn't planned anything out; he couldn't decide if he should just come out and broach the subject head on or start in one direction and kind of sneak it in.

During his deliberation, Gretchen asked, "Is Mo your real name?"

"Actually, it's Mordechai."

"Mordechai? Isn't that Jewish?"

"It is. My great-grandfather escaped a Russian pogrom and moved to Sacramento. He lived to 101 and died the year before I was born. I was named after him."

"That's fascinating." Gretchen finished her mimosa. "I'm sure you've heard about Dell's father, my estranged and soon to be *ex*-husband," she put down her glass. "It's been hard on both of us, and I've leaned on Dell more than probably appropriate. Anyway, that's what she wanted you to talk to me about."

Mo liked that this woman was direct.

"Before you arrived, we talked and it's all settled. Perhaps now we can move to other topics."

174

"Sure." The brunch was Dell's obvious ploy to set him up with her mother. Clever. Devious. Gretchen poured herself an unmeasured third mimosa. Mr. Samson immediately sobered. No matter how attractive and interesting Gretchen might be, getting involved with the mother of a student was a wretched idea, and dating a person who imbibed as much as Gretchen was even worse, so he kept the conversation strictly on Dell. After ten minutes, Dell returned and Gretchen excused herself.

"Your mother seems to understand the situation," Mr. Samson said.

"I'd been thinking that having you talk to my mom wasn't totally—you know—kosher."

Mr. Samson said, "Your father's not Jewish, is he?"

"German."

"Oh."

"Ironic," laughed Dell.

Mr. Samson said, "I had a Jewish grandfather."

"Really? What was that like?"

"Oh, you know, standard fare: big nose, owned a bank, murdered Christian babies for their blood to make Passover bread."

"And my grandfather had a funny little moustache, a red and black armband, and… sorry, that's not so funny."

"That's okay," Mr. Samson said. "It's harder to turn the Holocaust into humor."

"No. Some people are funnier than others. You're really funny. You kind of model yourself after Mark Twain, right?"

Mr. Samson was puzzled.

"Not so mysterious," Dell continued. "You have two posters of him. He saw society's problems. He could either rage against the hypocrisy and meanness with bitterness…"

"Which he did plenty of times," interrupted Mr. Samson.

"But mostly he used humor as his sword." Dell smiled. "Like you."

"Do I?" Mr. Samson had never seen himself Twainesque, but maybe Dell was on to something. He sometimes thought about writing satire to expose the hypocrisy in education. Maybe he would do that. There was a lot of material there. This dreaded brunch was turning out to be okay.

The two gazed at each other. Dell saw him clearly, clearer than Katherine ever had, perhaps even clearer than Maria. She saw him the way he wanted the world to see him, even though he had never known this was how he wanted to be seen. This was heady.

"Turn-about fair play." Mr. Samson felt the wall between them dissolving.

Dell cocked her head telling Mr. Samson she was game.

"Dell Westergard has two sides. The one she presents to the world, and the one she keeps hidden…"

"We all have that, Dr. Freud. Not exactly insightful."

"The side she shows to the world is the exceptional young woman. She is insightful, a first-rate scholar who plans on attending a highly-ranked college and then a career where she will positively impact the world. She is what every mother aspires her daughter to become."

Dell was at full blush.

"And that part of Dell is as true as the sun rising at dawn. The secret Dell is tougher to fathom. She is constricted by the persona she has created for herself; this Dell is not the perfect young woman, but to bring it forth might put all she has worked for at risk."

A bead of sweat formed on Dell's forehead below her hairline. He had said too much. He stood up.

"Go on."

"I should go."

"I want to hear more. It's only fair." She motioned for him to sit, and he did. He sat for a moment and considered. She had been honest with him. It was only fair. Still.

"Just say it."

"Okay." He paused and considered and then, "this Dell rebels against societal norms and morality; she can be devious and perhaps has a streak of self-destruction…"

"Stop!" Dell commanded.

"I'm sorry. I shouldn't have…"

"No, no." said Dell. "It's not you. It's me. You're per…I mean…I just…you know…it's hard to take in."

"Of course," said Mr. Samson. "Hey, I've got to go. If you could thank your mother for brunch that would be great."

"I will." Dell was on the verge of tears. Mr. Samson touched his hand very gingerly to her shoulder. "Listen, Dell. Are you listening?"

"Yes."

"It's the private part of a person that's intriguing. Embrace it. There are lots of perfect students. But to be that with an edge. That's…" Mr. Samson nearly blurted "a turn-on." Fortunately, he found the rights words, "the path to greatness."

"Thanks, Mr. Samson."

Chapter 25

A T REAGAN HIGH, Patricia Baldini was a cheerleader and senior class vice-president before attending Sacramento State as a business major. She desired a career at a Fortune 500 company until she heard a radio interview with Wendy Kopp, the founder of Teach For America. Patricia was driving home when Ms. Kopp explained how college graduates were making positive differences in the lives of inner-city youth who had been abandoned by the educational system. She pulled into the driveway, parked the car, and kept listening. By the interview's end, she was in tears. She had been born into privilege and never lacked anything, yet all she wanted was to own a big house, drive a BMW, and travel to Europe with her fiancé Jackson. Instead of giving back to the world, she was wasting her life. Ms. Kopp explained that happiness lay in service to others, to those who did not have the advantages she had. The message was clear. Upon receiving her diploma, the newly-wedded Patricia Haman became a teacher.

Mrs. Haman joined Teach For America and taught in inner-city Sacramento. To the classroom, she brought the discipline she learned in cheerleading. Up until her class, her students had been written off as stupid: unable or unwilling to learn. Her class was the first time where failure was not an option. She set the educational bar high, and she was relatively successful. More of her students increased their state scores than slid backwards. Following her two-year commitment, she returned to Dos Robles and taught in an elementary school. She felt frustrated that the administration and most of her fellow teachers did not place high expectations on every student. They were content to buy into the lie that students were on two different tracks and only the top students were worth placing educational burdens on. Mrs. Haman obtained her administrative credential in order to change that. Now in her fifth year at Reagan High, she knew the key to improving student achievement was removing deadwood teachers. Firing such teachers had been impossible because of union protection, but now things were different. With the latest federal mandate combined with favorable court decisions, tenure was no longer an impassable obstacle. If a teacher did not perform for three consecutive years, he was out. If she got rid of only one bad teacher, the rest would fall into line. Mr. Samson was the one. He favored better students and scoffed at Common Core standards and best teaching practices. He was content to let students do poorly on the SBAC.

Monday morning Mrs. Haman stood on the school steps greeting the students and smiling at the prospect of getting rid of that elitist narcissist.

"Anyone can teach a student who wants to learn," she liked to say. "A real teacher reaches those who don't want to learn."

At first bell, she patrolled the corridors haranguing students to transform themselves from members of gossiping cliques perched in front of lockers to motivated scholars on their way to class. Mrs. Haman didn't see anything funny about education and did not use humor to motivate. Students were expected to learn and they would. End of story. She was comfortable with her nickname "The Hammer." That's how she felt as she saw loose nails congregating in the corridors.

There would be fallout from Friday's game. She would summon Blake and Leon, the ejected players. She appreciated Leon's loyalty and bravery, but he needed to tone down his response to injustice. If there was another incident, she might not be able to save him. As for Blake, he might do better in the continuation high school once the football season was over. Mrs. Haman downloaded the game film and videos of Mr. Samson posted on the Internet. She needed a smoking gun. Of course a teacher assaulting student athletes was grounds for dismissal, but Principal King would protect him unless she found incontrovertible evidence that even he could not disregard. Minimally, the film would be one more piece of evidence that she had been compiling against Mr. Samson. Soon she'd have enough to go over the principal's head to the superintendent. On the other hand, she could simply wait for the year's testing to take place. The former would give her more pleasure, but the latter would be a better cautionary tale to hold over other teachers' heads. Either way, there would be an English position to fill for the upcoming year. That thought put an extra bounce in her fingers as she tapped on her keyboard.

Mrs. Haman was pleased with her actions during Friday night's altercation. She realized that once order was restored, the ejected players had to quickly be removed from the field. She found her counterpart at Carter High who whisked his players into a car while Lisa Rodriguez did the same for Leon and Blake. Mrs. Haman exhorted the head referee to quickly resume play as if nothing happened. These were two of the axioms that Mrs. Haman's educational philosophy depended on: discipline and the creation of normalcy. The more extreme a situation, the greater the need for normalcy.

It was clear to any objective observer that Mr. Samson had overstepped, criminally overstepped, especially in regard to Leon. A boy from the other team had punched one of the Reagan players and removed his own helmet as if to challenge the player to do the same. When the Cowboy didn't, the Carter boy tried to wrestle the other's helmet off. Leon stepped in to defend his teammate. Mr. Samson charged in and, instead of going after the aggressor, manhandled Leon. That this bully was not immediately getting the boot gave her indigestion.

Mrs. Haman made a point to visit classrooms Monday mornings. Earlier in the year, Mr. Samson had, for a short while, followed the curriculum, and she had named him Teacher of the Month. How she could kick herself for that. Now it was more than likely that he would be playing games or doing something inappropriate he would label teaching. She'd visit his second period class; if he wasn't able to clearly tie his "educational" activities to a Common Core standard, she would write him up.

Principal King appeared in her doorway.

"Morning, Trish. Recover from Friday night's craziness? Another one of those and I'm going to file workman's comp for PTSD. By the way, I didn't get a chance to thank you for helping get the game refocused."

"Not a problem; it was something that needed to be done, and I was happy to do it."

Principal King smiled and then, "If you were principal and you witnessed a staff member going far beyond the call of duty, how would you reward that person?"

Mrs. Haman blushed. The principal was referring to her in his oblique way. She tried to think modestly and said, "I think in such an instance, the person should be commended at the next Board of Trustees meeting and be given a small token of appreciation—say—a Starbucks gift card."

Principal King said, "I had the same thought on a commendation. Starbucks is a nice touch. I can pick up the card. Listen. I can't make next Thursday's board meeting, but you're providing an SBAC update, right?"

"Yes, I'll be there."

"Will you be able to present the commendation to Mo?"

Mrs. Haman's face dropped. Was this a joke? "I'd prefer not to present anything to Mr. Samson, if it's all the same to you."

"I see." Principal King stepped into Mrs. Haman's office and closed the door. "Trish, I know he's not your favorite, but he single-handedly stopped the fight from turning into a riot. Look at this as an opportunity to start the relationship afresh, like extending an olive branch.

Mrs. Haman was unmoved.

"Mr. Samson is getting a commendation next Thursday. You are going to be there; I am not. It will be a bad reflection on you if Coach Hall gives it since you are the senior staffer. But I won't insist. Your call."

Though she was mortified at the prospect of presenting Mr. Samson anything but a kick out the door, Mrs. Haman clearly understood her dilemma. If she didn't give him the award, it would seem that she had it out for Mr. Samson, and when it came time to fire him, he could manipulate this for a defense. "I'll do it, but giving an award to a teacher whose test scores are abysmal sends the wrong message."

Mrs. Haman grabbed a legal pad, a pen, and minced down the corridor clicking her stilettos. She was livid. King had set her up. Probably put up to it by Mendoza. She was certain King and Mendoza were having an affair, and she and Samson were friends. And then she had an idea. She would sneak in on his class. Her stilettos would not warn him. He would not have a chance to prepare. She put on her running shoes, put away her legal pad, and set her phone to video. She would capture his ineffectiveness. It was as if she was in Special Forces. Special Forces for education reform. It was nothing personal, but the sooner that man was gone, the sooner the school would be on the right track.

Mrs. Haman noiselessly glided through the corridor. She paused outside Mr. Samson's classroom and listened, video camera paused. Inside the classroom she could make out no shouting, no cursing, no sound whatsoever. They must be out. This would be a write-up if he took his class somewhere without notifying the office. She smiled as she tried the door knob. To her surprise, the door swung open into a classroom of students silently reading. Mr. Samson sat on a stool also reading. He didn't look up. With any other teacher, Mrs. Haman would have backed out and observed another class. But SSR usually devolved into texting and pretend reading. After a few minutes, they would forget she was there. Like a good predator, she would wait. False good behavior never lasted.

Five minutes passed. A couple of students rustled, but Mr. Samson refocused them. Mrs. Haman walked up and down the aisles to look at the books. Likely they were trash. If an entire class was reading *Harry Potter, Twilight,* and *Hunger Games*, that would be a sign that they were not being academically challenged. While not a write-up, she would definitely berate him. She was surprised to find Chloe Kelsey reading *The Handmaid's Tale* while Blake Thomas had his nose in *The Catcher in the Rye*. She was never impressed with this book's cursing, terrible writing conventions, and poor role modeling, but it was a standard in many high schools, so she could not make a note of it. When she became principal, she would replace it with non-fiction books that better aligned to Common Core standards. She walked by DeSean Williams. His test scores indicated a third-grade reading level, so when he was bent over *Lord of the Flies*, he could not possibly be reading it. The book was one of her favorites because it reflected her life philosophy: without strong authority, people turn to savages.

"How's your book?"

"It's okay."

"I haven't read it in a long time, could you remind me what it's about."

"It's kind of hard to explain."

"Oh," said Mrs. Haman. Clearly pretend reading. She shot Mr. Samson a "gotcha" smile, but he pretended to ignore her, his head in a book.

"These boys crashed on an island," DeSean started, "and they try to make rules, but this one kid, Jack, starts his own group, and now the two groups are fighting."

"Interesting."

Mrs. Haman was about to move on when DeSean added, "Want to hear something weird?"

"Only if you want to tell me."

"Promise you won't get mad or get any English teacher in trouble?"

"I promise." Could this be it? She lowered her head conspiratorially.

"When I finish this book, it'll be the first book I ever read. Weird, huh? I never read a whole book."

"That's wonderful," she said. Before she moved on, Mr. Samson announced, "Five more minutes." Mrs. Haman started out of the classroom but saw Cooper fiddling with his phone and stopped by his desk.

"I'm checking a text from my mom."

"May I see your book?"

Cooper dug through his backpack and produced *Holes*. She had Samson.

"What did you read today?"

"Uh," he nervously laughed. He and Mrs. Haman were now the center of attention.

"Alright," said Mr. Samson. "I see we're done. Take out your journals and write a paragraph summary of what you read."

Mrs. Haman headed out the door. Mr. Samson followed her into the hall and accosted her.

"What do you think you're doing coming in and disrupting my class? You and I have an agreement that I can teach as I see fit."

The effrontery took Mrs. Haman by surprise. She should be the one doing the grilling. "I have every right to come and observe what goes on in your classroom. Our agreement covers your 'curriculum' if you want to call what happens here 'education.' And I must say, I was not impressed by Cooper. Do you know he reads *Holes*? That's a *fourth* grade reading level, and he was not even reading it."

"I made him a deal. If he doesn't disturb the class, he can hang out when he's had enough reading."

"If he will not read, he needs another assignment. I will not have you abandon any student. And furthermore, I did not see your lesson objectives posted. I am sure that even *you* are aware that posting lesson objectives are best practice. How else will students know what they are supposed to learn?"

"Maybe they'll learn something I hadn't planned. They have brains just like us."

"You will post learning objectives on your board tomorrow."

"You didn't see Chloe and Blake reading? Open your eyes and see what's happening in front of you. Christ, you talked to DeSean about *Lord of the Flies*. Trish, posting objectives has nothing to do with learning. It has everything to do with administrators trying to get a 'Gotcha.' Best practice. Best bullshit. Look, I'd love to talk more, but I've got to get back and teach."

To Mr. Samson's back, Mrs. Haman said, "We will speak more on your lack of professionalism," and Mrs. Haman marched down the corridor. She missed her stilettos.

185

Chapter 26

MR. SAMSON WAS eating lunch and grading homework. He looked up at Esther writing her essay.

"How's it going?"

"Do you know where that quote is where Emilia tells Desdemona it's okay for women to cheat on their husbands if the husbands cheat on them?"

"Just a sec," Mr. Samson reached for his book.

"Try Act Four, Scene Three," Dell said walking into the classroom.

"Impressive," said Esther.

Dell gave a half-smile and then addressed Mr. Samson. "You're busy. Maybe after school I can drop by."

"Sure."

Dell left. Esther put her pen down. "She likes you."

"I believe you have an essay to write."

Esther picked up her *Othello* book and spoke while flipping the pages. "A woman can see."

Mr. Samson thoroughly agitated, twirled his chair to face Esther. "You don't have a lot of time, I'd get to work."

Esther returned to her essay. Mr. Samson couldn't concentrate on grading, so he ate his sandwich. Between bites, he stole glances at Esther. Was she right? And what about the totally unwanted feelings he sometimes had about his star student. And then there was the beautiful woman-child sitting ten feet away. He wasn't Humbert Humbert, *Lolita*'s sexual predator, but what was he?

"Mr. Samson," Esther said, her head bent over her essay, her hand scribbling across the page, "you're staring."

"I'm not staring; I'm thinking."

Esther ripped the page from her notebook and said, "My own work. Where do you want it?"

"Here." Mr. Samson held out his hand. Mr. Samson had half a sandwich in his other but wasn't hungry. He held it up. "Want it?"

"Sure," she traded essay for sandwich and sat down next to his desk. He perused the essay. Passable but superficial—something that needed to be done, not an opportunity to delve deeply into something worthwhile.

"I never had p.b. & j. with banana. Not bad."

"What do you usually do for lunch?"

"In and Out Burger, Subway, you know. Lots of times I don't have anything."

"How do you get through the day?"

She shrugged. "I dunno. Sometimes I don't have breakfast either."

Mr. Samson couldn't think of anything to say.

"I was kidding about Dell," Esther said.

"Sure."

Dozens of emails congratulated Mr. Samson on Friday night's game. He had come a long way since the Tracy Smith Facebook fiasco. Yet rather than being energized, he was sapped by the dismissal bell. The lunch conversation with Esther and a Hammer email demanding he come to her office before he left school made him ready for the weekend, and it was only Monday. He stood at the whiteboard writing the next day's agenda.

187

Dell stepped through the door, and Mr. Samson felt the armpit pinpricks that signaled the release of adrenaline; he willed himself to act normal. Esther was probably wrong, and even though he had yet to meet someone on OkCupid, he now had a clear idea of the type of woman he was looking for.

"Is Bible Dude too busy?"

"Depends. Did you want to discuss the Old or New Testament?" His voice sounded forced to him, but Dell appeared not to notice. "Go ahead and leave the door open. It'd be good to get some fresh air."

She sat down on top of her desk in the front row while Mr. Samson reviewed the agenda twice, thrice.

"That was nice having you for brunch yesterday."

"It was nice for me as well." He erased "America" and wrote "AMERICA."

"My mother apologizes for leaving. She wasn't feeling well and had to lie down."

Mr. Samson turned to face Dell. "Please tell her it was no problem, and I enjoyed meeting her, and…" Mr. Samson searched for a gentle way to say this. "Was that a typical morning of mimosas?"

"These months have been hard, but if you're thinking she's an alcoholic, she's not. Anyway, I want to talk about something else."

Dell was obviously in denial, but that barely registered in light of her desire to "talk."

She said, "I think Twain's view that civilization is inherently evil is too simplistic."

"You made that point this morning in class. Did you want to continue that conversation, or…" Why did he add "or"?

Dell blushed. "I really liked talking to you yesterday. You're the one person I feel so comfortable, so at home with."

For each word of comfort that Dell spoke, Mr. Samson grew increasingly uncomfortable.

"Dell, I have to stop you. I am your teacher, and you are a terrific student, and that is the extent of our relationship. If you'll excuse me, I need to prep tomorrow's classes."

Mr. Samson turned back toward the board, picked up an eraser, but there was nothing to erase. He put quotes around "AMERICA" and stared at the board hoping Dell would understand and walk away, both of them to forget this conversation ever occurred. But Dell's presence solidified.

"But why does our relationship have to be proscribed? Because society says so? There's been nothing wrong about older men and younger women since time immemorial. It's just a middle-class American taboo."

"Which happens to be a felony."

"Don't misunderstand me. I'm not talking about dating."

"Dell, I am really sorry. You have to leave." Mr. Samson walked to the door and stood there.

"If we like spending time with each other, what's wrong with that? I'm just talking about getting together for conversation. That's all. Really."

"This is an impossible conversation." Mr. Samson signaled with his hand that it was time for Dell to go.

"You were right about me and subverting social norms. What about you? If you like talking with me, what's wrong with going to a coffee shop? Besides," she smiled, "you owe me one."

Mr. Samson stared at this clever girl who was minimally his intellectual equal, probably his superior. Why couldn't they meet and talk? Other teachers and students did. Besides, Dell was more interesting than his Saturday night date.

Mr. Samson stuck his head out the door. The corridor was empty.

My God, what was he contemplating? This was wrong. But Charlie Chaplin was in his 50s when he married the 18-year-old Oona

O'Neill. Nothing wrong with that. Dell had a pretty face and a nice figure. Those awesomely beautiful women like Katherine or Esther were just trouble. Jesus fucking Christ, what was he thinking? Date a student? Gretchen would castrate him, Dewey would fire him, The Hammer would impale him with a stiletto, and Dell would need therapy for life. He'd wind up in prison, and when he got out, he'd have to live in a Ted Kaczynski cabin in the woods because he'd be banned from living in a city. This was insanity. Beyond insanity. The adrenalin pinpricks were now exploding bombs. But Dell specifically said *not* dating. Just conversation. Not a date. That was all. Period. Exclamation point!

But what if, and this was an "if" so far from reality, it was located in the last seat of the last row of the upper deck; but what if Dell was his "helper in opposition"? No, that was ridiculous. The Bible was filled with tons of crap. This was just another biblical falsehood.

But *if* she was the one, couldn't he wait for her to graduate?

No, no, no, NO!

Why were none of his books or poems telling him what to do?

But this was all ridiculous. He was making it all up. Dell just wanted to talk. She didn't want to date him, and he sure as hell was not going to date her. A conversation and a cup of non-caffeinated tea. He'd insure boundaries, and he'd drop the Mississippi River of hydrochloric acid into the bottom of the Grand Canyon and stick that between them as the first of multiple boundaries.

"I'll think about it."

Dell smiled and left.

Mo looked up Dell's student profile. She was 18-years-old. If he were to do the unthinkable (which he wouldn't) and be fired from his job and blackballed from education and dumpster diving for dinner, at least he wouldn't go to jail. Mo, who usually spent 30 minutes lifting weights after school, began at 5:30 and ended at 8:00.

Chapter 27

H IJO, DESPIERTATE," Javier's mother gently called from the kitchen.

He rolled over and read the clock: 5:15. From his bed, he watched his mom simultaneously scramble eggs, fry tortillas, and sort laundry. His father was already in the almond orchards. Javier silently got up, so he wouldn't wake his younger brother still asleep on the shared sofa bed.

"¿Chocolate caliente?" Javier shook his head and went out the front door where the last of the stars greeted him. He never grew tired of the night sky. It reminded him of the wonders of science and how astronomers figured out that the earth was just one tiny speck in the infinite universe. He wished he could be that smart.

The family dog, a 40-pound pit bull mix whose chief job was to keep the coyotes and raccoons from the chickens, greeted Javier. Javier scratched him behind the ear and then fed the chickens and Easter Dinner, the pig.

As he headed back to the two-bedroom house, he caught the scent of almond blossoms—sweet yet delicate, unlike the overdose of cologne and perfume that flooded the corridors and classrooms at Reagan High. If he ever met a girl who smelled of almond, he might say, "Hi, my name is Javier. Will you marry me?" Javier smiled at the absurd idea. He thought a lot about girls lately. Not that he did anything about it.

While Javier's father was a farm worker, his mother cleaned houses in Dos Robles. Between her cleaning houses for a living and her own house work, Javier didn't need to infer how she felt as if she were a character from one of the AP Lit novels. The slender body from the wedding pictures on the wall had squared; she moved slowly, deliberatively. Javier figured she was probably just a few years older than Ms. Mendoza, but she looked like she could have been Ms. Mendoza's mother. The only part of her that didn't look exhausted were her eyes. Every day those eyes reminded Javier that he was the repository of her dreams. He had long ago vowed to retire his mother from cleaning houses.

Javier's brother was out of bed and in the bathroom, so Javier folded the bed back into the sofa and sat down at the kitchen table to his eggs, bacon, and tortillas. The ancient, mottled-green, Formica table was the center of the household. In addition to being the dining table, it was the homework spot, the center of family meetings, and the occasional place where board games were played. Javier's father forbade television until all the children finished their homework. The family owned two battered laptops that everyone shared. They had no internet. Javier had a phone but no data; he accessed social media from the school library.

Javier had four siblings, but being first born male, he was the most privileged, shouldered more responsibilities, and carried more stress than his brother and sisters. Following breakfast, he, his brother, and school-aged sister waited at the road for the school bus. His mother and grandmother remained behind to clean and take care of the youngest girls. Later his mother would take the family's 2004 Dodge Grand Caravan minivan to town where she would clean houses. The van was kept alive by the secret ministrations that

Javier's father and uncle did on weekends and during the dead of night.

Javier climbed aboard the bus filled with farm worker children. Many farm worker kids held jobs, and they drove their cars to school. Javier's father forbade him to work during the school year; his job was getting into UC Berkeley to become an engineer. Like Javier, many bus riders were not citizens. Javier's parents hired a coyote when he was a year old to bring them from Mexico. His father despised the term "illegal immigrant."

"16 years I work 12 hour days, 6 day weeks. I love America. Without me, Americans don't eat. So how am I illegal?"

Javier sat next to Pedro. Javier might have spoken mostly Spanish at home, but his parents believed that assimilating into an American was as important to his success as studying. They went without in order to buy Javier clothes at Target at the start of every school year. For his part, he was one of five juniors who scored a perfect 5 on the AP Calculus test. Pedro, on the other hand, was clearly Mexican. He dressed like one, talked like one, and acted like a kid who just arrived from a Oaxacan farm. Javier liked Pedro because even though he was in the bajo classes, he was intelligent and not like the second generation Cholos who only cared about partying, cars, and girls. Though gangs were pretty much kept out of the community, the Cholos were wannabes. They were why white Americans looked at Javier and instinctively clutched their purses. Once while playing basketball with white friends in the park, he was the one cops stopped to interrogate. Sure the cops were racist, but if those punks weren't such Cholos, the cops wouldn't hassle him. If they were going to waste their lives drinking beer and smoking pot, they should go back to Mexico.

The Adventures of Huckleberry Finn was okay, but *The Great Gatsby* was the only school novel that he felt. Javier was no Jay Gatsby, the New York bootlegger who gave huge parties and obsessed over this dumb blonde. Yet Javier understood the striving of Gatsby to make something of himself. Gatsby reached out for the green light at the end of Daisy's dock. Like Gatsby, Javier was reaching for a green light. If you had brains and drive, you could make it in America. Javier liked Noah, but Noah was wrong to be down on the country. He lost his drive because he was brought up in the suburbs and took America for granted. He forgot his dad came from Vietnam with nothing but the drive to succeed. He forgot that America was the greatest country on Earth.

Javier read the board when he walked into AP Lit. They were going to read a poem called "AMERICA." It would probably be negative because, like Noah, Mr. Samson didn't love America. A lot of teachers didn't. Javier and his father had snuck back to Mexico when his grandfather died. He saw the poverty, corruption, and crime there. If Mr. Samson or Noah knew Mexico, they would recite the Pledge of Allegiance with meaning instead of mouthing the words or texting. Ironically, he, the undocumented one, was more patriotic than the citizens. Mark Twain would have appreciated that.

Though Javier occasionally participated in class, he was mostly an observer. He wasn't sure who else observed the thing between Mr. Samson and Dell. Dell and Javier shared three AP classes. She was at the top of the other classes as well, but she didn't stare at the other teachers. Other girls looked at Mr. Samson. The difference with Dell was that Mr. Samson looked back. Sometimes their eyes locked on each other. It was fleeting, but it was there, if you looked.

"This poem is a sonnet," said Mr. Samson as he passed out a sheet. "Sonnets are often, but not always, love poems. This is kind of, but not really, a love poem—maybe a love poem between a couple who don't know if they should stay married or get divorced."

Mr. Samson closed his eyes and everyone quieted down. It felt like church before the priest delivered a sermon. Javier liked how Mr. Samson recited poetry. When students read the poems, Javier often

194

didn't understand them, but Mr. Samson knew how to read a poem so it made sense. It was like the feeling he got when he looked at something beautiful: a sunset over the almond orchard in full bloom, Leon's car, a pretty girl. Hearing Mr. Samson recite a poem did to his ears what the other things did to his eyes.

"America" by Claude McKay

Although she feeds me bread of bitterness,
And sinks into my throat her tiger's tooth,
Stealing my breath of life, I will confess
I love this cultured hell that tests my youth!
Her vigor flows like tides into my blood,
Giving me strength erect against her hate.
Her bigness sweeps my being like a flood.
Yet as a rebel fronts a king in state,
I stand within her walls with not a shred
Of terror, malice, not a word of jeer.
Darkly I gaze into the days ahead,
And see her might and granite wonders there,
Beneath the touch of Time's unerring hand,
Like priceless treasures sinking in the sand.

Javier got goose bumps on his arms. It wasn't that these 14 lines of iambic pentameter were a warm cinnamon roll to his ears; no, the poem was a bucket of cold water dumped on his head because it explained America in a way he had never thought about.

Mr. Samson asked, "Javier, what do you think?"

"I think I get it." He felt the need to answer not only the teacher but to address the entire class, so without even thinking about it, he found himself standing. "My father brought us to America because it is the land of opportunity. I love America. It's the greatest country in

195

the world. But it's something else too. Something all Latinos feel. America hates brown people..."

Amara put up her hand and said, "And black. Claude McKay was black."

Hudson blurted out, "If Americans hated blacks and browns, then Obama wouldn't have been elected."

"No offense, Hudson, but you have no idea. You're white, and white people own this place. Do you have to prove you belong in an AP class?" Javier paused. He looked at Mr. Samson. "Even now, you don't consider me and the other Hispanics equal."

"That's not true."

"On the first day of school, you assumed the white kids, Asians, and Indians belonged. You looked at the rest of us wondering if we could do the work. We had to prove ourselves. And when it comes to difficult texts, you don't have the expectation that you have for the others."

Mr. Samson didn't speak, but Violet said, "It's not about race. He doesn't have high expectations for any of us except Dell."

Some kids laughed and Mr. Samson said, "Maybe on a subconscious level there's something to what you say. If so, I'm sorry. I'll try to do better."

Javier waved his hand as if he were fending off seconds of broccoli. "I don't blame you. It's always like that. You're actually better than a lot of teachers here. Anyway, the poem. The narrator is like steel that's tempered by hate. It makes him work harder. It's like that for me. I'm going to make it a lot farther than the white students who don't care about school. They think they're superior because they're white. They're like Huck's drunk dad who thought he was better than that black professor because he was white. It's ironic that California spoke Spanish before English, but I'm the outsider. McKay loves America, and he understands it's the bitterness that fuels him. That's the thing I never thought about until this poem."

"The power of poetry," said Mr. Samson. "What about the last four lines?"

"I don't know; maybe it's like America is going to fade away?"

"Exactly," Noah jumped in. "Just like *The Great Gatsby*. Fitzgerald believed the Roaring Twenties of partying wasn't going to last. McKay goes farther. He thinks America is going to fall."

"Yes," agreed Mr. Samson, "it's like McKay senses the promise of America juxtaposed against its racism creates a cognitive dissonance. It fueled McKay and now Javier, but McKay thinks it will ultimately destroy America because a country can't survive when so many of its citizens feel marginalized."

"No offense," said Hudson, "but illegal immigrants aren't citizens."

"So it's okay to treat us like shit." Up to this point, Javier had always been polite, even diffident in his classes, but the poem wound him up. He had never cursed in class.

Hudson swallowed and said, "I don't treat you that way."

"It's subtle. Last year you walked with me between classes to tell me why I should vote for you for president. Since then you haven't said a word to me."

Javier's voice was not angry and he smiled because Mexicans wrap their hard rocks inside soft tortillas.

Mr. Samson jumped in. "Okay, you see the assignment on the board. Let's see if you can take some of these fascinating ideas and write your own sonnets about America."

"Can we listen to music?" Poonam asked.

Samson nodded. Javier didn't have an Ipod, so Hudson moved his chair next to him and offered him one of his ear buds. Javier smiled and said, "Thanks, but I think better in silence. Maybe at lunch."

After 15 minutes Javier had:

Hispanic, Cholo, Beaner, Latino,
This is me proudly wearing my brown skin.
This country, it's the only one I know,
I get looks like living here is a sin.
I love the same movies like Spiderman.
I play baseball and I love apple pie,
And I don't want to war against Iran.
My mom works so hard she looks like she'll die,
So why do you think I don't belong here?
I love America as much as you.
I do not give you anything to fear.
I also salute the red, white and blue.
We are truly the world's melting pot
So let our colors blend and love her a lot.

After he turned in his poem and walked out at the end of class, he noticed he was more noticed by the others. A él le gustaba eso.

Chapter 28

ENGLISH 12 STUDENTS read an excerpt from Dick Gregory's *Nigger: An Autobiography* called "Shame" in which Gregory recounts a childhood incident where he bragged to his third grade classmates about his father until his teacher said, "Richard, we know you don't have a daddy." The shame of being called out by a teacher stayed with him for over twenty years.

Mr. Samson instructed the students to write essays about incidents that caused them shame. Unlike their *Othello* essays, Mr. Samson didn't need caffeine to slog through them; rather, he reached for facial tissues as he discovered the pain so many kids carried.

Abby wrote about getting leukemia as an eight-year-old and how she was too embarrassed to go to school because the chemo made her hair fall out. Blake remembered seeing his father grab the back of his mother's head and slam her against the refrigerator. When she slumped to the floor, Blake thought she was dead, and despite only being four years old, the fact that he couldn't protect her still "was an open gash filled with salt." Leon claimed he felt shame for breaking Jesus' jaw. Mr. Samson didn't believe him. DeSean wrote about how he hated gays until he learned that his favorite aunt was a lesbian. She and her partner had a better relationship than his parents had. Chloe felt shame about her dead father. He was a gambler, and the family was sometimes homeless. She used to pray that he would die. She even made a voodoo doll. When he was killed by a drunk driver, Chloe felt responsible. Q felt no shame and this essay was stupid; he wrote that people needed to "just get over it." Esther wrote about how as a little girl she had been vain about her looks, and how her vanity forced her family to move. She didn't give details. Cooper folded his essay, stapled it five times, and wrote on the outside *Do NOT read except if you don't get me in truble.* Mr. Samson assured Cooper that he would be the only reader and found out how Cooper turned into a stoner after his grandpa died because his grandpa was the only one who "gave a shit about me." He felt shame about being a stoner with no drive, but getting stoned made life okay. Kimi went to church three times a week; her shame was that she questioned some of the Church teachings like homosexuality being a sin. Mr. Samson wondered if her real shame was that she thought she might be a lesbian.

Mr. Samson teared up because so many of their young lives already had two strikes against them. He didn't see how he or anyone else could make any difference. School wasn't going to take these young people, erase their pain, and turn them into critical thinkers who would score well on standardized tests, go on to successful careers, and live the American Dream. If this was the goal of public education, it was and would forever be an abject failure.

And then he got it. He couldn't turn these teenagers into what the politicians and education experts desired, but he could bear witness to the traumas in their lives. There was nobility to that. For even the students who exuded confidence that they didn't need him or school or anything were mostly children covering up pain and shame with bravado. This insight was tempered with a second insight that though he knew more than a score of poems by heart and was conversant with dozens of classic novels, he was a charlatan because beyond being a witness, he didn't know anything about mentoring teenagers into adulthood. This was his shame.

200

It was six o'clock, and he was still at it. Dewey walked in.

"What are you doing?" Dewey asked.

He handed him Blake's essay.

"Wow," Dewey said. "That's good work, Mo. But it has a lot of errors. You might hedge that bet with Trish by reviewing basic writing conventions and grammar."

"I'm good."

"Mo, it's good to live for a principle, but don't die for one."

"I'm not going to die. What's up?"

"Coach Dowling lost his hitting coach, and he'd like you to take over."

"Wow."

"Is that a yes?"

When Mo walked away from the Portland Sea Dogs, that was it. To butcher a quote from Chief Joseph, his Nez Perce ancestor, he told everyone, "I will play no more forever."

"Dewey, I've been out of baseball for years. I don't own a bat. I appreciate the offer, but thanks anyway."

Mo gathered the unread memoirs that he'd take home and weep over. He slid them into his briefcase, but Dewey didn't move. He gave Dewey a sympathetic but tight smile and put his sweatshirt on.

"Look, Dewey, I don't do baseball anymore. You want me to take over the debate team, no problem. I'll advise the chess club, and I'm terrible. But baseball...too painful."

Dewey stood like he hadn't heard a word.

"There're plenty of guys from Davis or Sac State who could use the part-time work. I'm going home. I've got more essays to read."

Dewey put his hand on Mo's briefcase. "Just a day. Try it for one day."

Mo sighed. "One day?"

Dewey put out his fist; Mo ever so slowly bumped it.

Chapter 29

IF MR. SAMSON could remember how to hold a bat, he might give a pointer. Ryan Dowling was the only one who mentioned it during the day.

"Rumor is you're our new hitting coach," he said.

"Just for today. But I doubt there'd be anything I could teach you guys."

"Maybe it'll be like English and you'll surprise us."

At the end of school, Mr. Samson opened his briefcase and fished out his high school baseball cap. Even though he had been a college star and played in the minors, it was his high school team that came to mind when he thought about baseball. Trashbag, Ears, Lumpy, Willie, Red. Even though he hadn't worn the hat since the banquet following their high school championship game, it was probably the first thing he'd save if his apartment ever caught fire. Underneath the brim was the word "Beast" scrawled with a Sharpie by Lumpy. "So you never forget who you are," he said.

He made his way to the diamond. The boys were suiting up, so it was just Coach Jeff Dowling sitting in his all-terrain wheelchair studying a clipboard. Coach Dowling never acknowledged that he was handicapped, and he expected his players to never bring excuses; apparently they never did because in his ten seasons, the Reagan

Cowboys went deep into the playoffs eight times and were section champs twice.

"Hey, Coach," said Mr. Samson.

Coach Dowling looked up. "Glad you came out."

"I'd be lying if I said baseball didn't get me through high school."

"Same with me. I loved her more than girls, and I did love skirts. And then—well, you know—she about killed me, and I was so messed up I tried to finish the job. And then in an act of grace, she redeemed me."

"Coach, you're a poet," Mr. Samson said.

"Every emotion in your poems and every plot in your novels can be found here." Coach Dowling waved his hand palm up across the diamond.

This statement was true, and Mr. Samson had always known it subconsciously, and now it dawned on him how the odd couple of his early and late passions—baseball and literature—rather than being diametrically opposed like the god Janus pulling him in opposing directions, were intimate lovers leading him to himself.

The players jogged out to the field. Ryan led them in stretching.

"We graduated a lot of talent last year, but I think we can be competitive. Pitching should be decent, defense adequate, but hitting is marginal. That's where you come in."

"You might want to wait before offering me a contract. I haven't swung a bat in a decade."

"Fair enough. Take the batting cages and look at their swings. Probably a lot of rust from the off-season. And…" Coach Dowling grinned. "Afterwards, maybe you can watch the catchers throw. They chuck it to centerfield as often as second base. I remember watching you in the Big West championship game. You pegged three guys; each throw over the corner of the bag, four inches from the ground."

"That was a good game."

"You had an arm to match your bat. I thought you were going to the Big Show."

"Looks like they're ready for me."

"Okay, go get 'em."

The first batter to face the pitching machine was Ryan. There was no rust in his stance. His feet balanced, his body relaxed, his hands coiled behind his shoulder, bat ever so slightly circling not unlike a cobra ready to strike. Out of ten pitches, he hit six hard line-drives, two towering flies, and two sharp grounders.

"Not bad," Mr. Samson said.

"Any suggestions, Coach?"

"You have a swing I wouldn't think of tampering with. You have a private coach?"

"Yeah. But you had better stats than him. If you see something tell me, okay?"

And without doing a thing, Mr. Samson had been accepted as hitting coach. Ryan set a high bar with his A-plus swing; he was followed by a group of Ds and the occasional C.

Blake came up. He was focused, not a hint of class clown. His feet weren't bad, and his swing was vicious—too vicious—he got under five balls for flies, topped three for grounders, and whiffed two. He started out the cage. Mr. Samson said, "You ever hear of Sandy Koufax?"

"He's your grandpa, right?" Blake was not happy and didn't want to chat.

"The Dodgers drafted him because he had the Habanero of fastballs. The problem was he walked more than he struck out. Before one game this catcher, Norm Sherry, told him, 'Don't throw so hard.' That day he threw 7 no-hit innings."

The lesson seemed clear enough, but Blake gave Mr. Samson a blank look, shook his head, and headed toward the exit.

"Blake, don't try to kill the ball. Shorten your swing and square up the ball. Watch it meet the bat. Get back in there."

Blake stared hard at Mr. Samson and then stepped back to the batting box.

"Just meet the ball."

Blake hit 5 line-drives. As he left the cage, he said, "Thanks, Coach."

Mr. Samson almost choked on the lump in his throat. Why was he such a sentimental bastard?

Leon was next. Before stepping into the cage, he said without looking at Mr. Samson, "Don't bother, *Coach*. I know how to swing a bat."

While not as powerful or consistent as Ryan, Leon could hit. Mr. Samson would have told Leon to shorten his swing and get inside the ball, but he said nothing.

Chapter 30

MR. SAMSON WATCHED the steam rise from his tea. He sat across from Dell who cupped her hands around a strawberry smoothie. He checked the door whenever it opened. He had a story if a colleague, student, or parent walked in: Dell was consulting him about the Signet Classics Student Scholarship Essay Contest, and there were too many distractions at school for them. A legal pad and pen sat to the right of his drink.

The door swung open, Mr. Samson turned his head, and Dell loudly whispered, "Boo!" Mr. Samson jumped and then scowled at Dell.

"Are you sorry you came?'

"Of course." Mr. Samson sipped his tea. "You're not drinking your smoothie."

Dell stirred the red concoction with her straw and then scooted in her chair. Her knee grazed Mr. Samson's knee under the table. He jerked back, tipping the table, and tea sloshed over the rim.

"You said drinks and conversation. You said nothing about knees." Mr. Samson glared at Dell. She appeared confused until he broke into a small smile.

"Is this better?" Dell said and propped Mr. Samson's legal pad between her smoothie and his tea.

"Would you mind asking the barista for a two-by-three piece of plexiglass to insert between our knees?"

Dell responded, "Why don't we just strap sensors on them hooked up to electric shocks?"

"Good idea," added Mr. Samson, "and add a bell to ring with every shock."

"With all the bells at school, you'd need a knee replacement by spring break."

Mr. Samson laughed. "And your fast twitch muscles would be so strong, you'd win the section 100-meter dash."

"That wouldn't look so bad on my college app. Speaking of sports, I heard you got drafted to be a baseball coach."

"Just a little batting. It's good seeing Blake Thomas in a new light."

"Kind of like seeing me in a new light?"

Mr. Samson let that comment pass. An extremely overweight woman plodded across the room. Dell said, "Lupita Alvarez wears a scarlet letter like her. The modern shame isn't 'Adultery,' it's 'Obesity.'"

Mr. Samson nodded.

Dell said, "None of my classmates would have understood that allusion."

"Your generation isn't the most versed in classic American literature."

"That's my point. None of my classmates understand me. Even with Poonam I edit what I say." She paused. "But never with you." She locked onto his eyes. The light banter was over. His skin felt clammy. He drained his tea.

Dell seemed to understand she had touched his knee again and pulled back. "People don't see Lupita. They see a fat girl. Gay people are getting equal rights. Everyone knows it's wrong to be racist. But no problem hating the obese."

"There's a difference. People are born into their race or have the genetic make-up to be gay. But obese people can eat less and exercise more."

Dell plunged in her straw and sucked down her entire smoothie, ending with a loud slurp.

"Impressive."

"Lupita eats better than me but outweighs me by over a hundred pounds. My parents are slender, I'm slender. Her parents are obese, she's obese. You know, the "thrifty gene" hypothesis."

"The what?"

"Native Americans coming over the Bering Strait had to deal with an inconsistent food supply. It was literally feast or famine, so they became very efficient at storing fat..."

Mr. Samson held up his hand, and finished, "...so now that there's a constant food supply, descendants are genetically predisposed to obesity, and Lupita is—drum roll, please—Native American?"

"Exactly."

"My grandfather was a Nez Perce."

"Oh, great, now I'm lecturing a Native American about his genetics."

"No, no, no. I never heard of the thrifty gene. It makes sense. I'm glad you told me."

"Is your grandfather the reason for the ponytail?"

"Pretty much, yeah."

"I've never seen such a nice ponytail. It looks silky."

Another awkward silence. Mr. Samson looked into his tea cup to see if there was anything more to drink.

Dell said, "Last year my aunt had chemo; after her hair fell out, she wore a wig. On the first day of class, I wondered if you ever thought about donating your hair."

Mr. Samson shook his head and looked at his empty tea cup again. This "coffee date" was like being at a party where he didn't know anyone; he'd be more comfortable with something in his hands. "Scone?"

"No, thanks."

Mr. Samson excused himself to get a scone. As he stood waiting for his change, he thought how the lack of light banter mixed with intellectual boredom doomed his marriage.

When he returned, Dell said, "I really like *Brave New World.*"

The teacher was grateful the conversation turned from the personal to literature. He said, "It's hard to believe that more than 80 years ago, Huxley predicted a world of rampant materialism, drugs to decrease stress, and happiness chosen over the quest for truth—a world almost exactly like ours."

Dell added, "What scares me most is how everyone is the same. A world of no Lupita Alvarezs because the thrifty genes are screened out."

"I'm sure Lupita wouldn't mind being slender."

"I'm sure she'd like to look like a Victoria Secrets' model, anorexic with big breasts, but if you start modifying genes for weight, then what stops you from modifying for gayness? Or shortness? Are we moving toward a world where parents genetically engineer their children and create a homogeneous population of Alphas? The problem with homogeneous populations is they can't deal with new environmental stresses. Maybe sometime in the future, the thrifty gene will again be the way to evolutionary success. It may become sexy like in Rubens' paintings. But that's not the biggest problem."

"No?" Mr. Samson was captivated.

"The biggest problem is that you can't deviate from the social norm. There's no room for the individual. Anyone with different morals is destroyed, like Edna in *The Awakening.* It's a future in

209

which we're all sheep. Given what I see in the world, we can't wait to get there."

Mr. Samson stared at Dell. This high school girl was on track for a MacArthur Genius Award. She was perhaps the most interesting person he had ever met. Was coffee her ultimate goal, or did she want more? She definitely gave off the vibe. For the sake of argument, what if he was interested as well? Besides breaking the social norms she was so intent on not following and losing his career, a relationship with Delphinia Westergard would be short-lived. Once at Harvard or Stanford, she'd shack up with Mr. Samson's intellectual betters. About that he was certain. Yet, he could not deny their chemistry. She would graduate in less than six months, and then she would no longer be taboo or at least less so. Mo Samson was at an emotional impasse. That is until he gave his head one enormous shake. She was his student. There was absolutely no way he was going to entertain the idea of a relationship. End of story. Slam the door shut.

"What?" Dell asked.

"Nothing. Just thinking."

Dell turned blotchy red on her neck. "About me?"

"No."

"Oh." Dell looked disappointed.

Without permission, his foot slipped into the closing door to keep it ajar. "I never properly thanked you for the poem you gave me. It was a…a lifesaver."

Dell turned scarlet.

"Really?"

"Really."

Dell glanced at her phone. "Sorry, I've got to get going. I'll see you tomorrow." As Dell got up, her knee hit Mr. Samson's. Before he knew it, Dell rubbed his knee and was out the door. The rub remained on his knee long after she left, the years separating the two seemed inconsequential.

Chapter 31

OLIVIA JOHNSON LOVED her Tuesday and Thursday early morning Bible study. It had been a month since she broke up with Hudson. The two of them were sitting on her living room couch, her parents out for the evening. Hudson's right hand was fondling her right breast, and when his left hand started for her female part, she stopped him. She took his hands in hers and told him, once again, that sex was a sacred intimacy that she would only share with her husband after they were sanctified through marriage.

He tried to free his hands and said, "We've been going out for almost a year."

"Hudson, if you respected me, you'd stop."

Hudson broke away and stood up. "This is so stupid! A person wouldn't buy a car without test driving it, right?"

Olivia could not believe what came out of Hudson's mouth. How could he compare the intimacy between two loving people to driving a car? She knew for the past few months it was coming. And now here it was. It was over, and she told him so.

Both Youth Minister Chuck and her best friend Kimi provided comfort following the breakup, and Jesus, of course. Jesus was the anchor of her life; without Him she'd be adrift in the sea of the world. Jesus was her rudder, her ballast, and her map. Jesus was her everything.

"Good morning, my brothers and sisters in Christ," the minister began.

"Good morning, Minister Chuck," the 15 teens answered.

"Let us pray."

They bent their heads while Minister Chuck beseeched Jesus to bring strength to their study of His Sacred Word. As Olivia prayed, her breathing deepened, the tension in her shoulders lifted, and she felt the spirit of Jesus effuse through her flesh. "Effuse"? What a weird word, and then she remembered it came from that poem "Song of Myself." A strange feeling came over: weren't the goals of Bible study and AP Lit kind of the same? Minister Chuck used the Word to bring teens to Jesus while Mr. Samson used literature to bring students to themselves. She appreciated Mr. Samson, but sometimes she felt uncomfortable because he tried to make her question her faith. But hadn't her faith blossomed this year? Wasn't she stronger in Jesus? Though Mr. Samson had tried to kill her love of Jesus, he had only strengthened it.

"Today," began Minister Chuck, "let us continue to delve into Acts, Chapter 7 and examine the testimony of St. Stephen and his martyrdom."

After the reading, the class discussed the importance of testifying for Jesus. Olivia hoped that if she ever had the chance to testify, she would have the courage to speak up. People like Mr. Samson, Dell, and Noah were too smart for her to argue against. She remembered how absolutely petrified and speechless she was when Noah challenged her when she spoke about true Christians during a class discussion earlier in the year. She wished she had the confidence of the other kids. She wanted another chance to be tested to show her love and dedication to Jesus, but at the same time the thought terrified her. She could never do what St. Stephen did.

It was still awkward with Hudson. He bad-mouthed her at school and on all the social media. He thought he was so smart and everything, but he was just an immature boy. She tried to ignore him and wondered what she ever saw in him.

The book they just finished, *Brave New World,* was strange. It was about a future world where Jesus was replaced by Henry Ford. That was totally never going to happen. There would never be a world without Jesus. In this made-up world, having sex meant the same as going to the movies. Everyone had it with everyone. It didn't take a genius to see that this was where the real world was heading, but Praise the Lord, there were enough Christians to prevent a worldwide orgy from taking over everything.

Olivia drove to school with Kimi who also recently broke up with her boyfriend.

"Who do you think is the bigger jerk, Hudson or Andre?" Kimi asked. "Did you see the Instagram Andre posted of him standing between like five Hooter waitresses?"

"I am so done with looking at anything either of them post."

"Me too. And then there was his stupid Facebook invite to Cara for prom. He is such a jerk. Hey..." Kimi touched Olivia's shoulder. "You and me should go to prom!"

"Like a date?"

"Yeah, let's get dressed to the nines and show those jerks what real women look like!" Kimi laughed. Olivia kind of liked the idea except Kimi seemed a little too enthusiastic.

"Not like a real date though, right?" Kimi was her best friend, but sometimes she kind of got a weird feeling from her.

"No kissing. Just hand holding."

"What?"

"Kidding!"

"Let's start the Socratic Seminar," Mr. Samson said. A Socratic Seminar was when they sat in circle to talk about a book. Everyone had to say something. Olivia was anxious. Hudson would likely belittle anything she said.

The students pushed their desks to the outside of the room and made a circle of chairs on the inside. Mr. Samson spoke about time as the fourth dimension and "how a great writer throws back the curtain of time and is able to peer into the future to comment on the human experience that is always true no matter when the book is written. The classic science fiction writers are able to look at the trajectory of society and create a world that future generations recognize as their own. The dystopia *Brave New World* is Aldous Huxley's masterpiece that does this."

"I don't think it's dystopian," Hudson challenged Mr. Samson. "I'd have no problem living in a world with no war, everybody happy, and nobody sick. If something bothers you, take a dose of soma. And they have no hang-ups about sex."

Olivia felt his glare but didn't give him the satisfaction of looking at him. Why did he have to be so mean? Couldn't he just leave her alone?

"There is so much neurosis around sex," he continued. "But animals don't have it. Take bonobos. They have sex way more than in *Brave New World*, and they're totally happy. Sex isn't a big deal in our generation. Having friends with benefits doesn't make you immoral. What's the problem?"

Olivia wasn't shocked but disappointed that Mr. Samson nodded and said, "Hudson makes a strong case. Would anyone like to argue his point?"

Dell said that she viewed it as a dystopia because people lost their individuality and had to live by societal norms even if they disagreed with them; however, she said nothing to counteract Hudson's view on sex. It figured. In a world of "hook-ups" and girls giving blow jobs to boys whose names they didn't even know, then sex didn't mean anything more than shaking someone's hand. As a

Cowboy for Christ, Olivia saw that it was here, her moment to testify. She nervously raised her hand.

"You all know me," she began. "What I'm going to say isn't new, but I hope you can see it in your hearts to at least hear me." She wasn't sure if Hudson's face was disgusted or bewildered. "I am sure that having sex feels wonderful. One day I hope, with God's blessing, to have that experience, but I won't do it now. Maybe you're saying it's because I'm all Christian and everything. And you're right. That's who I am. But my reason for disagreeing with Hudson is not because of Christ; it's about dignity. The most intimate act between a man and a women is not the same as eating a bowl of ice cream. We are not bonobos. We are humans. If casual sex made the people in the book happy, then why did they all take soma? If they were so satisfied having sex every day, they wouldn't need anti-depressants. Teens have lots of sex. I might not be one of them, but I know. And I know that our generation takes more anti-depressants than any other group of teens ever. You might disagree with me, but you don't even need to be a Christian to see the truth: casual sex makes your soul sick."

Olivia felt hot in the face, embarrassed. The power of Jesus that had spoken through her was gone. She was spent. And now her classmates would see her as being even odder than before. Even if Hudson hadn't blabbed to everyone why they broke up, they'd know now. But she didn't care. She was a Cowboy for Christ.

Mr. Samson said, "The point you make about casual sex is excellent. While I can't speak for Jesus because I'm no authority on him, I'm certain that Aldous Huxley would have applauded." Mr. Samson slowly clapped his hands. The rest of the circle joined in. Even Hudson was peer-pressured into silently applauding.

Chapter 32

ENGLISH 12 WAS beginning a unit on short stories which would culminate in students writing their own. For Mr. Samson, reading 100 short stories was far deadlier than reading 100 essays. While the students normally wrote short essays because they had little to say, their literary works often were significantly longer with significantly less to say.

"Today you're going to write the beginning of a story which might become the seed of your short story. Let's brainstorm 15 words that could be good in a story and put them on the board. Who has a word?"

Blake raised his hand. Mr. Samson ignored him.

"Anyone?" Mr. Samson braced himself. "Blake."

"Shit."

"Let's keep the words school cool."

"You said our stories don't have to be school cool. All the books you make us read curse all the time, like Holden in that Catcher book."

"You can use any language to make your stories realistic. But I don't want Principal King walking in with 'shit' on the board."

"Okay, then 'Prostitute.' It's the world's oldest profession, so must be school cool."

Mr. Samson shook his head before writing "Prostitute" on the board in small, crowded letters.

"Hammered," DeSean called out.

Mr. Samson wrote "Hammer" and the class booed. He picked up an eraser and went to the word.

"It's okay, leave it," said DeSean turning to his classmates. "We can just use the past tense."

Cooper said, "Camel toe."

"What's 'camel toe'?"

The class laughed, but no one volunteered a definition.

"Fine I'll google it."

"Use Google images," Q suggested.

"Will I get fired?"

More laughter. Mr. Samson wrote the word "camel" on the board.

Q said, "Placenta."

"YOLO!" Cooper screeched.

Mr. Samson said, "How about some voices we don't normally hear. Abby?"

"Dog?"

Mr. Samson wrote "dog" in larger letters.

"Fabio?"

"On."

Mr. Samson rolled his eyes at this most basic of prepositions, but he wrote "on" in large letters directly below "dog." Blake's hand shot straight up as if he needed to go to the bathroom immediately to avoid an accident. Mr. Samson again searched the room, but no other hands were up. He nodded to Blake.

"Cat!"

Blake gave a Cheshire Cat grin. If there was a joke, Mr. Samson didn't get it. No one else seemed either, so he wrote in equally large letters, "cat" under "on." There were a couple of laughs, fingers pointing at the board, and the entire class broke into a paroxysm of laughter. Mr. Samson was clueless until he stood back from the board and saw the three large words. Once again his attempt to teach this class was subverted. Cell phones took pictures before he erased the offending preposition.

"Chloe."

"I don't know."

"Just say the first word that comes to your mind."

"I don't know. Call on someone else."

The class turned on Chloe demanding a word.

"Cupcake. Okay?"

"Pedro."

"Almond."

Five more words and the list was finished. Mr. Samson instructed the class to write the start of a story using as many of the words from the board as they could. He told them not to write something obvious but, "Surprise the reader. That's what makes a great story."

For fifteen blissful minutes, there was quiet as students wrote. DeSean asked Mr. Samson, "Does 'beginning' have two g's and one n or two g's and two n's?"

After the time was up, the students shared the stories with each other. There was consensus that Esther's was good, so she read it to the class.

Cupcake, a beautiful Siamese cat with blue eyes, was getting ready for the school dance.

"Young kitten," her mom sternly said, "You march those four legs of yours back upstairs and put on something sensible. No cat of mine is going out of this house looking like a prostitute."

"Come on, Mom," Cupcake complained. "Placenta's mom is letting her wear a strapless-fronted, camel-hair blouse."

"Well..."

"Thanks, Mom!" and she was out the door.

The dance was particularly crowded. There was tension in the air because a group of dogs had come to crash the dance.

"Dance with your own kind, or we'll call in The Hammer!" said Ms. Almond the nut teacher.

A hound named Butters said, "Why can't we be friends?"

Butters had his eye on Cupcake. A feeling overcame her that she had never experienced. "YOLO," she whispered.

"That's as far as I got."

"Nice," said Mr. Samson. "Do you want to keep going with it?"

"Yeah, It's about going out with someone you're not supposed to go out with."

"Sort of like Romeo and Juliet or Othello and Desdemona?"

"A student and a teacher!" Blake yelled. "Like Robertson and Tanya!"

Thankfully the bell rang, so Mr. Samson hoped no one noticed his   red,   sweating   face.

Chapter 33

IT WAS SATURDAY morning. The night before Mo went out with Maria's friend Jennifer. They went to a club in downtown Sacramento and had platonic fun, for neither Jennifer nor Mo was attracted to the other in that way. After a half-year, he had at least a dozen dates through OkCupid and another handful, like Jennifer, through friends. Yet, no one lit his fire. He hated to admit it, but the best times he had with a woman were his sporadic coffees with Dell. Once she brought a set of kitchen magnets that consisted of a hundred small magnetized words. They composed poetry which was terrible but so much fun. Then they recreated their favorite lines from *Monty Python and the Holy Grail* as if delivered by various teachers and students from Reagan High. Totally inappropriate for a teacher to collude with a student like that, but he laughed hard enough to spill his tea over the unblemished legal pad that he still brought. Of course, the coffee shop was the entirety of their relationship.

He picked up his phone and found a text from Maria asking about the night before. He texted: *Lots of fun, great woman, but...*

He looked over the pile of essays he needed to grade and remembered he had extra hitting practice in the afternoon because play-offs were just around the corner. So much for a day off.

A text came from Dell: *Hike Hidden Falls with Poonam, Noah, me?* Texts from Dell annoyed him. The nearly 2,000 texts between

Tanya and Robertson was his smoking gun. Of course, there wasn't anything untoward about his relationship with Dell; still, texts created a record.

As for a hike? He could use some exercise, it was looking to be a beautiful day, and observing the world's most unlikely couple would definitely provide entertainment. Why not? If they went early enough, he'd be back before practice. There was always Sunday to do the essays. Since the trailhead was near his house, he texted: *Ride bikes to my apt 3152 Los Pinos. 30 min?*

She replied: *K*

A half-hour later, Dell arrived alone.

"We meeting Noah and Poonam at the trailhead?"

"Some cheerleading disaster came up, and she couldn't make it so early. As Poonam goes, so goes Noah. Ready? Do you have an extra water? I forgot mine."

"Uh, sure. Be right back." Mr. Samson went into his kitchen to get another water bottle. What started out as an innocent outing was now fraught with moral hazard. A spring-time hike alone with Dell was definitely different than meeting at a coffee shop. The word *devious* sprang to his mind. Cheerleading disaster? Had she even spoken to Poonam?

"Nothing's wrong, right? Poonam and Noah really wanted to come. Do you want me to text her and see if we can put it off to the afternoon? I'm sure that would work."

"I've got baseball."

"Oh. Do you still want to go?"

Mr. Samson's choice was between what his head recommended versus what his heart desired. The head was safety. The heart was danger. He thought of the climactic scene in *Huckleberry Finn* when Huck had to choose between what society required him to do and what he knew was true in his heart. Huck believed if he went with his heart, he would condemn his soul to Hell. Huck went with his heart

221

because to go with one's heart no matter what the consequences was the sign of a hero.

Or a fool.

"Uh, sure."

The ride was without incident. As they locked their bikes at the trailhead, a red El Camino slowed down.

"Damn," Mr. Samson said. "Leon's car."

"We're not doing anything," Dell protested.

"It's how we're perceived. A picture of us is probably already online."

Dell took out her phone. "Not yet it's not. Want to go back?"

Poppies dotted the green hillside. The air still carried the just-rained scent. This wasn't a date.

"Shame to waste the day. Let's hike."

Mr. Samson and Dell kept a respectful distance from each other both physically and emotionally as they hiked to Hidden Falls. The trail more or less followed an intermittent stream up a hill dotted with oak, poppies, and the occasional buckeye. Redbud was blooming and both Dell and Mo watched their steps to avoid the shiny, potent green leaves of poison oak that was a heavy presence in places. Scrub jays squawked at the hikers, and the bright lapis back of a bluebird flying across the path stopped Mo dead in his tracks to stare. He thought he heard an animal coming from below. It seemed too quiet for a person; there were mountain lions in the area, but it was probably a deer or perhaps only a rock dislodged because the noise stopped. Nevertheless, he was glad he had a baseball in his backpack.

Hidden Falls wasn't much, so it didn't attract many visitors. It stood not even 20-feet high and wasn't a straight drop; rather, water dribbled over a half-dozen rocks. Still the ferns and wildflowers that surrounded it made it pretty.

Dell said, "There's a nice spot at the top. I brought some grapes and a book of John Donne poems."

Dell clearly planned this to be just with him, but as long as he knew what was up, it was safe enough he supposed. The trail turned left at the bottom of the fall and traveled a hundred feet before doubling back to the top. Dell thought it'd be more fun for the two of them to go straight up the falls. Dell led and carefully made her way up over the mossy, wet rock. Mr. Samson closely followed.

As Dell reached for a handhold, her foot slipped and she fell, tumbling straight into the arms of Mr. Samson causing the two of them to crash into a thicket of ferns.

Though surprised, they were clearly fine. Mr. Samson quipped, "Laurel and Hardy go rock climbing."

They both laughed, and Mr. Samson heard a camera click, as they untwined their arms from around each other. There was Leon Pruzinsky.

"What a pleasant surprise," Leon said.

Mr. Samson raised himself to one knee. "You followed us."

"Just on a lovely hike."

"Give me the phone, Leon."

"Right," he chortled.

"Leon!" Mr. Samson searched his pack with his fingers. "Serious. Give me the phone."

"See you at the batting cages." Leon turned to go, the phone held above his head like a championship trophy.

Mo was squatting behind home plate, and the runner was going. Mo could be fast asleep, he could be a teetering drunk, he could have a girl fall into his lap. It didn't matter. When a runner went, he reacted. In one fluid movement, he leapt to his feet and fired. The baseball knocked the phone from Leon's hand.

"What the fuck!"

Leon turned and charged. "I'm going to kick your fucking ass!"

Mr. Samson feigned left and sidestepped right. Leon tripped over a root and went sprawling. Mr. Samson stood over the prostrate boy.

"Dell, check the phone."

"He took two pictures, and—whoops—they're erased."

"Fucking bitch!" Leon got up and snatched the phone from Dell. He glared at Mr. Samson. "You are fucking finished!" and stormed down the trail.

Chapter 34

T URNING OFF THE *electric light he continued the conversation with himself, It was the light of course but it is necessary that the place be clean and pleasant. You do not want music. Certainly you do not want music. Nor can you stand before a bar with dignity although that is all that is provided for these hours. What did he fear? It was not a fear or dread, It was a nothing that he knew too well. It was all a nothing and a man was a nothing too. It was only that and light was all it needed and a certain cleanness and order. Some lived in it and never felt it but he knew it all was nada y pues nada y nada y pues nada. Our nada who art in nada, nada be thy name thy kingdom nada thy will be nada in nada as it is in nada. Give us this nada our daily nada and nada us our nada as we nada our nadas and nada us not into nada but deliver us from nada; pues nada. Hail nothing full of nothing, nothing is with thee. He smiled and stood before a bar with a shining steam pressure coffee machine.*

When Samson passed out the two-page "A Clean, Well-Lighted Place," Hudson was encouraged by its length. Everything they had read in this totally lame class was either stupid or made no sense. Unfortunately, this story turned out to be both. Two waiters wait for an old drunk to leave a café. One of them kicks out the drunk and goes home. The other one goes to a bar and has his "epiphany" which Samson called, "one of the most profound paragraphs of the 20th century." Right. What did Samson know? That ponytail made him look like he was 150 years late for Custard's last party.

It was early April, and Hudson suffered from senioritis. It had been a decent year, more or less, but it wasn't what he thought it'd be like. Most people didn't care that he was student body president, and being president was mostly stupid. He planned awesome rallies, but the students didn't care, so mostly nerds volunteered for the games. Once a month there was a student council meeting that dealt with stupid stuff like carwashes. He thought the president could do things that mattered like bring soda machines back to school; instead, he got to break the tie over whether the prom theme should be "Shoot for the Stars" or "Saturday Night Fever." Big Whoop. At least after he dumped Olivia, his social life got going. He went out with a sophomore who knew how to have a good time, unlike Olivia who wasted a year of his life. What he ever saw in her, he couldn't say. He wasn't religious at all. Now he had this freshman girlfriend. She was totally hot and no hang-ups. Olivia had no idea what she was missing. He was going to Chico State in September, so he'd still have his girlfriend here when he came home on weekends. Of course, what happens in Chico stays in Chico.

"Handsome!" hissed Violet. "Samson is waiting."

"What?" He hated being called that, especially by Violet. If she thought piercings made her hot, she was an idiot. She looked like the offspring of a Hippie and a Goth. He couldn't stand being within five feet of her.

Hudson searched the room. Eyes were on him. His rested on Dell. She was looking a lot better recently. Kind of the look of a girl getting banged. Maybe Samson. Why not? Lots of teachers did. Maybe he'd be a teacher for a couple of years and bang some virgins. How bad would that be?

"Can you explain the paragraph, Hudson?" That bastard Samson again.

"Why don't you ask Dell? Everything you need to know, I'm sure *she* has the answer."

Dell blushed. Hudson might be onto something.

"What's nada?" Olivia asked.

Javier said, "It means nothing."

"Everything is nothing." Hudson said. "That's the meaning of the *most* important paragraph of the 20th century. Any stoner could have written that."

Hudson was pleased; he had shown how this piece of junk was a waste of time. Poonam raised her hand. Hudson couldn't figure out why Poonam who could get practically any guy in the school was banging Noah. Hudson was smarter and way better looking than him. An Asian rasta? C'mon. Plus, Hudson had a future. Noah was going to ride a bike to the food co-op and bag groceries all his life. Hudson was going to major in business. He'd start some kind of startup, sell it for a few million, and then run for office. Start at the city council and then move up to Congress. Who knew how far he could go?

Poonam said, "Out of all the dark things you've made us read, this is the darkest. There's no hope. Why don't we just kill ourselves?"

"Hemingway committed suicide," Noah said.

"Big surprise," Poonam said.

"Try to think of it like this," Samson pontificated. "If there's nothing waiting for us at the end of our lives, then we have total freedom to live our lives however we want. That favorite of teen terms, YOLO, would really mean something."

"There's another thing," said Noah. "The title, 'A Clean, Well-Lit Place.' The waiter knows that there isn't any god and there isn't any afterlife. This is it. So to comfort us from the nothingness that awaits us, we need clean, well-lit places to feel good while we're still alive."

"Nice," said Samson. "Let's extend Noah's insight into an essential question: Is Reagan High a clean, well-lit place? In other words, is it a place where you feel good and protected from the harsh outside world? Write a paragraph on that."

Hudson scoffed at the question. Of course Reagan High wasn't a "clean, well-lit place," and he started to write, but as he wrote, he had to admit that for all the stupid classes, pompous teachers, and weird people, he liked school. His friends were here. He could practice politics and leadership. And it was better than being at home with his parents who fought all the time. He wished they would just divorce already. If high school was a place where he felt good and protected, then it must be like that for everyone.

After ten minutes, Samson asked, "What do you think, Hudson?"

"School a clean, well-lit place? Someone must have slipped some soma in your tea." Everyone laughed; Hudson so owned this class.

Chapter 35

BEING BLACK AT Ronald Reagan High School didn't mean a thing. DeSean Williams had all sorts of friends from all sorts of colors, and he was co-captain of the football team. He almost believed that America was pretty much post-racist with Obama as President and blacks totally kicking butt from Oprah to Dr. Dre to Lebron. DeSean's grandmother told him stories of growing up black in the South, and at school he learned about lynching, the KKK, and all that kind of stuff. But it was pretty much history. He had a job at A&F, the world's premiere preppy clothing store. They didn't care what color someone was as long as they had great perfect teeth and six-pack abs. Yet even when he wore his nicest clothes, a helluva lot nicer than what most whites wore, and cruised through mall stores, employee eyes always followed him. The week before while shopping in Sacramento, he saw fear in two white girls' eyes before they crossed the street to avoid him. And while none of his white friends ever got pulled over unless they were speeding, he'd been stopped in his car three times for nothing and disrespected each time.

English 12 was a great class. He could get crazy with his friends, and he even finished his first book, *Lord of the Flies*. It was about how people needed government or else society would fall apart. But he already knew that, so the book didn't teach him anything. In fact, reality was a lot more complicated than the book because if you were black, the police, who were the hand of the government, could be just as out of control and evil as Jack. If DeSean ever wrote a book, he'd write about that.

In a way, English 12 was kind of like *Lord of the Flies*. Samson wasn't a typical teacher dictator, so the class sometimes went crazy. Another good thing was that kids in other English 12 classes had to practice for the SBAC test, but Samson didn't do that at all.

Now they were doing this play, *A Raisin in the Sun*. It was about a black family who got some insurance money and were figuring out what to do with it. They bought a house in a white neighborhood, but the whites living there didn't want them because they were black.

On the first day, Samson asked, "Who's going to play the protagonist, Walter?"

Blake said, "Got to be DeSean."

"Because I got the right skin color?"

"Hell," said Blake, "I'm more black than you, bruh. It's just cuz you so good looking."

"Up to you," said Samson.

"Whatever."

By the end of the first scene, DeSean discovered that he was good at playing Walter. At the start of each following class, Samson asked for volunteers for the other roles because it was clear that DeSean owned Walter. Each evening DeSean read the play at home, so he'd be ready.

Today DeSean was extremely ready. In the play, Walter went apeshit that his mother didn't give him some of the insurance money to open a liquor store. So he got hella drunk. His sister, Beneatha, was playing and dancing to African music when Walter stumbled back on stage.

DeSean made a mixtape of African music for the scene. He also brought in a bottle of Smirnoff filled with water. He let Samson check it out before class began. Samson told him no, but DeSean begged and Samson caved.

Samson put on the mixtape and Beneatha, played by Abby, was supposed to be getting rid of her assimilationist present life and looking back to her African past through song and dance. Abby didn't volunteer for the part; Samson volunteered her. DeSean waited off-stage for his cue.

Instead of singing and dancing, Abby delivered her lines in a monotone. The air conditioning drowned out her voice. As for dancing, she crossed her arms and leaned against the whiteboard with her face in the script.

On his cue, DeSean staggered onto stage clutching his bottle. Cell phones went from texting to video mode.

DeSean pumped his arms and screamed: "Ethiopia stretched forth her hands again!"

He took a swig from the bottle, wiped his mouth and crouched down like he had a spear and stalked about the room miming that he was hunting: "Flaming Spear! Hot Damn!"

Abby perked up and mildly shouted: "Flaming Spear!"

DeSean jumped on a table, yanked open his shirt, and yelled: "Owimoweh!" He took a long swig from the bottle.

The class went insane, but DeSean took no notice. He was Walter, a powerless black man beat down by life. His only comfort came from the bottle which gave him the courage to act like a man. He staggered atop the table. And then…

"Mr. Samson! I am shocked and outraged! DeSean Williams come down from that table and button your shirt! What is that in your hand?"

Haman stood in the doorway, balled fists resting on her waist, and anger burning from the bottom of her heels to the top of her dyed mane. DeSean stumbled off the table and fell to the floor.

"What the hell do you think you're doing!" Samson yelled at Haman. His anger matched hers. This would make an excellent play.

231

"I will not have you raise your voice and use that kind of language with me!" Haman yelled back. "Students with their shirts off! Alcohol in the classroom! This is beyond a Notice of Unprofessional Conduct! You are finished here, sir! You are finished!"

DeSean scrambled to his feet and held out the bottle to Haman. "It's only water."

Samson calmed down. "With all due respect, Mrs. Haman, we were simply acting out *A Raisin in the Sun*. If you look at the stage directions, it says, *He pulls his shirt open and leaps onto the table*. I think you were taken in by DeSean's incredible performance. It was extremely lifelike."

"DeSean's a beast!" Blake yelled.

"It's water, for real," DeSean said. "Check it out."

Haman looked at DeSean, then at Samson, and then for a reason DeSean couldn't figure out, she stared hard at Leon. She turned back to Samson. "Good day, Mr. Samson."

Haman clicked out the door, and the play continued. At the end of class, DeSean, Ryan, and Blake walked out of the room.

"Don't you think it's weird that The Hammer came?" Ryan said.

Blake said, "Someone texted her."

An epiphany came to DeSean. "It's Leon, dude. They both want to can Samson."

"That's bullshit," said Ryan.

"No, I saw her give Leon the stink eye. He texted her, but we weren't doing anything wrong."

"That's not what I mean," Ryan said. "It's bullshit that Leon wants to get rid of Samson."

"I know," said Blake, "He's a great hitting coach, and his class is friggin' insane."

DeSean nodded. He didn't hate English as much as in the past.

232

Chapter 36

S USAN, THE SCHOOL secretary, called from the outer office. "Don't forget, staff meeting in ten."

Dewey surveyed his dozen Post-it notes arrayed along the edges of his computer monitor. His desk held document piles from the blueprints for the new stadium restrooms to the resumes for Truck's English position to the Board of Education meeting packet. He needed to ask Rotary to serve breakfast the first day of SBAC testing. He was going to need another special ed teacher, so he wrote another Post-it and stuck it on the middle of monitor. He should have been on that at least a month ago. Glancing at his iPhone, there were 53 unopened texts. He'd start on them at the staff meeting. The ASAP folder of his To Do App had 22 items. He could farm a half-dozen to Trish and a couple to Susan. He didn't bother looking at the Long Term To Do list. That would be disheartening.

Dewey took a swig of lukewarm coffee. His blood-to-caffeine level was not a 50-50 mix, but still, he wouldn't want his doctor to know the actual ratio.

If he didn't need to pay alimony, he'd be back in the classroom and coaching football. But there were benefits besides the pay, such as being the center of things. He had enough dirt on students and teachers that could fuel ten years of sit-coms or hard-hitting dramas. Often the sit-coms and dramas were the same incident, and he enjoyed ruling a minor kingdom; though like a king, he had to watch his second-in-command. Trish had friends on the Board of Education that were not his fans, so he had to be more solicitous to her than he would have liked. But what Dewey loved most was working with teachers. These selfless individuals were dedicated to teens. Many had given up opportunities in more lucrative fields. Yet they could be prima donnas. If someone ran out of copies, it was the Hindenburg exploding. If a janitor didn't vacuum a room, it was the Titanic sinking. And then there was Mo. What the hell was Dewey going to do with him? Because of that idiotic bet, he wasn't doing test prep. Instead of reviewing grammar, he's got a half-naked DeSean Williams waving a bottle of vodka over his head.

The irony was that he agreed with Mo; the SBAC wasn't worth the bytes it was processed on, but if Mo didn't get his scores up, he'd have no choice but fire him. And if the school as a whole did poorly, Dewey would have to circulate his own resume.

"Susan!"

The door opened and Susan stepped in.

"You rang, Boss."

"Anyone calls about kids drinking alcohol and running around naked in class, tell them they were acting out the classic play, *Raising the Sun*."

"DeSean's a pretty convincing drunk."

"Susan."

"Don't worry; I got it. By the way," she added exiting, "It's *A Raisin in the Sun*."

"*A Raisin*," he mumbled to himself. "Okay, now to motivate teachers to kick some test butt." Dewey straightened his tie, took a deep breath, put on his game face, and headed to the multi-purpose room.

Walking across the quad, he noticed a dead limb on an oak. He added "call facilities – oak" to his To Do list. The cracks on the walkways were tripping hazards. No matter how hard he tried to stay one step ahead of the chaos, the stuff that bit him in the butt was almost always something he couldn't foresee, couldn't even imagine. But Susan was right: DeSean did have acting talent.

The teachers milled around the multi-purpose room. They had the look of April. Like the students, they were ready for summer. He overheard plans about camping trips, European vacations, and house projects; not one mention of anything vaguely educational. Dewey would have liked a ten-week break as well. He'd be lucky to squeeze in three. He sighed. At least he'd see his son.

"I know we're all busy, so I'll make this short. Only one item on the agenda: SBAC, but first let me remind you that spring is here, and I'm seeing lots of flesh. We do have a dress code. Okay. Testing. Mrs. Haman, are you ready."

"Absolutely. May I get some help passing out test procedure booklets?"

Dewey picked up a pile and after passing them out, he went to the back row and took out his phone. Already, three texts about Mr. Samson's class. He'd have to talk to Mo.

"Anything you'd like to add, Principal King?"

Dewey raised his head. 30 minutes had passed.

"I've gone over procedures, Principal King."

Dewey didn't like her implying that he was engaging in off-task behavior. Hell, testing was her job. Dewey didn't like Trish, but she was efficient. She did so badly want to bust Mo's balls. He really needed to talk to him.

"That's great, Mrs. Haman." If the staff looked beat at the start of the meeting, now their collective pulse was one beat north of comatose. He turned to the staff. "I know the test feels like a burden, but it's our one opportunity to see how we're meeting educational objectives as measured against other schools. It's an imperfect tool, but for the most part, it's a pretty accurate way to find out what students know. Anyway, it's what we have, and it's important to Dos

Robles that our students do the best they can. To that end, the Rotary will be providing breakfast on Tuesday."

Free food usually got teacher attention. Dewey noted fewer teachers texting. Time for the last push.

"If everyone would try to bring snacks during the testing, that will be a big help as well. Hungry students don't test well. We have four days to go. Between now and next Tuesday, I want you to focus on test preparation. If that means postponing other areas of curriculum, you have my permission. Just by showing that you care will indicate to the students how important the test is. Any questions? No? See you tomorrow." Dewey walked over to Mo, and put his hand on his shoulder. "Got a minute?"

Mo made a show of improving his posture, loudly cleared his throat and deepened his voice to imitate Dewey. "Mo, while I appreciate your—uh—shall we say unorthodox approach, I'm not sure that having students dancing on the tables without their shirts and waving vodka bottles over their heads is the best way to teach the Common Core. Not to mention all the phone calls I have to field to cover your ass."

"Not bad," Dewey replied, "but seriously, Mo. These kids are at a public school. You aren't making YouTube videos. Okay?"

"Sure, Dewey, I get it."

"And if I walk in during the next four days, might I see some preparation for the SBAC?"

"Absolutely."

Dewey didn't believe him. Maybe he could appeal to Mo's sense of compassion.

"You know I'm in the crosshairs too. My job is as much on the line as yours."

"I know, Dewey. My students are ready, but I'll do some practice problems as well. Really."

Maybe Dewey could get a job in the district office. Decent money and a helluva lot less stress. Maybe lousy scores would be a blessing in disguise.

"Dewey, you look kind of beat. You should go home."

"My day isn't nearly done."

"That's why you get paid the big bucks."

Mo flashed a huge smile to which Dewey managed a grin. He did like Mo, but his job would certainly be easier if Mo was gone.

Chapter 37

TWO WEEKS FOLLOWING the hike, Mo was still discombobulated by it. Dell and he barely exchanged a word on the walk out. Ditto on the return bike ride. In class, Dell had been trying to connect, but he had rebuilt and added mortar to the teacher-student wall. Yet he missed her company. Besides the fun, she understood him, and he her. Sometimes at night he mused about waiting for her to graduate. Of course that was stupid, immature, and absolutely not going to happen. As for Leon, his animosity was more palpable than ever, but no one noticed because it was common knowledge Leon Pruzinsky hated Mr. Samson's guts. Once Dell came to class fifteen minutes before the bell to talk about a presentation. While Dell and he spoke, Leon popped his head into the classroom. Clearly, Leon was stalking them.

Now as Mo stood over his sink draining pasta, he chuckled at Leon wasting his time trying to get another gotcha photo. His thoughts shifted to a conversation with Truck who advised Mo to do SBAC prep.

"Why fall on your sword?" he asked Mo as the two stood at the men's room sinks.

"Are you doing test prep?"

"I'm outta here; it doesn't matter for me."

"If you weren't, you'd do practice questions?"

"Absolutely."

"Yeah, sure."

Mo expected Truck to avert his eyes or at least give a sheepish grin, but he soberly looked Mo full in the face.

Mo said, "So you're saying good teaching isn't as effective as test prep?"

"Look at your scores the last two years."

"Aren't you the one who preaches that progress happens when someone stands up to the bullshit conventional wisdom? You more than anyone know that improving education by incessantly testing is the biggest load of crap foisted on American kids. I'm just proving that good teaching trumps all the bullshit that politicians and alleged education experts shove down our throats."

Truck clapped thrice. "Wonderful speech. I'm going to engrave it on your sword." He put his hand on Mo's shoulder. "Seriously, it would be a shame to lose you."

"Don't worry," Mo said, "I'm doing practice questions."

Mo dumped the pasta into a bowl, spooned in pesto, and took his dinner to the kitchen table where his laptop sat. The night before, Katherine sent an email announcing her upcoming marriage. She wanted him to be the first to know, so he wouldn't hear it from someone else, and she hoped he would come to the wedding. Mo wasn't surprised by the email; nonetheless, it knocked him down. He was jealous. Mo logged onto a porn site which afterwards made him want to chuck the machine out the window.

Now as he ate, the machine that held all his embarrassing secrets and screw-ups sat on the table silently mocking him. It was stupid to feel pissed off at an inanimate object, but there it was. Despite his irritation, Mo logged on and between bites perused OkCupid. As always, there were plenty of faces greeting him from cyberspace. A Rocklin pharmacist caught Mo's eye. Unfortunately, he couldn't summon a chipper persona to write a witty reply, so he closed the laptop, and there staring at him was the manufacturer's logo, Dell. He needed to get her out of his head. She was taboo and more destructive than alcohol, and he could only imagine how destructive he was to her. If he acted stupid, he could ruin her life.

Mo considered. Why could he shake alcohol but not Dell? Alcohol patched his pain with oblivion. When Mo started teaching how he knew he should, alcohol held nothing for him. But Dell wasn't a patch; perhaps she was a set of wings with whom Mo could soar.

Mo brought his bowl to the sink. "Total psychobabble."

The doorbell rang.

"Go away!" He was in no mood to talk. The bell rang again.

"I said, 'Go away!'"

It rang a third time. Somebody was going to be on the wrong end of a tongue-lashing.

He yanked open the door.

"Dell?"

"Look!" Dell held a fat envelope in her outstretched hand.

Mr. Samson surmised, "Stanford?"

"Harvard!"

"Wow! That's amazing!"

The two stood on either side of the threshold.

"Can I come in?"

"Uh…sure…of course…come in."

Mr. Samson held the door as Dell bounced in. For the first time in his memory, Dell wore perfume; it was a floral scent. Strong.

"Can we celebrate?" Dell handed Mr. Samson a bottle of sparkling apple juice and unzipped her fleece jacket to reveal a tight black bodice that accentuated her breasts and clung to her torso revealing a curvature that captivated Mr. Samson. Instead of her usual Levis, Dell sported a short, and undeniably sexy, red skirt atop her long, well-shaped legs.

"Have a seat; I'll get glasses." Mr. Samson retreated into the kitchen. Up until now, his actions had no ramifications; of course, he had been stupid for not quashing the relationship at the start. Dell was now throwing the center of her lineup at him. The time was here for Mr. Samson to play the adult and decisively put their illicit relationship to an end. He never should have gone on that hike. He shouldn't have gone to the coffee shop. He was sorry he had let it get this far. He had acted wrongly. Now he was forced to explain the impossibility to Dell. He was not looking forward to this conversation.

Yet as Mo Samson stood at the kitchen cupboard, he was paralyzed, for at the level below his ethical stance, Mo saw Dell as a woman. And then like a beanball, it hit him: Dell Westergard was the reason none of the OkCupid dates succeeded. She was the high bar no others could reach.

Mr. Samson stood in the kitchen attempting to summon his moral umbrage and put a stop to what he was considering.

End…it…here.

Yet wasn't Dell his helper in opposition? Didn't that make this love?

He brought down two wine glasses from the cabinet. He could not be rash. If he were to act, not only would he likely be fired, but he would lose his teaching credential. At least Dell was 18 and he wouldn't go to jail. Dell. What about her? The story usually ends with the hero and heroine living happily ever after. But that was just bad fiction or an American romantic comedy. In reality, it was a sure bet that they wouldn't last, and she would suffer. He'd screw up her life royally. How could he live with that?

"Need help?" Dell called from the living room.

"Coming."

Mr. Samson returned to the living room. "I can't believe it," Dell said.

"I can," Mr. Samson replied and shakily set the glasses on the table. "Shall I do the honors?" He picked up the bottle.

"Sure."

Mr. Samson popped the cork and filled the glasses. Handing one to Dell, he toasted, "To your incredibly bright future."

They clinked glasses.

"I couldn't have done it without you," Dell gushed.

"Wrong. This is all you."

"You might think you only wrote a letter of recommendation and edited an essay. But it's been so much more." Dell put her glass down and looked into Mr. Samson's eyes. He felt copious and equal measures of dread and exhilaration. "I mean, you're always there for me. I can talk to you about anything."

"Does your mother know?"

"I texted her. She's out of town for work."

"Oh."

There was an awkward moment of silence.

Dell and Mr. Samson went to put their drinks on the coffee table at the same time, glasses knocking into each other, sloshing apple juice onto the table. As Mr. Samson sprang to get a sponge, the end of his ponytail whipped around his side and brushed through the spill.

Mr. Samson picked up the end of his hair in his hand, and said, "Sometimes it's more trouble than it's worth."

Dell reached for her handbag and pulled out a pair of scissors. "You could always..." She playfully snipped the scissors at Mr. Samson, "donate it."

Mr. Samson chuckled at the scissors and contemplated his hair. What do I need it for anyway? For a game 15 years ago? Maybe cutting it would signal a new beginning. He looked Dell over. He would not let society dictate to him how to teach; he would not let it dictate to him how to live.

242

Mr. Samson signaled for the scissors. They were dull. He went into the utility drawer and brought out a sharp pair. He handed them to Dell.

"Serious?"

"Serious."

Mr. Samson sat at the kitchen table and Dell cut his hair. Afterward, he shaved his head while Dell called out the names of famous bald people from her cell phone.

"You want to know something...Mo?"

"Mo?"

"Can I call you that?"

"Uh...okay."

"Bald is sexy. That's my devious side talking."

Mo wiped his head with a towel.

"You look even more handsome."

Dell tentatively laid the tips of her right hand on Mo's head.

"It's so smooth. Feel it."

Mo placed both hands on his head. She was right. Smooth. He felt good. He felt right. As he moved his hands on his head, he touched Dell's hand. It was soft and smooth and strong. Their hands opened a portal between them. Mo felt himself slipping down the rabbit hole; where he'd come up might be out of his control.

He didn't care; he was following his heart.

Mo gently took Dell's hand and moved it from his head. There was no resistance. He stood up, took up her other hand, and the two of them faced each other as lovers. She tilted her head and closed her eyes.

The entirety of Mo's life had brought him to this moral quandary, this divergence of his heart against his head. Heroes followed their hearts.

He gazed at Dell's face and squeezed her hands. At the squeeze, Dell parted her velvet red lips expectantly, and after months of soul

243

searching and moral outrage that had left Mo Samson teetering whether to swing or take the pitch, he knew. Unlike Huckleberry Finn, he was not a hero; he was weak; he was a coward; he could not follow his heart.

Mr. Samson released Dell's hands, placed his on her shoulders, and straightened his arms.

"I'm sorry."

He let go of her shoulders and walked to the other side of the room.

"But I love you," Dell said. "And I know you love me. Remember how you told us how strong Edna from *The Awakening* was? She was willing to sacrifice her status and family for love. Then there was Robert, the man who loved her. He wouldn't break social conventions for love. You called him weak, a coward. Remember?"

"Yes."

Dell's face was a mixture of anger and distress.

"Well?" she demanded. "Are you Edna or Robert?"

Mr. Samson grappled for the right words. "You are an amazing young woman, and I value our friendship, but it cannot be; it is not love."

Dell grabbed her purse and the envelope and fled the apartment.

Chapter 38

PILLOWS PROPPED BEHIND her, hands folded over her stomach, Dell sat on her bed and stared at the poster of Klimt's "The Kiss." She didn't pick up the phone when the attendance robocall reported her absence. She ignored texts from Poonam and her mother. She didn't answer when her father called to congratulate her. Had *he* texted or called her, she would have thrown the phone in the garbage to keep company with that fat envelope.

Dell wasn't hungry; she wasn't thirsty. If an earthquake brought down the house, she would have remained right-angled, hands still folded.

Since the first day of high school, Delphenia Westergard had been a laser focused on gaining acceptance to one of America's elite universities. Whenever she pulled an all-nighter or forced herself to ace a boring honors class, it was the thought of Harvard that got her through. For the four years of high school, she averaged five hours of sleep a night during the school week. When her parents tried to intervene, she said, "The competition isn't sleeping; I'll sleep later." If her parents knew how much coffee she drank, they might have switched the house stock to decaf. Had they known that she occasionally resorted to pills to fuel an all-nighter, they would have sought professional help.

He was right. She was devious. And the bottom line was that all her work, everything, was for naught. None of it mattered. She wasn't going to attend Harvard. She wasn't going to do anything. She was going to stare at "The Kiss" forever.

Had she misread the signs? Poonam often accused her of being socially obtuse. Maybe she was, but here she was certain. He lied. He loved her. She knew it. And she loved him. For all her accomplishments, for all her essays about women grabbing power in society, and even her acceptance to Harvard, she surprised herself to discover that what she desired most was in "The Kiss"—intimacy.

She came home from his apartment, propped herself on her bed, and stared.

In the late afternoon, her mother came home, cutting short her business trip when Dell didn't answer texts or phone calls.

"Dell!" she yelled from the front door and burst into Dell's room to find Dell wearing her "naughty" outfit that Dell gave her a hard time about whenever she wore it.

"What's going on? Why didn't you answer the phone? Why are you wearing my skirt?"

"It's just a cold. My phone ran out of juice. I thought it was cute."

"Have you been crying?"

"Just a lot of sneezing. I'm okay."

Dell's mother made soup that Dell didn't touch until she threatened to make a doctor's appointment. Though almost 24 hours had passed since the celebratory apple juice had passed her lips, she had to force herself to choke down the soup.

Her mother wanted to talk, but that was impossible. Her mother would call the school and then probably the police. She couldn't talk to Poonam. She'd think it totally gross and tell everyone that he was a pervert. Dell was going to have to bear the burden herself because the only person who could have possibly understood was him.

246

Dell didn't emerge from her room for a second day. Her mother stayed home to cook and care for her. And then at dawn on the third day, she was over it. She tore down "The Kiss." It was an idealized view of love that didn't exist. She fished the acceptance envelope from the trash, showered, dressed, ate, and headed to school. She didn't hate him; rather, she felt sorry for him because he portrayed himself as strong, as not constrained by middle-class bourgeois morality. But he was a social sheep like practically everyone else. He would not risk his social status to pursue what he really wanted. He was Robert. He was weak.

Dell was Edna. She wasn't going to let social mores dictate how she was going to live. The irony was that during her sequestration, she realized that she was a lot more like her despised father than her beloved mother. Though she hated her father for what he did, he created his own moral code as would she.

In fact, Dell was glad that Mr. Samson had not kissed her. Their relationship would never have worked. She was already beyond him; he would have held her back. Maybe he knew it as well and that was why he lied about not loving her. Dell had awakened and found compassion for him. Now as a reborn person, she was ready to return.

Poonam accosted Dell in the hall.

"Where've you been? How come you didn't return my texts?"

"Sorry, I was really sick."

Poonam laughed. "Noah said that once you got into Harvard it was adios to us little people of Dos Robles."

Dell laughed too. "I should have called. I'm sure I would have felt a lot better a lot faster if I did."

"No worries, but I have to tell you about your favorite teacher. The two days you were out, Samson's been weirder than usual, if that's possible."

"Oh?"

"Oh my God! Not only did he cut off his ponytail, but he's totally bald! But that's nothing. He's such a jerk. Remember "Ode to a Drowned Cat"? He did it again; forgot we already read it. When I told him, he looked at me funny—like he was trying to remember who I was—and then out comes, "R-r-right, didn't you write an ode to a revolutionary?" Can you believe he'd embarrass me in front of everyone? Like I'm ever going to tell him anything again. Totally clueless. Yesterday at the end of class he comes up to me and asks if I knew where *you* were. Like I'd tell him anything. I said, 'Why don't you call her and find out?' and he totally freaks. I mean the guy is *sweating*. It was so weird, like I don't know, but it was like…"

Dell felt like she was punched in the gut.

"Oh my God! That pervert came onto you! What did that he do?"

Dell hugged Poonam and wept.

"That bastard! I'll kill him!"

Dell pulled herself away and said, "No. No. He didn't do anything. That's the truth. I'll tell you everything, but not now. I want to go to class."

"You totally do not have to go to that man's class."

"Poonam, Mr. Samson didn't come onto me or do anything. That's the truth. I'm okay. I want to go to class."

Poonam had a quick word with Noah when they entered, and then she sat in her old seat next to Dell. She placed her desk slightly in front of Dell's as if she would throw her body between Mr. Samson and Dell if he so much as looked at her funny. Dell was touched by Poonam's loyalty, though it was unnecessary. Mr. Samson wasn't interested in Dell. And even if he were, it didn't matter. Earlier in the year, she told Mr. Samson women no longer needed men to complete them. Now she was that woman. He had made her what she desired to be.

Mr. Samson began class with, "I would be derelict if I didn't prepare you for next Tuesday's SBAC." He projected a photo of a rubble-filled, urban war-zone. Parachuting onto the landscape was a battalion of zombies. The text underneath the photo read: *Dos Robles 2020 if students don't reach 60% Proficient on the SBAC.*

Dell laughed with the rest of the class. She and Mr. Samson briefly caught each other's eyes. She wanted to let him know that there weren't hard feelings. She was a lot tougher than he thought.

"The only thing missing from the picture," said Dell, "is the zombies' first meal: the heads of teachers with low test scores."

Mr. Samson turned to Dell for the first time. He looked both grateful and confused, if that were possible. He recovered with, "That's why I cut my ponytail. I didn't want a zombie to choke on a long strand of hair."

"Lovely visual," Violet said.

"All kidding aside, it is true that these tests count for both the school and Dos Robles, so please try your hardest. I know you'll do fine."

Dell said, "As long as no students have vendettas and want to get rid of you." Mr. Samson slightly narrowed his eyes at Dell. This was fun.

Poonam said, "Of course this class *totally* loves you, but in English 12 there's Leon Pruzinsky…"

"Don't forget Blake Thomas," added Dell.

"Cooper Henderson," Poonam said.

"Q!" Noah called from the back.

"Okay, okay! Ha, ha. Very funny. I get it. You guys just do your best. That's all I ask. My god, what's gotten into all of you?"

"We're just trying to be helpful," Dell said.

"Alright, now that we've more or less prepared for the test, I've got a powerful poem for us."

Dell raised her hand. "It hasn't gone unnoticed that your English 12 classes have way more fun than the AP Lit classes have. I think if we had some fun today, we'd do better on tomorrow's test."

"That's right!" Poonam agreed. The rest of the class vigorously nodded their heads.

Mr. Samson looked put upon. He was not used to insurrections in AP Lit. Nevertheless, he did not dismiss Dell outright. "Miss Westergard, any *fun* suggestions?"

"How about a drama game?"

"Samson can play a famous bald guy like Vin Diesel!" Hudson yelled and the class erupted.

"Or Tyrese Gibson!" Poonam added.

"Winston Churchill!"

"Mao Tse Tung!"

"My baby brother!"

Dell had tapped into a year of pent-up energy which the class unloaded on Mr. Samson. Between fits of laughter, Mr. Samson nodded a touché to her as he took the ribbing. She had established her power. They were even, almost.

Chapter 39

DESPITE DELL'S REBELLION, Mr. Samson was glad to see her. He barely slept the prior nights, worried what she might do. He knew he hurt her, and if part of the recovery was for him to be the butt of an hour's worth of derision, it was a bearable cost.

Onto English 12. He began with, "We need to spend today preparing for the SBAC. Open your journals and answer the example questions on the screen."

No one moved. DeSean asked, "What about the play?"

Blake led the class in, "The play! The play! The play!"

Mr. Samson put up his hand. "We aren't doing anything until you do as you're told." Tier One students didn't need practice because their curriculum covered SBAC; Tier Twos needed to cram.

"You told us we weren't going to do practice questions," Esther complained.

"You said the test was bullshit," Cooper added.

Leon mumbled, "Fucking douche bag," loud enough for Mr. Samson's benefit.

"Look, it would be good to at least see what the questions are going to look like. I'm sure you'll all do well because the test affects the school as well as Dos Robles. Many of you will live and raise families here. One of the best things you can do to keep this a strong community is to ace the SBAC. From purely enlightened self-interest, you need to do your best. That's why we're doing a little practice."

Q grumbled, "Let's get it over with."

"That's the spirit!" Mr. Samson said and projected the following on the screen:

> "So I do not think that it is altogether fanciful or incredible to suppose that even the floods in London may be accepted and enjoyed poetically. Nothing beyond inconvenience seems really to have been caused by them; and inconvenience, as I have said, is only one aspect, and that the most unimaginative and accidental aspect of a really romantic situation. <u>An adventure is only an inconvenience rightly considered. An inconvenience is only an adventure wrongly considered.</u> The water that girdled the houses and shops of London must, if anything, have only increased their previous witchery and wonder."

The underlined piece is which of the following literary devices?

  a. hyperbole
  b. paradox
  c. euphemism
  d. synecdoche

"Write down your answer and a one sentence explanation."

DeSean laughed. "Samson, what did you smoke? We don't know any of these words. I'm not even kidding."

"Yes you do. We've talked about all the terms except for synecdoche. That's when a part of something is substituted for the

252

whole. You see a nice car and say, 'nice wheels,' but you mean the whole car is nice. Get it? Who can remind us what hyperbole is?"

Not a hand stirred.

"Esther?"

She shrugged.

"Q?"

"No idea. Couldn't care less."

"Ryan?"

"Something like an allusion?"

Mr. Samson had never been mightily impressed by this class' intellect, but had absolutely nothing sunk in? Were Maria, Dewey, Truck, and—gasp—The Hammer right? The only way for students to get this stuff was to pour it into them every day? He tried three more questions. They didn't know a thing. Even if Noah Chu didn't miss a single question, Mr. Samson was looking at a third straight year of lower scores and would be fired. He had mightily miscalculated and was way, way too late in the game for even an ace closer to help. Why trouble them anymore?

Ten minutes later, scripts in hand, DeSean and Esther were standing in the front of the room. Somehow, a dozen students with off-periods surreptitiously entered and lined up against the back wall to watch. Just as DeSean had become Walter Younger, Esther had morphed into the elderly Mama. Mama had taken some of the insurance money to put a down payment on a house in a white neighborhood. The Youngers would be the first black family there. Walter took the rest of the money and "invested" it with a con artist who skipped town. A representative from the white neighborhood had previously offered to buy the Youngers' house at an inflated price in order to prevent them from moving in, and Walter had kicked him out. Now broke, Walter has changed his mind.

Mama: Hijo...

"Son." Mr. Samson interrupted. "The line is son."

Esther blushed. "Oh, right, sorry. For a second I kind of became my mom. *Son...*"

"Hang on," Mr. Samson interrupted again. "You really became your mom?"

"Just for like a second."

"Think you could ad lib Mama's lines into how your mother would speak?"

"I guess, but this play isn't about a Hispanic family."

"True art transcends race."

DeSean said, "You want us to be Mexicans?"

"If you're not up for it, we don't have to, or someone else can try."

"Samson, you really did smoke some bad shit. In case you forgot, I am an actor. You want me to be Younger, Lopez, Wang, Goldberg—it don't matter because I am Walter. Mama, your line."

Esther looked at Mr. Samson who shrugged and opened his palms to the stage.

> Mama: Hijo, you come from 5 generations of farmworkers slaving away on other people's farms, scratching out livings on less than minimum wage with one eye always watching for La Migra. But nobody—nobody—in this family ever let somebody disrespect us by giving us money to tell us we weren't good enough to live on their calle. We've never been that poor.

Walter: Well, we are now. Mama, this ain't no Hollywood movie. This is the barrio. We need that dinero.

Mama: Hijo, how's your heart going to feel?

Walter: Great. I'm going to feel great. I'm going to look that pendejo in the eyes and say, "Okay, man, you want to keep us out, just give me that fat check, and you can have your shitty little house, and you won't have to live next to some greasy Mexicans who'll stink up the neighborhood with their beans and junky cars parked on the lawn. Just give me the money..."

Mr. Samson called, "Stop!"

"You can't stop us here!" DeSean shouted at Mr. Samson. "This is the—you know—what do you call it—of the whole play."

Mr. Samson ignored DeSean and addressed the class, "Is Walter doing the right thing?"

The class collectively groaned, but Mr. Samson knew if he didn't stop to magnify the moral dilemma, the students might miss it. No one responded.

Mr. Samson's eyes alighted on a scowling Leon.

"Leon, is Walter morally right to take money over pride?"

Leon sneered, "Morals are for the weak."

"So you agree with Walter?"

"Sure do."

DeSean faced Leon. "You'd take the money?"

"Dude, they'd burn down his house. It's a no brainer."

"I wouldn't take it if it were a million dollars."

"Well, you're a fool."

Mr. Samson was rooting for DeSean, but Leon was his intellectual superior. He was about to lend a small hand when DeSean said, "Sometimes you do things because they're right. That's morals. Don't pretend you don't have them. When Noah got hit at the Carter game, *you* led the bench onto the field. You knew you'd be tossed, but you still did it. No one called you a fool, and if Walter rejects the money, no one would call him a fool either. That's all I got to say."

"You right, Walter DeSean!" Blake shouted and the rest of the class nodded. A couple clapped.

"Leon?" Mr. Samson asked.

"What?"

"Rebuttal?"

"You trying to rub my nose in it, Samson?" Leon practically spat out the words.

"No, I…"

"This isn't about Walter and it's not about DeSean. It's about me and you. Isn't it?"

Mr. Samson was taken aback. But he was the teacher and would rise above Leon's bait. Instead he spoke to the class. "DeSean and Leon have taken opposing views on the specific question of the importance of standing up against an injustice if it means taking a personal loss. DeSean agrees with Mama, Leon takes Walter's side that there is no injustice worth a personal loss. Open your journals and write what you believe. Back up your position with evidence from your own life."

At the start of the year, the students would not have even removed their journals from their backpacks. He would have to explain the assignment again. And a third time. Then he would need to explain that rather than being a burden, the writing was an opportunity to explore something interesting about themselves. Then he would cajole. Finally, he would threaten detentions, and the students would open their journals as if their fingers were dipped in molasses. The letters would appear on the page at the rate a mason chiseled letters in stone. By the end of the assignment, the majority of journals would have no more than two sentences scrawled in indecipherable script. But now was different. Even though they wanted to see the play, except for a petulant Leon, even Cooper's pen was trotting across the page.

As they wrote, Mr. Samson was despondent that he'd likely get fired. Of course it was his own fault. Still with the exception of Leon, he loved his students; he had even come to appreciate Blake. During the quiet of their writing, he had a hair-brained idea of moving to Cambridge. There'd be nothing keeping him in Dos Robles; after all, it was a boring exurb. It was good to shake up one's life every now and then. Maybe he'd audit classes at Harvard. Maybe get a master's degree in literature. And maybe, just maybe, he and Dell would have a future.

The students began chatting with each other signaling the end of the journaling, and Mr. Samson awoke from his ridiculous daydream.

"Back to the play!"

Chapter 40

FOR A 62-YEAR-OLD MAN riddled with cancer, the alarm clock is never a welcome sound, especially if the man is a teacher about to administer the Common Core's SBAC test.

"When this one fails, what'll the next one be? The 'Is Our Children Learning Initiative'? Thank God I won't be around for that."

Mick's wife, Nina, had wanted him to retire three years before when the melanoma last went into remission. He agreed and each fall he told Dewey that he was retiring, but he could never bring himself to sign the papers. There was an ignorant generation who needed Dr. Truck to give them words of encouragement, kicks in the pants, or both, administered simultaneously. Now it was back, and he signed.

Mick sat down to a breakfast of oatmeal, orange juice, coffee, and a salad of five medications. He lifted the coffee, breathed deeply of the Kenyan roast, and stared at Nina whose head was buried in the *Sacramento Bee*.

"What?" Nina asked without lifting her eyes from the page.

"You're the best wife ever."

"You're the most full of it husband ever. Eat or you'll be late."

Mick grinned. Nina was the most insightful woman he knew, and after forty years, he still wanted her in the same way as when he first laid eyes on her. Nina glanced up at Mick and loudly turned the page.

Mick contemplated the cup in his hand. He had indulged in and had given up a score of vices over his life. All that remained was coffee. The luscious, silky, earthy drink was as delightful as any whiskey he had ever sipped, and he had been catholic in his tastes.

"Wouldn't it be nice to open a coffee shop next year? Bay windows, overstuffed chairs, and laminated short stories and poems for the patrons. We'll call it, A Clean, Well-Lit Literary Café."

Nina smiled crookedly at him. The café had become a daily ritual. Mick took a bite of oatmeal and picked up the sports section.

"Mick, wouldn't it be better if you told them?" He put down the paper. "I don't understand why you keep it a secret from everyone. At least tell Mo."

"You tell people the cancer's back and everyone starts treating you nice. I couldn't abide The Hammer asking how I was feeling. And then there's the perverse ecstasy that it's you climbing the scaffold not them." Mick picked up the paper and reread the first sentence of an article about Ryan Dowling. "I will but not yet."

"No one will be 'ecstatic.' Besides you aren't 'climbing the scaffold.'"

"Course not. Anyway, even babies live under the Sword of Damocles; it's just that while the sword is tied above most people's heads with a stout rope, the one over mine is unraveling twine."

Nina's face drooped. He attacked his oatmeal with vigor. "I'm too much a curmudgeon for the Grim Reaper. He's got way easier pickings."

Mick finished and picked up the pile of unread essays that he brought home. He no longer had the energy or care whether MLA format was correctly followed or if "there" and "their" were mixed up. It didn't matter. Unless one was going to be an academic or a writer, who cared if you were guilty of the greatest writing transgression of all, the use of "you" in an essay? So what did matter to Dr. Truck? With death as his mentor for over a decade, he came to understand that you can't fully live unless you know that one day you'll die. With the knowledge of death as a companion, life is lived with immediacy. If Dr. Truck could somehow get his students to understand the paradox of mortality, he'd consider his career a success.

During prep, he'd scan the essays. Those that kept his interest got A's. Those spelled in recognizable English received B's. Those whose syntax he had no desire to decipher got C's. Even before the cancer, he didn't give F's. If he failed a 10th grader in English 10, the student would retake the class as an 11th grader. If there was one guarantee to a dysfunctional class, it was having upperclassmen in a lower level class.

That wasn't the full story. He didn't fail the ne'er-do-wells because he too hadn't given one shit about high school. His teen years consisted mostly of riding dirt bikes, listening to music, and getting stoned. After receiving his diploma, he worked in a bike shop and married Nina, his high school sweetheart. By 20 they had two kids, and he had to make real wages, so he became a trucker. Twenty nights a month he was on the road. That's when the drinking got out of control. One day a book on tape of Kurt Vonnegut's *Slaughterhouse Five* found its way into his cab. The week before he was sharing a 12-pack of Bud at a rest stop with a fellow trucker, and they compared their sordid high school experiences. Mick recalled that he had a teacher who thought Mick might enjoy Vonnegut and loaned him a copy of *Slaughterhouse-Five*. Mick felt guilty because he never opened it.

Mick slipped the tape into the player. Not only did he finish the book on his run to Wichita, but on the way home, he stopped at the library and checked out the entire Vonnegut books-on-tape collection. With the help of AA, books replaced alcohol.

During his tenure at Reagan, it had become harder for literature to speak to kids reared on cable TV, the internet, and video games.

The more ignorant the kid was, the more problems the kid had, the more Dr. Truck invested in him. Though he loved and had a Ph.D. in literature, the books were secondary. He used whatever worked.

As Dr. Truck rode to school on his motorcycle, he debated when he would tell Mo the cancer was back and had metastasized to his bone marrow. He should tell Mo, immediately resign, take Nina for a trip to Hawaii—God, she deserved it—and then take advantage of California's right to die program. He wouldn't allow her to change his diapers when the end neared.

Over the years, Dr. Truck learned that the best way to deal with the ubiquitous administrative crap that took more and more time in a school day was to savor the sublime teaching moments that most days held. This day his moment happened before the first bell. He took off his helmet and noticed Cooper Henderson staring at his motorcycle. Cooper was his student two years prior. In addition to the fact that he was a stoner, he was obnoxious, loud, couldn't read worth a damn, and wrote just as well. And he was a dick. Dr. Truck invested heavily in Cooper but could find no key to unlock him. He couldn't even give him a C, so Cooper got one of the two Ds he meted out. Probably just a matter of time before he wound up in prison.

"Like it?" Dr. Truck asked nodding at his motorcycle.

A tiny light flickered in Cooper's eyes and then was gone.

"You ride?"

"My grandpa taught me on his Kawasaki 500."

"This one has twice the horses. Think you could handle it?"

Cooper stared at Dr. Truck. The doctor held out the helmet.

"You got a license, right?"

"Yeah." His hands were shaking.

"Don't get a ticket and be back in ten minutes."

Cooper hopped on the bike and revved the engine. Dr. Truck gave him the thumbs up and Cooper took off. Dr. Truck was stupid;

Cooper was likely stoned, but he didn't care. Maybe he'd will the motherfucker to Cooper. That'd be something.

Cooper returned on time, cracked a smile, mumbled a thanks, and the two of them went their separate ways as if nothing happened.

But if that was Dr. Truck's moment of the day, he supposed it was the apex of Cooper's month.

The multi-purpose room was a high-anxiety vortex as teachers came for their testing materials. Funny thing was that while the rest of the teachers appeared as if they had mainlined triple espressos, Mo, the only teacher whose job actually was on the line, appeared to be remarkably calm. Maybe he had accepted his fate, like Truck accepting death. That was wisdom. None of that Dylan Thomas raging against the dying of the light or in Mo's case: the losing of the job.

Truck counted his tests, signed the affidavit that he wouldn't cheat, and decided he'd tell Mo after school. Truck carried the tests to his classroom in a small, plastic file box. Jobs, political careers, and property values came down to pencil marks placed in boxes by teenagers who didn't give a single, solitary shit about the SBAC. God Bless America's educational system and its multi-billion dollar testing corporations.

Once the students were seated with tests in hand, Dr. Truck read from the script and they began. 90 minutes were allotted for the test. Of the 33 students, 29 were finished after 30 minutes. Though Truck signed the affidavit promising he wouldn't peek, he did. The readings and questions were tough. He figured he himself armed with a Ph.D. would need at least an hour to do the test justice.

"So it goes," he muttered summing up the test, its ramifications, and his life. He would reread *Slaughterhouse Five* before dying.

After school, Truck stepped into Mo's classroom. Truck pulled from his leather jacket two Lindt chocolate bars and slid them across the desk.

"Life's too short to waste on Kisses. This is the real shit."

Mo opened the Extra Dark, took two squares, and passed the bar back.

"Good choice," said Truck. "Dark chocolate for dark days. How'd it go?"

Mo shrugged. "Who knows? Did I tell you how Noah Chu gave the test his middle finger last year?"

"Good for the Vietnamese Rastafarian."

"I asked him to consider trying this year. You know, not for me, but for the greater good of Dos Robles. Today, there was an absent student, so I had an extra test. Turned out to be the same version as Noah's. I perused the first part..."

"That my friend is illegal..."

"And unethical. But I walked by Noah; he answered the first five correctly. He's going to be Advanced."

"Increasing Mr. Samson's scores enough thus insuring his continual appointment at Reagan High. Well done!"

Mo's posture sank. "Noah did his part, but my English 12 students...they didn't learn a damn thing this year. I should have hammered them with grammar and vocabulary from Day One."

"But what about lighting their fires and all things Yeats?"

"I know. I taught the way I wanted to, and after I get fired here, if I ever find another job, I'll do the same. And yet now that the SBAC is over, I'm filled with regret."

"The nagging conscience—Siamese twin of the overbearing parent. But, hey, chin up; you're not dead yet. You've got Noah."

"And Leon Pruzinsky. He would purposely score a zero to see me canned, but the Marines don't take recruits who test below Basic."

Truck grinned. "Hah! The little bastard has to try. So you made it."

Mo shrugged and broke off another piece of chocolate.

Truck cleared his throat. "Melanoma's back."

Mo froze with the chocolate square two inches from his open mouth.

"I won't sugarcoat it, and I definitely don't want sympathy. It's bad. Most likely six decent months before I'm a drooling invalid. Nina and I are going to Hawaii the day school's out."

Mo remained frozen.

"Best to give it to you straight. That's the way. Get the shock over and then enjoy your chocolate."

"Two bars won't be enough."

"Mo, it's okay. I've been living on borrowed time for ten years. I got to see two grandchildren born and taught 'em both to ride bikes. I had a great run with Nina. You'll drop by for coffee afterwards, right? She really likes you. She'll want company."

Mo looked like he was going to be sick.

"Hey, I'm the one with cancer."

It was funny how the dying more often than not comforted the living.

"Since it's time for coming clean. I've got one. I almost had a relationship with Dell Westergard."

"Oh." Truck was surprised but not shocked. These things happened. He broke off a square and slowly started chewing. He'd let Mo talk.

"It was really stupid, I know. I thought that I might be in love with her."

"And were you?"

Mo reached for the chocolate, but Truck pulled it away.

"The answer please. Did you love her? *Do* you love her?"

"Of course not."

Truck cocked his head. He wanted more.

"And she? How does she feel?"

"She was in love, but I told her I wasn't."

"She's 18?"

"She is."

"At least you didn't have to worry about being fitted with county clothes."

"Idiotic, huh?"

"Mo, you're a gifted teacher, but you try so hard to fail. Is that why you quit baseball? Coach D told me you had the talent, and you threw it away. Now, you tell the SBAC to go fuck itself and almost sleep with a student. Why?"

"Chocolate."

Truck passed him the second bar.

"What makes a good teacher?" Mo asked and then answered. "The ability to relate to a teenager. And teens have been fed a lifetime of movies and books that view the world as good versus evil. And then there's the biology. The prefrontal cortex isn't finished developing until you're in your twenties, so the grays of nuances and compromises are mostly lost on them. Everything's black and white. Yet compromise defines the adult. To the teenager, compromise is a euphemism for hypocrisy…"

"The Holden Caulfield syndrome," Truck said.

"I think I never learned to compromise. Maybe that's what makes me—as you say—both a good teacher and self-destructive."

An aspect of being terminally ill was that it purified one's thoughts and emotions. Gone was the dross and all that remained was elemental ore.

"I'm going out on a limb. So here it is: Despite what you just said, you still think you might love Dell Westergard. Could be you're even contemplating pursuing a relationship after she graduates.

265

Subconsciously, maybe you even want to get fired, so you can go east with her."

"Are you reading my mind?"

"The almost dead know all. Let me add one more layer. 18 isn't too young to fall in love. That's how old Nina and I were when got married."

"What should I do?"

Truck signaled for the chocolate. "This orange is okay, but I'm a purist. Dark chocolate straight up."

"Truck!"

"Mo, what do you need me for? You know the answer."

"I want to know what you think."

"Forget it. There are two questions that only Mordechai Samson can answer. One, is he in love with Delphenia Westergard, and if so, is he prepared to follow her to Harvard?"

Mo stood up and walked to a desk in the front row that must have been Dell's. He stared at it for a good half-minute, and then lifted it into the air and turned it so it was facing the back wall.

"I am not in love with my student."

Truck said, "Had to be. Could never be love because no matter what your relationship was/is/will be, there'll always be the power differential. It'd be different if you were an incoming freshman meeting her in the dorm. But you're not."

"Truck, you're spot on. That helps a lot. I'm serious. Thanks."

Truck chuckled, "How awesome is it that I'm counseling you."

Mo jumped up. "Shit! Here I am with my stupid little life crisis, and you're..."

Truck waved Mo off and said, "Your crisis is as legit as mine. I'm good. It's a blessing I won't live to be a tottering old fool. I've had a great life. I've dealt with mortality and am good with nothingness. You're still figuring out the whole shebang. You'll find a woman who's not taboo, and live happily ever after. Or if you fuck

266

that up, you'll have more fodder for that damn novel you've been threatening to write ever since you swaggered into Reagan High."

The two men hugged. He'd miss the messiness of life.

Chapter 41

MARIA ENTERED THE classroom agitated.

"Mo, I don't know how to tell you this." Her face was pale and her eyes welled.

"What?" Either Truck dropped dead in the middle of class or Maria had Stage 4 breast cancer. "Just say it."

Maria grabbed two tissues and dabbed her eyes. "I want to tell you before Haman does. I got the SBAC results. You dropped half-a-percent. I'm sorry."

Even though his lack of test preparation was the educational equivalent of tilting at windmills, and even though his English 12 students were clearly going to set the far left boundary of the bell curve, at his core, he thought he could subvert the system, especially with his Noah ace. But here it was. Stabbed through the heart with a number 2 pencil.

"Jesus fucking Christ."

"I know. But I made a phone call, and Carter High will have two English openings next year. You won't even have to move, so we can still do Friday tapas. Carter's a good school." Maria sniffled. "I'm so, so sorry. I don't know what to say."

Mo pushed back his chair and wanted to give Maria a hug because she looked so distressed. As he stood, he felt lightheaded and put his hands on the desk to steady himself. Clearly he was taking this harder than he imagined he would.

"You okay?" Maria put her hand on Mo's shoulder.

"Yeah. I'll be okay. I guess I made my bed here. Those Carter spots sound good. Thanks for checking them out."

"Oh, Mo, these tests are so stupid! You're a great teacher. Everyone knows it." She took Mo's hands and squeezed them. "I've got a meeting now, but I'm around. Let's talk later. Okay? You going to be all right?"

"I'm good. Really."

"All right, I'll let you finish your lunch. Don't leave without stopping in, okay?" and Maria was gone.

Mo trekked around the classroom. Besides the carpet's sour-milk aroma, when the AC clicked on, the unmuffled motor put out as many decibels as a small airplane. When the ambient temperature dipped below 40-degrees, the heater often spewed arctic air. Under the onslaught of years of dry-erase markers, the whiteboard's default was a light grey. The ceiling occasionally leaked. Though OSHA might not approve of this as a workplace, Moe had taught nearly 10,000 classes in room 201. He'd spent more time in this 30-by-25-foot space than all the baseball diamonds he'd played in put together. He was going to miss this piece of shit classroom. Before his eyes welled-up, they alighted on one of his placards: "Our greatest glory is not in never failing, but in rising every time we fail. – Confucius." Could Mo rise? Should he apply for a Carter position and keep his head down until the drumbeat over test scores ceased, when teachers would be evaluated on different metrics, such as the number of students they inspired?

Did Mo even want to rise? A new career might be a better bet. He was still young. Out of all the professions that needed college degrees, teaching was the least respected with the worst remuneration and a helluva lot of work. He quit baseball and survived. Maybe

Truck was right; perhaps he'd rather fail than compromise? Would that be so bad? Lumpy had a profitable commercial real estate business in San Francisco. He could join him and work fewer hours, make tons more money, and, best of all, no education bureaucracy to deal with.

Mo returned to his desk and began typing his resignation; he wouldn't give The Hammer the satisfaction of firing him.

"Got a minute, Mr. Samson?" Dell walked in. In the three weeks since he cut her off, Dell had thrown fastballs at his head. If it was anyone else, he would have fought back, minimally doling out a few detentions. Instead, it was as if he had pinned a "Dell, kick me" sign on his back. And she obliged. Yet, the past two days she had softened. The old Dell was returning. Maybe that's who wanted to talk.

"I want to apologize for being such a jerk in class."

"I have no idea what you're talking about."

"Are you kidding? You haven't noticed that...oh, ha ha."

"Apology accepted."

"I really am sorry. I just...you know..."

"Dell, if I were in your shoes, I'm sure I would have done the same. Probably worse. But I'm happy to have you back on my team. You're a formidable opponent."

"Thanks. I guess I didn't understand—you know—how impossible it was, but now I do."

"Don't take it all on your shoulders. It takes two to—uh—make a misunderstanding. So no more correcting my grammar when I'm lecturing?"

"But it's so much fun." She laughed. "Okay, next time you have a split infinitive, I'll just raise an eyebrow. Deal?"

"Deal."

Dell extended her hand which Mr. Samson shook.

"There is bad news though," Mr. Samson said. "I got the SBAC results. Third year of negative growth."

Dell took a moment to absorb the information then exclaimed, "Oh, Mo!" and threw her arms around him. He let her hug him. It had been awhile since he had been embraced. He hugged her back. "You're such a great teacher! It's my fault! If you hadn't spent so much time with me."

"Untrue," he replied. "This is about how I teach."

The two remained embraced. In the sublime silence, he heard the click of a camera. In the doorway stood Leon.

"Patience rewarded."

The teacher and student dropped their arms and jumped back.

"Wa-a-ait for it...good," Leon said while fiddling with his phone. "Picture sent to Mrs. Haman. Now you two have a nice day."

He waved, turned, and left.

Dell yelled, "Leon!" and took a step after him. Mr. Samson grabbed her wrist.

"It's done. There's nothing you can do."

"But that picture will make people think we're a couple. It could get you in trouble."

"I was typing my letter of resignation when you came in."

A devious smile appeared on Dell.

"What are you going to do after you leave?"

"Carter High has some openings."

"You could move to...Cambridge."

"Dell, we both know that would be a terrible idea."

Dell addressed the floor. "I know."

"I need to finish this letter, okay?"

"Okay."

Mr. Samson returned to his chair, but he was unable to articulate a clear thought with Dell standing there. Vice-Principal Haman clicked into the classroom. Dell scooted out the door. Mrs. Haman closed the door after her.

"Mr. Samson..."

"Mrs. Haman," Mr. Samson interrupted. "Don't bother. I got the SBAC results. I'm typing my resignation." He swiveled the monitor, to show the vice-principal.

"Though I am never happy to see a teacher leave, I am sure you will agree that your unorthodox 'methods' do not benefit the students as they do not prepare them for the intellectual demands of the 21st century workplace..."

"Trish, no lecture. You won. I'm resigning as of the last day of classes."

"I am afraid, Mr. Samson, that will be impossible given the picture I have just received. You will clean out your desk now, and I will personally escort you off campus."

"Is this a joke?"

"I'm placing you on administrative leave..."

"You can't do that. That's Dewey's call."

"Principal King is escorting the Academic Decathlon team to Milwaukee for Nationals. The district lawyer will contact you within the next day or two. That's all I can say. You probably want to contact your union's lawyer."

"You've got to be kidding. Teachers hug students all the time. Trish, even for you, this is insane."

"There are only four minutes until lunch ends, so if there are things you want to take, I would get them now."

"No. This is totally ridiculous. I'm not leaving. Not for this."

Mrs. Haman reached for her walkie-talkie. "Would you please send security to room 201."

"There is absolutely *nothing* going on between Dell Westergard and me. That hug was innocent."

"Was it? Look." Mrs. Haman showed Mr. Samson the picture. Mr. Samson's offending hand was on the lower back. "That, sir, is a grope. Oh, and one piece of advice, Mr. Samson. I do not recommend erasing text messages. Your phone will likely be subpoenaed."

272

Mr. Samson was frozen by disbelief. Sure, he had blurred the line between him and Dell, but he had never done anything untoward, unethical, or illegal. It was he who stopped anything from happening. Though there was nothing salacious in the text messages, an investigator would discover their coffee dates. That couldn't be good. And then there was the Tracy Smith thing from the start of the year. Given that the Robertson scandal was still fresh, he realized that though he was innocent, there was a distinct chance he might lose his credential. Haman wasn't content with him losing his job through sinking test scores; she had to royally screw him. That woman was no bitch, she was a cunt.

The school's security officer came into the room, and Mrs. Haman said, "Mr. Samson, you have three minutes."

He went to his desk. The only things he wanted were his two baseball caps, his high school cap and his coach's cap. He contemplated for a minute and then jammed the Cowboys on his head.

They started for the doorway. "Oh, by the way." She stopped and pointed to Mr. Samson's whiteboard. Mr. Samson, confused, followed her index finger to one of his hand-made posters. "'Education is not the filling of the pail, but the lighting of a fire' appears to come from a source quite prior to Yeats. Google it."

Math teacher Tom Hanson walked in.

"Sub plans?" he asked.

"Show a movie. I've got a bunch in the cabinet. Try…*The Fugitive*." To Mrs. Haman he said, "I don't know what's going on, but something's rotten in Dos Robles."

"After you, Mr. Samson."

"This game goes to you, but the series is not over."

Chapter 42

WITHIN A DAY, the photo was at the center of a social media firestorm. Mo Samson's defenders far outnumbered his accusers in online debates as to whether or not he was a sexual predator. The next day, *The Dos Robles Gazette* ran a front page article with a first line: *Former Yuba County Teacher of the Year, Mordechai Samson has been put on paid administrative leave following accusations of improper behavior with a female student.*

"That's it," Mo said, "Carter High will never hire me, and even if I keep my credential, I'm done. The Hammer knows her business."

The union lawyer assured him that he was in a strong position since the evidence was "completely without merit," but he added a caveat. "Unfortunately, given the media attention on anything with the whiff of teacher misconduct, I can't offer any guarantees."

Dell signed an affidavit that their relationship was platonic, that he had mentored her and helped her prepare her college essays. While Dell's affidavit was certainly better than her testifying against him, a student's word of defense carried considerably less weight than a student accusation.

Mo Samson might have been fond of teaching beforehand, but as soon as his career was in jeopardy, he realized that he would never work in real estate; all he wanted to do was teach. Minimally, he needed to get back and finish the year and see his classes through graduation and be with the baseball team during playoffs.

He asked his lawyer to file a motion allowing him back while the investigation continued.

"My advice is to do nothing. If you don't antagonize the district, they may be more willing to drop the suit. If they see this through, it'll be expensive and even if you're exonerated, it could be costly. You're on paid leave. Why not just enjoy time off?"

"Enjoy the time off? Where's the justice!"

"It's how the system works."

So Mo sat in his apartment and read. He searched for the literature that would give voice to his injustice. He reread *To Kill a Mockingbird* and *Black Boy*. On the scale of injustice, even if he were to be found guilty of a crime and needed to register as a sex offender, his circumstances couldn't compare to the profound injustices heaped upon American Blacks. He reminded himself of the nobility of suffering, but that was just rationalizing his shitty situation. In a moment of weakness, he bought himself a single Arrogant Bastard. He opened it, poured it into a glass, and stared at its bubbles for a long while before tossing it out. He believed he had reached a point where he could drink alcohol and not fall off the wagon, but if he ever were to take that route, it would be from a position of strength, not in the condition he was in.

He refused to let himself go; he continued to shave, workout, and do laundry, though he was not optimistic that he would be absolved of wrongdoing, and he beat himself up over his relationship with Dell. Seeing a student outside of school, even if it were just for coffee or a hike, was a serious breach of trust that society had bestowed upon him. As he shaved, he took a hard look at himself. Maybe despite the fact that he despised her, The Hammer was right. Maybe he had been wrong, not only with his relationship with Dell, but that he didn't expect as much from his Tier Twos. In fact, why did he categorize them at all? They weren't lesser students. They were different students. He should have invested more in them. He should have tried different strategies. Maybe she was right; Mo Samson was unfit to be a teacher. Mo's hand shook and he put his razor down. Was this an epiphany? An epiphany that he was not as good of a teacher, as good of a person as he thought, not nearly as good.

Mo's knees weakened and he grasped the side of the sink and then let himself sink to the floor. He sat cross-legged and his head sank into his hands. This was worse than when he gave away his baseball gear; it was worse than when Katherine told him she wanted a divorce. Those were terrible times, though in neither of them did he feel that he wasn't a good guy at his core. But now he wasn't sure.

Mo wallowed on the floor long enough for the bathroom mist to dissipate. He put his hands back on the sink and lifted himself up. He was getting his just desserts. He looked at the razor. Good thing it wasn't a straight-edge. He looked again in the mirror. Self-hatred stepped aside to allow a second epiphany in: He'd been Teacher of the Year. Lots of students came back after graduation to tell him how much he had mattered in their lives. Not only was he not a bad teacher; at his core he was a not a bad guy. All he needed to do was to recalibrate his student relations and expectations. He could do that. He would become a better teacher, a better person.

Mo racked his brain for a baseball metaphor to explain the balance a good teacher needed to maintain between establishing closeness while ensuring a distance. He struck out and could only come up with the lame tightrope walker image. Though he wobbled and temporarily lost his balance, he would have made it had The Hammer not cut the rope.

Mo finished shaving and wiped his face. "Humans," he said to his reflection. "Twain got us right. We're one screwed up species."

Mo grinned. No matter the outcome of his case, he'd survive.

Chapter 43

MARIA MENDOZA'S FAMILY had been Central Valley farmers for over a century. Until her generation, the expectations of the family were for sons to go into the family business and for daughters to marry well. Maria's mother had different ideas. Maria was bright. She would attend UC Davis and become a doctor, an engineer, or a lawyer. She would not settle as someone's housewife.

Maria did well in school and fulfilled her mother's dream of being the first female Mendoza to attend UC Davis. A quarter of organic chemistry cured her of any desire to be doctor. She did well in calculus, but she wanted to have fun in college as well as study, so engineering was out. Her freshman summer, Maria worked in a Sacramento law office; the law was way too dry for her.

One evening Maria volunteered to translate at Dos Robles High School during their Back to School Night. She found that she counseled the students and their parents as much as she translated. She loved it. The next day she declared her major and became a high school counselor in order to do for others as her mother did for her. Counseling was not only helping students get into good colleges. It was helping young people chart their paths to reach their goals. It was keeping them on the path when they strayed. It was befriending them and getting them specialized help when needed. She made about half the salary of an engineer, but she would never trade her job for anything, not even a husband.

Maria had married her college boyfriend just before she took a position at Reagan High. From Day One, she averaged 60 hours a week at work. Out of frustration that she never came home earlier than 8:00 PM, her husband made her choose between him and her career. Within three months of the wedding, they annulled the marriage. Maria occasionally dated and had pseudo-boyfriends such as Dewey. She had no desire to get serious. Perhaps someday, but she was too busy. She sometimes fantasized about Mo, but she would not jeopardize their friendship.

Regarding Mo's current situation, she thought, "If he would have played ball with Haman, even a little, then none of this would have happened. I've never known such an insufferably inflexible man in my life."

She had worked on Dewey to get him to go over Haman's head.

"I know Mo's innocent," he said, "but the Robertson thing almost cost the superintendent his job. Believe me, there is nothing more that I'd love than for this thing to go away, but he's going to see it through unless there's something incontrovertible that proves Mo and Dell had nothing going on."

"How about her affidavit?"

Dewey shook his head. "I saw the texts between him and Dell. Not the brightest thing to be having coffee with a student, but no smoking gun. Unfortunately, it's not enough to call the investigation off."

Since the picture surfaced, Haman had ratcheted up her power a dozen notches. She strode through the school as if she were the principal. And since the school's overall test scores weren't exactly stellar, it was not inconceivable that Dewey might be canned and Haman become principal. If that happened, she'd try for a job at

Carter. Whenever Maria heard Haman's heels, she retreated to her office. She couldn't look at her complacent, despicable face.

"You busy?" Esther knocked on Maria's door.

Maria pointed to the couch. "What's up?"

"Nothing."

"Just want to hang out?"

"Yeah, I guess."

"You think any more about what we spoke about?"

"About being a school counselor?"

"Yes."

"You really think I could do it?"

"You'd be great."

"I don't have money for college."

"There's lots of scholarship money out there."

"I doubt it'd be enough. I'll take a couple classes at a community college and be a medical assistant."

"The pay's bad and you'll be bored. You're so much more than that."

Esther shrugged. "So it goes."

"So it goes?"

"So it goes. Dr. Truck gave me this book last year, *Slaughter House Five.* Ever read it? So it goes. It kind of sums it all up. Life ain't a bowl of cerezas."

Maria grinned for the first time in days. "No, it's not. You know, for an 18-year-old woman, you know a lot about life. That's why you need to be a counselor, or minimally go to Sac State and find something that you can sink your teeth into. Forget medical assistant."

"You never give up."

"Just doing my job."

"I hear you, Ms. Mendoza, and if I had the dinero, it'd be different."

Esther turned to Maria's wall of pictures.

"Which one's the oldest?"

"You mean besides the one from my junior prom?"

"No way! Where's that?"

"Near the top on the right. You have to find it."

Esther stood up and closely scanned the pictures.

"Uh, Ms. Mendoza?"

"Yes?"

"I know this is kind of personal, but did you and Mr. Samson ever *date*?"

"What? No! Whatever gave you that idea?"

Esther reached up on the board, gently removed a picture, and placed it on her desk. It was a picture of Mo and Maria hugging. His hand was low on her back, lower than where his hand was on Dell.

"Oh my God!" Maria hugged Esther. "This is great! You may have saved Mr. Samson!"

"It's only because his sub is terrible. Do you really think this can bring him back?"

"Esther, not a word to anybody. I've got to make some calls."

"No worries. I know how to keep a secret."

Maria knocked on Mo's apartment door.

"Maria?"

"Mo, listen! Esther was in my office earlier…"

"I did not have sex with her."

"What? No! Don't be stupid. Listen. She asked me if you and *I* ever dated. I told her absolutely not…"

"You said it like that?"

"No. I said, 'I'd never date a child molester.' Would you shut up and let me finish. Anyway, she discovered a picture of you and me hugging at graduation two years ago, and guess what? Your hand is lower than in the picture with Dell. You're exonerated!"

"Serious?"

"Dewey already met with the superintendent."

"What about The Hammer?"

"When I left, she was pacing the office. For the first time ever, those stilettoes were music to my ears. Mo, I am so happy for you! I knew she and Leon set you up."

"So there is a God," Mo said.

"Well, at least there's an Esther."

Chapter 44

O N HIS RETURN, Mr. Samson said to each class, "This is our last poem; I'm sure this news may make one or two of you ecstatic. It's a powerful poem; when I first heard it, I changed majors from business to English. Two books take their titles from its lines, though its meaning is something that's been argued over since it was written nearly 100 years ago."

In previous years he would say, "It was written by the same man who wrote that," and point to the "Lighting of a Fire" placard. This year, he simply began:

'The Second Coming' by William Butler Yeats

Turning and turning in the widening gyre
The falcon cannot hear the falconer;
Things fall apart; the centre cannot hold;
Mere anarchy is loosed upon the world,
The blood-dimmed tide is loosed, and everywhere
The ceremony of innocence is drowned;
The best lack all conviction, while the worst
Are full of passionate intensity.

Surely some revelation is at hand;

Surely the Second Coming is at hand.
The Second Coming! Hardly are those words out
When a vast image out of *Spiritus Mundi*
Troubles my sight: somewhere in sands of the desert
A shape with lion body and the head of a man,
A gaze blank and pitiless as the sun,
Is moving its slow thighs, while all about it
Reel shadows of the indignant desert birds.
The darkness drops again; but now I know
That twenty centuries of stony sleep
Were vexed to nightmare by a rocking cradle,
And what rough beast, its hour come round at last,
Slouches towards Bethlehem to be born?

"The falconer is authority, and the falcon is the individual," Noah stated.

Abby said, "I think the falcon is like a teenager and the falconer is an adult. To find our true selves, teens have to break free of our parents."

"The falconer is like poverty; the falcon is ambition; in America if you have the will to succeed, you can soar," said Javier.

"Maybe the falcon is like immigrants coming here to get away from violence in Mexico?" Pedro suggested.

"I think the falconer represents social mores while the falcon is your heart," and Dell looked at Mr. Samson significantly.

Poonam said, "It's what Noah's been saying all year; the capitalist world can't hold its contractions together and is falling apart."

"The center can't hold is about how America is becoming more politically divided," said Hudson. "The Republicans and Democrats hate each other's guts. I'm not saying I'm better than Obama, but I do get everyone talking at student council meetings. That's how you get the center to hold."

"The middle class is shrinking. Jobs are going to be tough to get when we graduate. That's what my dad says," said Violet.

"America and Mexico are the same," Esther said, "The rich keep getting richer, and the poor keep getting poorer. Mexican rich are drug thugs. American rich own Wall Street. They both buy politicians."

Cooper held up his backpack and pointed at the big A with a circle around it. "Anarchy and chaos!"

"There's going to be war," DeSean said.

Leon added, "America can kick anybody's butt."

"Don't underestimate your enemy," Ryan said.

"It's going to be a non-symmetrical war with terrorist groups and cyber attacks," Q said. "If you know what you're doing it's not hard. If I wanted to, I could totally hack the school's computers."

"The blood-dimmed tide is already here," Violet asserted, "especially on animals. Last year 20,000 elephants were killed for their tusks."

Chloe said, "And hunters kill animals just to put their heads on their walls like they're all macho or something. It's totally gross."

"Kids aren't even innocent anymore," said Amara. "I saw a show about child soldiers in Africa. They're like ten years old."

Lupita said, "The best people are quiet. They see what's going on, but they don't do anything. We need to speak up."

"It's the worst people like me who don't know nothing that are the loudest!" yelled Blake.

"You're not the worst, just the loudest," Esther amended.

"The Second Coming will be the end of days, and true Christians will be blessed forever," Olivia stated.

"My minister says that the Second Coming is when Jesus returns to earth and judges us," said Kimi. "I don't know…it's kind of hard to believe."

"Jesus is coming and boy is he pissed," said Cooper.

"What's Spiritus Mundi?" asked Javier.

"Spirit of the World," Mr. Samson answered. "Yeats thought it was the source of all inspiration."

"It's the Sphinx!" Violet shouted.

Lupita said, "Maybe it's baby Jesus waking up, and it could be he's not that happy."

Violet said, "The sphinx is mad because Jesus' cradle woke him up."

"He hasn't woken yet." Javier said.

Olivia said, "Bethlehem is where Jesus was born."

Dell said, "Yeats feels there is going to be a new world because the old ideas don't work anymore. We need new moralities."

Noah said, "He thinks the new world is going to be bad. I agree."

"All the 'great minds' predicted the future was going to be bad," said Q, "but we live longer, eat better, have better technology, less disease than any generation in the history of the world. The future is going to be great. Poets and all the 'great' writers are pessimists. They just don't know how to have a good time. Instead of crying that the world sucks, they'd be better off, we'd be better off, if they stopped whining and had some fun."

"This poem sums up the negative stuff we read all year," argued Poonam, "like the world is falling apart, and we don't stand a chance. But I know we'll pull ourselves through it like we always do. Maybe next year, you can have some hopeful poems and books to balance out all the negative."

With the exception of Q and Leon, the students seemed happy with themselves and the class. Though Mr. Samson would only teach one more week at Reagan High School, he was satisfied with the academic year.

Chapter 45

JUANA SANCHEZ WAS born in Colorado. The money in the States was good, but her parents' Sinaloa village was home. Every summer the family returned to Mexico. Their dream was to make enough money to build a beautiful house and return for good. Juana loved Mexico because life was more fun there. Though the United States called itself the "land of the free," Juana felt freer to be a kid south of the border where she could run with her friends without parents and other adults always in the way. People were more accepting of each other in Mexico, and the primary motivating forces in America, money and popularity, were toned way down in Sinaloa.

Juana, however, was anything but a normal Mexican girl. Even as a first grader, men stared at her. When she was 13-years-old, her mother entered her into the Sinaloa Beauty Pageant. She won first place and 10,000 pesos. Her father planned to use half to build a fountain in the courtyard; the rest was for Juana's education fund. She was going to be a doctor.

One week later, a man wearing a tight-fitting Ralph Lauren Polo with the number three on the sleeve came to the front door carrying a dozen red roses. Her father's hand shook as he read the card from El Rey, the undisputed leader of Sinaloa's most powerful drug cartel. *Esteemed Don Sanchez, It would be a great honor for me to take lunch with the lovely Juana Sanchez in the company of her parents following Sunday's church service. Please indicate to my associate if that would be acceptable.*

Juana's father forced a smile on and nodded to the thug. If El Rey wanted Juana, what could he do? Of course they didn't want to give their daughter to that pendejo, but if they refused, the entire family would be in danger, not only in Sinaloa but at their Greely, Colorado residence; El Rey's reach was long. Juana's parents stayed up all night and decided that the best terrible option was to relocate and reinvent the family north of the border. With the help of Mr. Sanchez' kindly boss at Swift Meat Packing and Juana's prize money, they moved north of Sacramento. To be certain that El Rey could never find them, the family changed their surname to Lopez and Juana became Esther. Esther knew never to talk about her former life. Even in the safety of Dos Robles, the past was taboo.

The pride Juana took for her looks was transformed to vexation in Esther. As a child, Juana was demure, the Mexican way for a striking young woman to behave. Esther was boisterous. Boys and men still stared, but she was desensitized to the lecherous looks; guys thought her stuck up because she gave them tongue lashings when she felt their eyes inappropriately on her.

Paradoxically, the brash Esther was a secret-keeper. Not only about the past, but she was the repository of her friends' secrets, and sometimes at parties, people she hardly knew told her the craziest things. She took pride in her gift, especially after Samson told her that her name in Hebrew meant "secret." Even though she resented Samson busting her essay, he was a good teacher. He didn't teach what he was told to teach; he taught what he wanted. She supposed that was why she liked Blake; he lived his own life. There was no other reason to go out with the white equivalent of a Cholo, though he did make her laugh with his antics, and he was sweet to her without fawning.

288

Esther sat in the baseball stands with Chloe, so they could watch their boyfriends. It was the section semifinals. Every time Blake came to the plate, he'd look at Esther, catch her eye, and tap his bat to his helmet's visor. Blake was the second best hitter on the team.

"God, what a dork," Chloe said.

"He's got a double and single. What's Leon done?"

"I don't even like baseball."

It was the bottom of the fifth inning. The Cowboys were up 5-3.

The Woodland Wolves' pitcher walked the last batter on four pitches. The first pitch to Blake was in the dirt and got by the catcher. The runner advanced to second and the Wolves' manager came to the mound. Samson called Blake over and the two of them conversed in front of the Cowboys' dugout.

"You know, he isn't that bad looking," Esther said.

"Who? Blake?" Chloe looked up from her issue of *Vogue*.

Esther pointed with her nose. "Samson."

Chloe put her magazine down. "Samson? You're *looking* at Samson?"

"I'm not *looking* at him."

"Mr. I'm-so-cool, I can recite a poem. What was that one today even about?"

"About how the world is falling apart."

"Whatever." Chloe's eyes went from Samson, to closely inspect Esther, and back to Samson. "I know someone whose life's going to fall apart." She closed her magazine. "Want to hear something?"

Esther shrugged. The less you pretended to care, the more people told.

"You have to promise not to tell, not even Blake, *especially* not Blake."

Blake was back in the batter's box. He hit a deep fly to left. Esther got to her feet, but the fly was caught ending the inning.

"Promise?"

Esther sat back down. "Do I ever tell Blake anything?"

Chloe laughed and then sobered up. "I'm not supposed to tell."

"So don't."

Chloe inched closer to Esther and looked around to make sure no one was listening. She whispered, "Samson's going to get fired..."

"Not for that picture."

"No, for something else. His test scores. Leon told me."

That wasn't much of a secret. If it were true, everyone would know within a week once school got out. There was more. Had to be. Esther was impatient for Chloe to continue but didn't want to scare her off, so she picked up Chloe's *People* and examined the cover.

In an even softer whisper that forced Esther to bend close to Chloe's mouth, Chloe continued, "Leon was in Mrs. Haman's office right after the SBAC test. You know she's his aunt?"

"Course." This was news to Esther.

"And there was this pile of answer sheets." Chloe looked around again, then, "Mrs. Haman said, 'These are the SBAC tests for Mr. Samson's Period 1 class. The top one is Noah Chu's. He bragged that his scores would surprise me this year. Last year he scored Far Below Basic. I saw his test,' she pointed to the pile, 'his first answers were right. He'll probably test Advanced. But if somehow he scored Far Below Basic, no one would raise an eyebrow. Leon, you know how Mr. Samson is harming our students and Reagan High. Even without any help, his test scores won't rise, but just to be safe, Noah should score Far Below Basic.' She picked up the next six tests and added, 'Just for insurance, five answers changed randomly on each of these would be good. I'll be at a special ed meeting for the next 30 minutes. Leon, are you with me?' She held out a pencil for him, and he did it."

"Pendejo," Esther cursed under her breath.

"You promised." Chloe looked alarmed that she told.

"You can trust me."

The girls didn't mention the cheating or Samson for the rest of the game. The Wolves went ahead. In the bottom of the seventh, Leon struck out with bases loaded. Ryan came up after him and hit a two-run double to win the game.

Chloe said, "Another bad game for Leon. Like I don't care, but he's such a jerk after. Whatever. Tell him I had to babysit." Chloe started off towards the parking lot. "You and Blake coming to my party Friday, right?"

"Course."

"Okay, see ya later. Don't forget; I had to babysit."

Esther couldn't believe what The Hammer and Leon did to Samson. He didn't deserve it, but what could she do? It was a secret.

The team left the dugout, and Blake was on his way to her.

"What did you think of your stud boyfriend's performance? 2 for 4, 2 rbis, and 2 runs. We're going to win section…What the hell's wrong with you?"

Blake stared at Esther. She had to look away.

"Nothing. I'm just tired."

"Bullshit. What is it? Me? Look you're not supposed to be polite when you slide into home. It's not, 'Excuse me, but may I *please* touch the plate with my toe?' No, it's, 'get the hell out of my way, or you're going down!'"

Blake smiled and tilted his head to try and catch Esther's eye. Esther smiled. "It's not you. You're great."

"Damn right! I'm the best thing that's ever happened to you!"

He beat his chest and hollered. Esther was used to tuning out Blake when he preened. Her eyes followed Samson walking from the field.

"You're tossing me for Coach S?"

Esther suddenly started bawling.

Blake dropped his baseball bag, took her into his arms, and kissed her tears. "What? What? What?"

291

Esther shook her head before burying it into Blake's chest. She sobbed, "Life always sucks; I just hate it."

Blake stroked her hair. "Sometimes it's easier when you tell your awesome boyfriend your problems."

"I can't. I promised."

Leon walked up and scowled, "That fucking ump put me in the hole with two shitty called strikes, so I had to chase that low outside pitch. They let any dick-wad behind the plate."

"We won," said Blake. "Forget about it. You know, you might work with Coach S on your swing."

"Fuck that pervert. He doesn't know shit." Leon turned to Esther. "Where'd Chloe go?"

"Babysitting."

"Yeah, right. Whatever. I'm out of here."

Leon headed towards the locker room.

Blake softly pushed Esther to arms' length and said, "Leon said that promises are for pussies."

Esther frowned. "Leon said that?"

Blake grinned. "You know Leon."

"Well, if that's what he said, then I guess it's okay to tell you because it's about him." And she told.

"Damn. Leon's been after Samson all year. First the picture; now this total rat fuck."

"Poor Samson," said Esther.

"Fuck that. You got to tell the King."

"I can't."

"You got to. Esther, you know why we're going to win section? Coach S. Last year I hit .285, this year it's .355. It's like that for everyone. Anyway, you can't keep a secret to cover a crime. It makes you an accessory. Dear Dad spent 7 months at Folsom because he didn't rat on his friend, this a-hole meth dealer."

292

"But if I say anything, Chloe will know, and then Leon will know, and I don't want Leon pissed at her and then me. He is seriously violent."

"King can make up some bullshit like he saw the tests had too many erases or whatever. Anyway, fuck Leon and double-fuck that cunt Haman. That is so fucked up."

"I can't, Blake. I shouldn't have told you."

Esther took a step back and waved her hand in front of her face. "You need a shower," and she turned away. Blake grabbed her hand and twirled her to face him. "Blake, let go. I told you. I can't. I know it's fucked up. But I can't and won't do it."

"What about that poem today? You know, 'The Second Coming.'"

"The one where you yelled, 'I'm having a second coming'?"

"Yeah, that one. It said the best do nothing, while the worst screw the world over."

"It didn't say that."

"That's what it meant. So it'll be on you if you do nothing and let a good guy get royally screwed."

"So why don't *you* tell him? It's on you as much as me because now you know too."

If he was so intent on saving Samson, let him do it. Blake pursed his lips. She did enjoy leaving her loudmouthed boyfriend speechless. "Well?"

In an unusually calm tone coupled with an uncharacteristically slow delivery, Blake replied, "In case you've forgotten, I am Blake Thomas. Not the class valedictorian. If I say to King, 'My girlfriend told me something that her friend learned from her boyfriend,' he'd think it was another Blake prank, and toss me out of his office. I'd probably earn a detention for bothering him with stupid shit. No, my sweet girlfriend, you're the chosen one."

"I can't."

For an interminable five seconds, Blake silently stared into Esther's eyes. And then he said, "I'm not stupid, Esther…"

"I never said you were."

"When we started going out, I asked you about where you came from. You gave some bullshit answer like, 'The past is past, I don't want to talk about it.' And I respected that. There's a lot of shit in my own past that I don't want people to know. So I'm never going to ask about yours. But consider this: maybe the reason you magically appeared in Dos Robles out of nowhere without a past was just for this. It's not an accident you're here, and it's not an accident out of all the people in the school, Chloe chose you to tell. Some secrets you can't keep, this is one of those. Look, I'm going to take that shower. When I get out, I'll walk with you all the way to the office door. Okay?"

Esther pursed her lips.

"Okay?" Blake wasn't going to leave unless she agreed, so she nodded her head, and Blake headed to the locker room.

Esther headed home unsure of what to do.

Chapter 46

PARENTS AND SIBLINGS filed into the stadium carrying balloons, homemade congratulatory signs, and leis made of bite-size Snickers. A carnival atmosphere permeated the air as both parents and students felt a mixture of ecstasy, incredulity, and enormous relief that after 13 years of public education, the graduates would walk the stage.

200 empty chairs flanked both sides of a temporary dais set up in the middle of the field. Behind it were 100 more seats reserved for school staff and local dignitaries. A mix-tape played in the background. Earlier in the week, students brought favorite music to the counseling office. In the absence of Mrs. Haman, who was on administrative leave, Ms. Mendoza arbitrated what was acceptable.

Truck and Mo stood with the rest of the staff in the shade of the gym to protect against the sun. The lid of four 50-quart coolers filled with ice and water bottles opened and closed with the pop and pace of pre-game batting practice. Mo pulled out two and handed one to Truck.

"You think The Hammer changed your scores the last two years as well?"

"No, I don't think so. The cheating wasn't about our mutual dislike. She saw two years of bad scores and decided I was a bad teacher, especially since I was so in her face about teaching my own way. I'm guessing she's smart enough to know that there are enough variables at play to introduce a randomness in the scores, and she figured I might get lucky and increase my scores, and then she'd be stuck with me. She did what she did because she thought it was best for the students."

Truck nodded. "So what do you think? Were you lucky or does all things Yeats work for standardized tests?"

"I have no idea, but even if my scores tanked again, I'd still proclaim that regarding education, Yeats is who we should follow, not SBAC question developers." Mo lifted his water bottle, "To Yeats!"

Truck said, "To my final graduation," and clinked water bottles with Mo. Mo wondered if Truck was referring to his retirement or the likelihood that by this time next year, he would be dead.

Truck said, "Can you believe Cooper Henderson is about to receive a document proclaiming to the world that he's a high school graduate?"

"Of course," Mo added, "he'll need to stop by your house, so you can read it to him."

Principal Dewey King and the counseling staff marched down the lines of the excited graduates gowned in orange for the boys and white for the girls. Each student unzipped his or her gown, so the staff could check for contraband. Mo followed with a steel pail. Each graduate dropped a folded bit of paper into the pail. Then the staff marched in a ragged formation to their seats. Though commanded by their boss to walk and sit with decorum, there was much joking, for they had survived another year of high school, served up another graduating class, and were looking forward to their summer, and for the post-50 crowd, counting down another year toward retirement.

At the first note of "Pomp and Circumstance," everyone rose, and the graduates entered the stadium using the cadenced walk they practiced earlier in the day.

"This, my friend, is the future," scoffed Truck. He shook his head. "I tried."

But Truck's eyes were wet as were Mo's.

Hudson Anderson opened the ceremony. Lupita Alvarez sang the national anthem. Principal Dewey King encouraged graduates to continue their studies. Dell gave her valedictorian address in which she exhorted her peers not to be limited by societal barriers; rather, "Test in your heart if something is right. If it is, that is the path to take."

At the end of Dell's address, she announced, "Mr. Samson will now introduce the commencement speaker."

Mr. Samson made his way to the front. Dell and he shook hands. No electricity sparked from their fingers. Their eyes met and Dell smiled without a hint of jovial wickedness. There was nothing improper between teacher and student. Mr. Samson placed the pail under the lectern and announced, "Dr. McGuire, affectionately known as Dr. Truck, has taught thousands of students over his twenty-one year career at Reagan High. But he has taught more than students. He has taught both me and my colleagues not only what it means to be a teacher who touches lives, but how to live every day with intention and panache. Unfortunately for our community, Dr. Truck is retiring, so this is our last chance to hear from this master teacher."

Mr. Samson moved aside and a standing ovation greeted Dr. Truck.

"Thank you, Mr. Samson." Truck removed his speech from his gown, flattened it on the lectern, put on his spectacles, and started in an uncharacteristically shaky voice.

"It has been a prodigious honor teaching at Reagan High. I love the school and the students and will sorely miss my life here. I have one last lecture to deliver, but not to worry, I've instructed Principal King to bring out a shepherd's crook if my ramblings exceed five minutes." Truck looked at both sections of students and commenced. "What is the difference between student and teacher? Of course there is the obvious that teachers have more knowledge, at least in the subjects we teach. In the students' eyes, the main difference might be that teens are exceedingly—to borrow a young person's expression—more dope than teachers since, through no fault of our own, we are adults.

"I offer another difference: the trajectory of our lives. Student lives are linear. Beginning in kindergarten you ascend each year to the next level never to return to the naps of kindergarten, the class pets of 5th grade, the proofs of 9th grade geometry, and—from what I hear—the madness of English 12…" Truck smiled at Mo standing on the side of the dais. "Students are arrows shot into the world. Yesterday you came to school, today you receive your diplomas, and tomorrow you'll get on with your lives. In contrast, teachers' lives are circular. Each August, we begin the school year and together with our students we ascend the mountain of knowledge. Come June, we reach the summit, more or less. During the summer, teachers return down the mountain alone to meet a new class waiting to ascend. Not the agony of Sisyphus but the same idea."

"Though there are these differences between student and teacher, between teen and adult, our similarities are greater. Perhaps the most essential one is ignorance. The stork deposited each of us on our parents' porch without explanation. Who am I? How shall I live? What gives my life meaning? Some of us ignore these questions and live unreflective lives, but many of us seek answers, and as most high schoolers know, adults are often no closer than teens in answering life's existential questions."

Truck looked to Mo and said, "Though I am honored to be called a 'master teacher,' the truth is that inside this old and somewhat failing body lives a teenager who struggles every day to try and make sense of the wonder, the beauty, the horror, the absurdity of life."

Truck returned to his prepared remarks. "This world which we have all been thrust into without a guidebook contains goodness on one side balanced against evil on the other. Unfortunately, the sides are almost always intermixed and determining what is true is rarely easy.

"High school is the crucible where existential and moral questions are explored and debated; it is the place where the teen begins the journey to adulthood. It has been an exciting career to share this journey with you. Sometimes I am able to provide insight to you; sometimes it is you who teach me something I've never considered. I love this job because of your optimism and passion. I love this job because even though I am trying to answer the same questions as you, my adult cynicism and passivity weigh me down. You students remind us how to live the full palate of human emotions and to grasp the immediacy of life. The truth is that I teach for me as much as for you, for being a high school teacher is an antidote against cynicism. There is no philosopher's stone or elixir of life, but teaching high school is the path for someone who wants to remain young at heart."

Truck took the pail and with a loud thud set it atop the lectern. "When Mr. Samson started here, he introduced himself by quoting William Butler Yeats, 'Education is not the filling of the pail, but the lighting of a fire.' He told me that he was here to light fires. I suggested that he keep two pails in his classroom. One to contain facts to heap on the students; one to hold evidence of student fires that were lit. Being a novice teacher in the company of his seasoned elder, he did so, and I did as well. It seemed a weird enough idea.

"While students practiced marching this morning, they all were given a slip a paper and invited to write down a fire that was lit in them during high school. They are all here."

Dr. Truck produced a lighter, removed one slip from the pail, lit it, and held it aloft. He continued, "Burning the slips symbolizes our hope that your fires stay permanently lit." He placed the burning slip into the pail and the others caught. The fire climbed above the rim for a few seconds before being replaced by a bright orange flame—compliments of a powder provided by Ms. Quast, the chemistry teacher—which rose two feet above the pail.

After it went out, he said, "So as I go off into the sunset, I leave you a final hope…"

Dr. Truck paused to make sure he had everyone's attention, but he needn't have bothered; for the entire address, everyone in the stadium strained forward.

"…that as you age and suffer the slings and arrows of life, you retain the optimism, passion, and can-do spirit of your youth. Or if you can't remember the feeling, do what your teachers did and join our ranks. Teaching is a noble profession, and we need the best and brightest our country has to offer. You most likely will never own a Ferrari, or a timeshare in Aspen, but the satisfaction of working with kids outweighs everything I've ever done in my life. And I've done a lot.

"And now I believe Principal King has some parchment he wants to award you."

Following the receiving of the diplomas, and the moving of the tassels from the right to the left, and the throwing of the mortar boards, and the walking out to Queen's "We are the Champions;"

students, parents, and teachers congratulated each other and said their goodbyes.

Jeff and Ryan Dowling were the first to find Mr. Samson. "Congratulations, Ryan," Mr. Samson said. "Have you decided what you're going to do? $900,000 is a lot of money."

"I'm not sure. What would you do?"

"I would never presume to know more than Ryan Dowling. You have a good shot to make it to the Bigs, but playing football at UCLA will probably be more fun than playing in the minors, and they'd be idiots not to let you swing a bat in the spring. You're young and have time. A college education is a good thing."

"That's exactly what I told him," said Jeff. "By the way, I want you to be the first to know; I got an offer from UC Davis. You want the Cowboys?"

Mr. Samson opened his mouth wide in feigned disbelief; then he laughed. Earlier in the week, he had accepted Principal King's offer to take over the team.

Violet Brown waved for him to come over.

"What did you do to your hair?" Mr. Samson looked aghast. Violet sported a head of blown-dry brunette hair.

"Ha-ha." Violet made introductions. "This is Mr. Samson who thinks he's a stand-up comic. This is my mom and dad, and you of course remember my sisters: Allie and Candice."

"Of course." Mr. Samson had not only forgotten their names, he had hardly a memory of either girl. He wished each student held a permanent spot in his heart, but all the students and all the memories that were such a central part of his life during their one year together tended to blend and gray over time. He wondered how long Violet would remain Violet before becoming another ex-student whom he could barely recall.

Mr. Samson moved through the adoring families and saw that he himself was already on the periphery of their lives. The arrows already left the bow. He caught sight of Noah and Poonam. He shook his head at the improbable couple. Without the glue of school, Mr. Samson figured by July they'd be finished.

"Coach S!" Blake clapped Mr. Samson on the back. Esther stood beside Blake smiling. Blake held up his hand for Mr. Samson to see his championship ring. "What do you think?"

"Large."

Blake said, "I decided on Consumes River College, so I can play baseball. I'll call you when I need English help, okay?"

"Uh, no. Bother your English professor."

"But Samson, you're the best teacher ever."

Mr. Samson barely heard Blake, for he was focusing on Esther. The day before, Maria informed Esther that she was the recipient of a new scholarship for students planning to enter the field of school counseling. Maria did not tell her that the scholarship was funded by Mr. Samson, and this was the first and last time it would be awarded.

"Congratulations on your scholarship, Esther," Mr. Samson said. "When you're ready to transfer to a four-year and need a letter of recommendation, I'd be happy to give you one."

Esther smiled. "You'd write one for a plagiarist?"

"I'll download one from the internet."

The three laughed and hugged good-bye.

And there was Dell and her mother.

"Mr. Samson," Mrs. Westergard began, "I want to thank you for all you have done for Dell this year." Mrs. Westergard didn't look particularly thankful. Aggressive was a better descriptor for her tone as she stood between her daughter and Mr. Samson. Perhaps she was unconvinced of the platonic nature of Mr. Samson and Dell's relationship. After all, Othello killed Desdemona on sketchier evidence. "You must," she continued, "must come over for dinner before Dell goes off to Harvard."

Mr. Samson was bemused by the invite, but it was clearly pro forma. She didn't want him coming, and he would never go. "I'd love to," Mr. Samson replied.

He wanted a final word with Dell, but she spoke first.

"You're a great teacher and a good man, Mr. Samson. I'll never forget you."

For a last moment he and Dell were alone staring intently at each other.

"Other students I wish luck. You don't need it. You'll slay them in Cambridge."

Mr. Samson choked up as he hugged Dell. He could feel her willing her eyes to not tear.

"How about a picture?" Mrs. Westergard was impatient for them to let go. They complied and then—as if his great moral struggle never happened—Dell was gone. For a moment he tried to look four years ahead. Might there? No, never. He would move on as would she.

Mo eyed Maria crossing the field making her way out. It was time for him to go as well. Maria wanted to meet for sushi. She had some news. He was pretty sure it was over between Dewey and her. Who knew? Mo and Maria? Nah, it would never work.

"Mr. Samson!"

An unfamiliar student stopped him. She smiled broadly and put out her hand. "I'm Megan Warren. I'm going to be in your AP Lit class next year. I wanted to introduce myself and let you know that I like poetry a lot."

"Nice to meet you. I'll look forward to having you in class." He shook her hand, and then she disappeared into the crowd of revelers.

Acknowledgements

This book would not be possible without the guidance of Pamela Ronald, John Hill, and Raoul Adamchak whose tireless readings of drafts helped shape the story. Elisabeth Kauffmann provided editorial polish. A tremendous thank you to Phyllis Gallagher for her boundless enthusiasm and belief in the book.

About the Author

Matt Biers-Ariel has been a teacher for 30 years. He is an empty-nester living in Davis, California.

His previous books include:

Solomon and the Trees

The Seven Species

The Triumph of Eve and Other Subversive Bible Tales

The Bar Mitzvah and The Beast: One Family's Cross-Country Ride of Passage

35820453R00183

Made in the USA
Middletown, DE
17 October 2016